REGAL REWARD
A BLACKSTONE NOVEL: BOOK ONE

Elaine Violette

Regal Reward
Copyright 2016 Elaine Violette
ISBN: 978-0-9966821-2-1

This ebook is licensed for your personal enjoyment only. This ebook may not be reproduced, resold, stored or transmitted, in any form, electronic, mechanical, photo copying, recording or otherwise without the expressed written permission of the author. If you have enjoyed Regal Reward and would like to share this book with another person, please consider purchasing an additional copy for each person. Writing a review of the author's work is especially appreciated. Thank you for respecting the hard work of this author. All characters in this book are fiction and figments of the author's imagination. Regal Reward was previously published by Cerridwen Press/Ellora's Cave.

Cover Art by Harris Channing
Cover model photo complements of Lunaesque Creative Photography

Dedication

For my mother, Millie Santos Noyes, who passed away on September 22, 2014. Thank you, Mom, for showing me through example the true meaning of patience, perseverance, and faith.

Chapter One

"I REFUSE TO move from this spot, Gerald. Your pleading is futile."

"Please, milady, consider the danger!"

"I'll not leave Beatrice here to be mauled by some wild animal and have her babes eaten up. Why, she's just given birth." Marielle looked down at her cluster of pets, her hands clasped firmly about her trim waist. "Oh, look! There's another one beneath Bea's hind leg..."

Marielle smiled as her faithful hound cleaned her pups and welcomed the new little one as it nuzzled its way into the crowded horde. The dog, swollen with her impending litter, had taken to the hills earlier in the day and they'd gone in circles trying to find her. Now with night closing in, she regretted being the cause of Gerald's anxiety. The evening dampness caused his arthritic bones to ache and she could see his discomfort as he limped back and forth scanning the shadow-draped woods.

"Milady, return with me. We'll send the grooms to find her. She'll be back home in no time at all."

"And, dear Gerald, when they arrive, they'll be carrying you back also. Your limp has worsened. You can not stay out any longer in this night air waiting for a search party. You need to direct them. Bea chose a safe, secluded spot under this big oak and I'll not leave her.

"But, Milady, your father will have my head if any harm comes to you."

"The night will protect me." Marielle patted Gerald's arm and smiled, hoping to placate him. "The grooms need only to keep a sharp eye for the stone markers we've placed near the road. You'll see. I'll be home with our new little family soon enough. I'm truly sorry for pushing you to continue searching past dinnertime, but we've found them. I wouldn't have had a moment's rest worrying about Bea's whereabouts. You must understand."

"Knowing you as well as I do, I most certainly understand. As your caretakers, Matty and I have coddled you and your behavior tonight confirms it. If only your mother was still here. You would not have been allowed to prance about the estate unsupervised since you were old enough to wander."

"Both you and Matty have been wonderful caretakers, but this night I must care for my pets. Do not fear. You know I've walked and ridden about the estate lands in perfect safety. This night will be no different from any other. Now, off with you. I'll not hold you accountable if my father rages."

"If your father took more interests in your whereabouts…" Gerald mumbled, then caught himself. "Since I cannot change your mind, here…take my cloak to fend against the night's chill and my knife too," her servant grumbled. "Pray, do not move from this spot and keep alert to any sounds that might warn you of intruders."

"I will keep it securely by my side," Marielle promised.

"It's not right, milady, not right at all," Gerald replied, shaking his head as he wrapped the cloak about her, turned and slowly limped away. He knew if he stayed a search party might take hours to find them. "Oh, milady, this is most unsettling, most unsettling…"

Marielle listened to her servant's voice fade into inarticulate mumbling as the distance grew between them. *How could he possible think I would leave Beatrice alone? Let my father rage. He most likely hasn't even noticed my absence. Poor Gerald. I should have set out on my own to find Bea. I've only caused him more worry.*

Having made peace with her decision, she wrapped the cloak snugly about her and struggled to find a comfortable position against the ancient tree trunk. Her cherished dog, nestled between two gnarled roots, slept blissfully with her new brood.

The sounds of night became more distinct and despite her efforts to stay awake and alert, her eyes grew heavy and sleep took over.

York Blackstone stood above the sleeping miss nestled beneath the large oak, rubbing his chin. He and his partner had recently stopped a carriage that held all sorts of rewards. The wealthy occupants were most generous and amendable, despite the one who attempted to run off into the woods. York couldn't blame him. Having followed the carriage from the gaming house, his pockets held the most sizable win.

As he and his partner Braum headed homeward at a comfortable trot, the moon's glow created a dim spotlight over the strange bundle. While his partner watched the road, York checked out the site, surprised to see the young woman wrapped in a heavy cloak. As he moved stealthily around the tree, he was even more surprised to realize that she was completely alone except for a dog and its new litter snuggled next to her.

While he meditated on what to do with her—he certainly couldn't leave her in the woods without protection—she began to stir.

MARIELLE SIGHED AS she sifted through the strange dream that interrupted her sleep. She stirred, unconsciously wrestling with the tightly wrapped cloak. Her green eyes, glazed from sleep, opened, attempted to focus. The full moon cast an eerie glow on a shadowy figure before her. Boots, high boots, worn, supple. While her mind tried to make sense of the dream, her eyes followed the lines of the boots upward from the sight of leggings stretched taut against large, muscular thighs to the stranger's bulging manhood.

"Oh my..." Marielle's eyes bolted upward. A mocking smile met her horrified gaze. The moon's glow created a ghostly aura around the tall stranger's mass of charcoal hair and broad shoulders. For a brief, profound second, Marielle thought she beheld the image of a god or a devil. The effect was surreal, until the sound of deep laughter broke into her terrifying trance.

Another voice joined in, jolting her into full awareness of her surroundings, where she was and why. Gerald's warnings and the events of the day swirled in her mind. Her glance flew to Bea then scanned the darkness for Gerald or her father. Her body instinctively shrank deeper into the folds of Gerald's heavy cloak while forcing herself to look directly up at the tall stranger and into the blackness of his eyes. This was no dream. She tried to speak, but no sound escaped her lips.

A gruff voice broke the silence. "York, I think we've found us a tasty morsel to dine on tonight."

Marielle's head snapped toward the sound to see a shorter, stockier man crouching, leering, his squinting eyes almost hidden by full cheeks.

Her body shook involuntarily. Despite the tremors, she ignored the shorter man and glared at the taller one just addressed as York. "What are you doing here? You're trespassing on my father's land. His men are on their way, will arrive at any moment…you must leave, *now!*" Marielle reached protectively toward Beatrice who'd begun to growl in a low, steady rumbling as her litter of pups, looking more like squirming mice, snuggled against her damp, speckled coat.

The tall stranger reached down slowly, smiled and patted the dog's head. Beatrice quieted and returned to cleaning up one of the pups. Marielle watched, momentarily paralyzed at the stranger's audacity and her pet's meek response. She gripped her fists beneath the cloak as her anger took hold. "Who are you? My father, Lord Henley…he'll have your heads for trespassing. You must…"

"*Silence*," the tall stranger snapped, then gave her a crooked smile as he bent down closer, meeting her glare. His voice softened. "I find your inane chatter annoying."

"Wh-what...?" she sputtered. "You have no right to speak to me in that tone."

Her attempt at boldness drew more laughter as she watched the tall stranger turn to his partner to mock her. "We've found ourselves a spunky little fox, Braum. A lady of the estate and she even comes with her own hound."

Marielle suddenly remembered Gerald's knife. She reached beneath the cloak for the leather scabbard only to have the shorter man, Braum, grab her arm and pull the cloak aside. Finding the knife, he sneered, waving it before her face.

"What else might you 'ave under that cloak?" He reached down to grab the cape. Marielle lashed out, clawing. She grabbed his arm and bit fiercely into his flesh.

"You little witch," Braum howled, pulling back and wincing in pain. "I'll do more than..." He lunged towards her, but was instantly pulled back. York's hand caught his collar, yanking him up and away from Marielle.

"Leave her be," York ordered while his partner stumbled, cursing as he fell back into a nearby bush. "We've come upon much more than a tasty snack. We may be able to secure our future with this midnight miss."

Marielle, fearful but fuming, attempted to stand but became tangled in the long cloak. Stumbling over a gnarled root, she tripped, grasping at what she could to block her fall. Her palms landed on York's steel-hard chest. Without firm footing, she lost the battle for balance. Her hands slipped further down his frame over his belt to the bulge beneath.

York's breath caught in his throat, his manhood reacting, rising to the occasion. "Ooh, my sweet, if that is what you're after, I will be happy to oblige."

"*Despicable demon*," Marielle hissed, pulling at the cloak and wrapping it more securely about her.

"Such language, you behave more like a wench than a well-bred lady," York jeered, while admiring her courage. "I would have thought, though you seem quite young, that you'd be more refined and with such beauty, even in the dark, certainly worthy of more ladylike actions. Might I ask why you're out here alone in the middle of night and without a guardian? I promise you, we'll do a much better job of keeping you safe."

Marielle wrapped her arms more tightly about her ignoring his query.

"The chattering miss has grown silent," York said, still smiling down at her. I find that much more agreeable. Now, I think it's time that we were off."

"Off? Off where? You must leave. I am safeguarding my pet and her litter. My father's men will arrive at any moment and you'll pay for trespassing *and* your crude behavior."

"Then we should be on our way. I refuse to leave you here unprotected," York countered, while leaning down to lift her off the ground.

Marielle tried to pull away only to have the

stranger lift her up effortlessly and toss her, like a rag doll, over his shoulder. Struggling against his powerful hold, she pounded his back. "*Put me down.* Do you hear me? I cannot leave Beatrice... *Please*, I must stay with her. Let me go!"

"Braum, grab a horse blanket and some rope. Make a harness for the animal and its brood. We'll bring them along. It seems the young lady takes her responsibilities quite seriously."

His partner shrugged his shoulders, muttering as he followed York's direction. "While my partner makes your charges comfortable, you, Miss Henley, will ride with me."

Marielle screamed, slamming her fists into his back, but to no avail.

"You may choose to ride upside down or right side up, whichever you prefer, but you will ride with me, so I advise you to stop struggling."

Marielle barely heard him as she screamed hoping someone might hear her in the darkness. The stranger heaved her onto his stallion and mounted, adjusting her flailing body. The ribbon that held her hair unraveled, releasing her thick, auburn curls that now fell recklessly brushing the ground.

Staring down into the darkness, fear crawled through her until she thought she might retch. Her attempts to push her body forward, away, grasp at the brush nearby, succeeded only in amusing her captor as her derriere, padded with petticoats, squirmed wildly.

"You don't seem to be enjoying the view, Miss Henley."

"You animal, you..." Against her will, tears sprang forth as her face rubbed against the horse's firm side.

In an instant, York lifted her, settled her firmly between his legs, her body pressed against his chest while his free arm clasped her waist tightly.

"I suggest you calm down and stop your babbling, or I'll gag your mouth shut."

"You wouldn't *dare*."

Hearing her iron will emerging, York pulled the black scarf from around his neck, preparing to use it if needed.

Marielle covered her mouth with her fists.

"That's much better. I see you're a fast learner." He pulled the reins, easing his horse closer to his partner. "Braum, is everything attended to?"

Having lifted Bea, Braum was busy grabbing some of the pups that had loosened their hold on their mother's teats. Once he'd gathered them all, he wrapped them securely in the blanket, placing the pups atop their mother. He tied the heavy bundle to his saddle, leaving an opening large enough for air to circulate. "Aye, the pups are secure," Braum grumbled as he mounted his horse.

Bea, her pups now hidden in the makeshift sling that hung half off the horse and partly on Braum's lap, whimpered. Marielle tried to call out her name, but their fate was out of her hands.

"We should o' stayed on the road and minded our business, Yorkie," Braum said as he pulled at his horse's reins. "We were havin' a fine night. Now, we're loaded down with trouble. A little play would o' been enough. We don't need anybody followin' us home."

"Let's be gone then, before we're forced to entertain unwelcome company." York said as he led his horse onto the main road.

Marielle attempted to wrench away from York's firm hold. He in turn, held her closer. As he picked up speed, she felt his body move rhythmically in the saddle. Being a rider herself, she could tell that he was an expert horseman, sure of his movements, despite the extra weight of his passenger. Screaming or fighting, she realized, was futile.

As they rode further away from her home, she prayed that someone would come along, another rider, or, perhaps a carriage returning to the country from a night in London. She heard nothing except for the sound of the horses' hooves and York's steady breathing. Scattered thoughts crept in. Numbing fear held a tight grip. She worried about Bea and wondered if the pups would be alive when they arrived at wherever they were going. Her back, stiff from her attempts to stay rigid and away from her assailant, ached.

York sensed her weariness, as well as her stubbornness to make herself more comfortable. He pulled Marielle to him and rested her upper torso against his chest. He was accustomed to keeping his mind on his purpose, but the softness and scent of the young woman he tucked into his arms was disconcerting and stimulating.

"Rest, my midnight miss. You won't come to any harm this night."

Marielle tried to protest, but knew she had no options. Fighting him only sapped her strength. She must save it for the opportune time when she could find a means of escape. She tried to keep her eyes on her surroundings, but the time seemed endless. As time passed, despite her grandest efforts to stay alert, her eyes grew heavy.

With York in the lead and Braum following close behind, they traveled through the night. As they drew closer to their destination, the sights and sounds of a new morning replaced the darkness. An ethereal coral glow emanated from the horizon casting off drapes of heavy mist that covered the distant mountains. York pulled the reins taut and led his horse into the brush and down through a gully.

Marielle woke with a start. She tried to lift her head only to have him push it down while he bent his own head over hers. Only a muffled squeak escaped her lips.

"Keep still or the brush will scratch you like cat's claws. We're almost there," he whispered hoarsely.

His faced was pressed so near to her own that Marielle could feel his breath on her cheek. They passed through a wooded area down an uneven, stone-stubbled path, causing the horses to tread with an unsteady gait. Soon a rush of fresh mountain air brushed Marielle's face.

York loosened his grip, allowing his captive to lift herself up and view the surroundings. The horses knew their way as they followed a creek that threaded through the rocky plain leading to a larger stream. He covered her head once again as they turned into more brush.

As soon as Marielle felt the cool air again, she squirmed from his grip. This time she could see a small thatched-roofed cottage in the distance with smoke curling from the chimney. The serene picture-book landscape softly lit by the new dawn was breathtaking. Simple beauty lay before her but she refused to allow herself to appreciate it. She adjusted her thoughts to the bleakness of her situation. The reality of the moment was no longer a hazy nightmare, but shone clear as glass. She felt powerless and knew it was useless to plead for release, but she could think of no other alternative.

"Where have you taken me? You *must* let me go. How far from home am I and where is Beatrice?"

"When your tongue wakes up, it chirps and flutters like mother birds skittering in the grasses to find food for their young," York teased as he brushed aside her tousled curls.

"I beg your pardon," Marielle hissed, pulling herself away from his grasp.

"I beg you to hush and save your strength for more productive exercise. Your dogs are safe and have been well behaved on our journey. Braum's left us many times through the night's ride to scramble our tracks and he's returned with the dogs in tow. I suspect he's become accustomed to the extra weight and may even have grown attached to his cargo."

The hint of satisfaction in his voice only increased Marielle's irritation. She grumbled something unintelligible as they rode up to the porch of the small cottage.

Meanwhile, Braum rode up behind them, dismounted and tethered the horses while a younger version of York stepped out on the porch, his eyes widening in wonder as he spotted Marielle.

"Well, big brother," Martin exclaimed, "I'm not certain whether your night's journey was a success or not, but it sure looks like a heap of trouble to me. Could it be you've found us a maid to tidy up the place?"

"Not a bad idea, Martin, but I'm considering other plans for this prim package."

Marielle tried to protest but before she could utter a sound, York lifted her up into the younger man's arms.

"Ah, light as a feather yet well rounded if my arms do not deceive me," Martin said, grinning.

"How dare you. Put me down!"

"She's a hot spark of fire too. Where on earth did you find her?"

"Be patient. Right now I could use a hot cup of coffee." York led the way through the cottage door. "Once we're rested, I'll tell you all about our profitable adventures. Braum, bring in the mutt and her brood. Then find old George to rub down the horses."

A freshly fed fire warmed the cottage and the rich smell of strong coffee permeated the air. Martin carried Marielle, despite her protests and once inside, stood her on her feet. She pushed him from her, but her legs, unsteady from the long ride, caused her to lose her balance. He grabbed her by the waist to steady her.

"Don't touch me! I am perfectly able to..." Unable to keep her knees from weakening beneath her, she reached out for support, unconsciously grasping York's arm.

"Ah, haven't had enough of me yet?"

Regaining her balance, Marielle gave him a look that could fry bacon. She pushed away and took a few steps before spotting Beatrice and her pups. Braum had placed them near the fire wrapped in the horse blanket. She could see the pups squirming and suckling while Bea busied herself with washing each of the scrawny babes. She rushed to them and bent down to count each one. She sighed with relief. They'd made the trip safely and when Marielle stroked her head, Beatrice seemed content. She marveled at their ability to adapt, despite the circumstances.

Her own insides were turning cartwheels and she feared she might be sick. Her predicament was beyond belief and what of her servant? *Poor Gerald, he'll be so distraught and will most likely blame himself and Father — he'll never forgive him for leaving me.* She stared up at her captives, her fists clenched. It was obvious they were not considering her distress, but only their own stomachs.

The men were comfortably seated around the large table that filled the center of the room. Marielle looked about, noticed a small bed along one wall and a washstand nearby. A large black stove with a few pots that hung above it and an open-shelved cabinet with assorted dishes took up another wall. An open door revealed a pantry to the rear of the small cottage. Turning about, she noticed the large front window that looked out onto the front porch. In the distance she could see overgrown grasses, wild flowers and clusters of trees that wound about an open field. The mountains she'd seen earlier were now splashed with sunlight.

Sitting on the worn rug, her arms tightly clasped around her knees, she continued to examine her surroundings. Two worn, but comfortable-looking chairs were placed near the large stone fireplace, with a small table and lamp between them. Off to the left, a half-opened door revealed a small bedroom with two roughly made beds. She guessed that was probably the extent of the living space. It was neat, warm and would be considered welcoming if it weren't for her dire situation.

Her gaze returned to the men sitting around the table. The younger man, whom they called Martin, sat engrossed as her two kidnappers filled him in on their night's exploits. Angered by their conversation, she returned her thoughts to Beatrice's needs. Concern grew, outweighing her fear. She stood and walked to the table interrupted their animated conversation.

"I request water and rations for my pet. She is, no doubt, thirsty and probably starved."

"And, so are we, love. I suspect that you are not up to fetching water from the well or helping with breakfast." York stood too close, his words and expression taunting.

Marielle took a step back, her breath caught. His formidable presence filled the room. Then she stopped, held her ground and challenged him with a frosty glare.

York didn't miss her repositioning, her recalculation. He admired her courage. She knew how to stand against fear and he understood the force of will behind it too well. He smiled, glanced over to the animals. "Actually, your dog and her new family have settled in quite nicely. I think they are going to enjoy their stay."

"Aye," Braum cut in, "as long as they don't begin to get underfoot. I may be forced to stomp on 'em or toss 'em out for the wolves though they ain't much to feed on. Of course, the bitch will be a bigger mouthful."

Marielle clutched her throat ready to snap at him, but held her tongue, recognizing his distasteful humor. Instead, she watched silently, surprised at York's actions as he searched for a bowl and filled it with water from a nearby jug. She would not allow them to intimidate her, nor feel any gratitude for her pets' care. This man riddled her mind, one minute a brute, yet in another, almost human.

While York set the bowl down near Beatrice's head, he brushed her arm. She backed away, narrowed her brow, glared, as he smiled knowingly.

This was the first time she could actually observe him in the light of day. She had to admit to herself that she'd never seen a man quite as handsome. His eyes, so black in the night, in the light of morning were the deepest blue she'd ever encountered, his dark lashes, thick and long. His hair, the color of mahogany and still damp from the night air, fell in reckless waves about his face. Wet curls clung to the nape of his neck. She guessed he was probably in his late twenties, perhaps older. His face reflected a naked strength she'd not seen before. His lips, she'd noted earlier, were beautifully formed. The deep cleft in his chin, now covered with at least a day's stubble only enhanced his sensual masculinity.

She couldn't help but notice, for she'd been kept too isolated on the estate to meet men other than the work hands and, of course, Richard her betrothed. Despite her precarious situation, her captor's few acts of kindness left her with an unsteady sense of security for the time being.

As she watched York out of the corner of her eyes, she readjusted her thoughts. *I'm a prisoner. He is a ruthless kidnapper, a highwayman. His appearance proves that good looks do not make a gentleman but may only hide the cruelest of men, as her Aunt Cornelia had often said.*

She looked down at her wrinkled gown, the dirt on her hands and the scratches, surely from her attempts to fend him off. *Why, my thoughts are as disheveled as my appearance. I must find a means of escape.*

She'd given little thought to Richard, her betrothed, until now. *Oh dear heavens, what will he imagine? He's most likely rounding up all his men and my father's men are probably scouring the woods. I must believe that they will be able to follow their tracks.* As she made useless attempts to evaluate her dilemma, York held out a glass of cool water.

"You seem to be in deep thought, my sweet. I can feel those lovely green eyes of yours piercing into me like hot coals. Mine may begin to smolder with lust if you keep staring at me like that."

Marielle's face glowed crimson.

York, aware he'd humiliated her, reached out with the drink urging her, in silence, to take it.

Her first inclination was refusal, but her thirst won out. She took the glass, begrudgingly. The water was cool, refreshing and she could turn away to hide her embarrassment. He was right. She'd become mesmerized and lost in her thoughts as she took in his appearance. *It must be exhaustion. It had to be.* Her thoughts swirled as if at sea, her mind doing battle with her senses.

York noted the change. Her guard was down. He reached out, took her arm, felt her stiffen, but urged her to come to the table. "Come, eat some bread and cheese. You must be as hungry as your pet."

Marielle grasped at one of the large chairs to pull herself up and away from his touch. "I need to take care of private matters," she managed, almost politely, setting the glass down on the table.

"Ah, yes. You might want to freshen up before breakfast. I'll accompany you to the pond."

"You *must* realize I have need for time alone. Please, you have humiliated me enough."

"I worry that you might do something foolish if I left you to yourself," York replied, "but I'm sure that you wouldn't want to become lost in this valley or to have your pups suffer from lack of your tender care."

Marielle bristled at the truth of his words. She couldn't run off, leave Beatrice. She had no idea where she was or where to find help. She needed to think, consider a plan and wait for an opportune time.

Chapter Two

LORD HENLEY PACED back and forth in front of his large cluttered desk. Gerald had broken the news of Marielle's disappearance and tried to explain why he returned without her. No explanation could appease her father.

Once Lord Henley stopped raging and accepted the dismal news, he wasted no time ordering some of his men to search the estate lands, others to search the countryside, another to fetch help from the neighboring estates. Then, with great reluctance, he sent a messenger to bring the news to Lord Craymore and his son, Richard. When he could think of no other action to pursue, he collapsed in a chair, his head in his hands.

Gerald stood by, head bowed, waiting to be dismissed.

Lord Henley finally looked up. "Where could she have gone? Why were there no signs of a struggle, or worse and how could the animals disappear too?" He glared at Gerald, continued to question. "Are you sure that you returned to the right spot? Forgetfulness comes with age. Perhaps in the dark you lost direction. How else would she and the dogs have disappeared without a trace?"

How Gerald wished that to be true, but he knew differently. He'd never forget seeing Beatrice lying beneath that massive oak and Marielle by her side, stroking her.

"My lord, we found her ribbon right at that very spot, but it is strange that the animals have disappeared too. I am mystified. Assailants surely would not be bothered with a dog and her new litter."

"Could she have been kidnapped?" Lord Henley winced as he gripped the arms of his chair. "Oh, what have I done, what have I done? My beautiful child, I've given her so little since her mother died. I confess I found it difficult even looking at her at times. She reminded me so much of my dear wife. Now she could be lost to me forever too." Lord Henley pushed himself up from the chair and began pacing again.

Matty, Gerald's wife, who'd been listening near the open door, had been waiting for the opportune time to move to her husband's side in support. Noting the pause in her lord's interrogation, she interrupted. "You must stop those morbid thoughts, milord," she blurted out. "Forgive me. I step above my station, but I cannot let you torment yourself. It is true enough, more time spent together would have been a blessing for the both you and Marielle, but we do not always know what is needed when our minds our clouded in misery."

"Please, my dear. I don't think he needs to hear..." Gerald attempted to hush his wife, but his wife's glare silenced him.

"Let me have my say, Gerald." She turned back to Lord Henley. "Whatever has happened, I cannot but think if Beatrice and her pups are with Marielle, she is unharmed. No wild animal could have taken them without leaving remnants of its... Oh, dear." Matty turned away and looked wide-eyed at Gerald, before turning about and continuing. "Whoever has Marielle or wherever she has gone, I've no doubt we will know soon enough. She couldn't have carried the animals herself. Why, Beatrice alone is a handful to be sure. Whoever has Marielle, if she is had and not wandering about somewhere, is surely not a heartless person."

Gerald smiled at his wife, thankful for once that her gift of chatter seemed to be helping to ease the tension that had consumed the dark library. He reached out to her, but she had more to say.

She stared up at Lord Henley as she continued her diatribe, her elbows jutting out to her sides, her hands grasping her full aproned waist and her fingers flared out above her rounded hips. "You must get hold of yourself, if you will forgive me for saying so, milord. Marielle might walk through the door at any moment with a perfectly plausible reason for her absence. That girl has never ceased to surprise me. Perhaps villagers came along and found her, took her to their home for refreshment and rest and will return with her shortly."

Master Henley glared at Matty, a glimmer of hope in his eyes. "Yes, that must be it! It's only been a few hours. She may be resting in one of the small cottages. I will go myself and question the villagers. The two of you keep an eye out and if she returns before I do, send the stable boy to find me. I appreciate your good sense, Matty, though I cannot say the same for your husband."

He turned to Gerald and waved his finger in

the air. "There is *no* excuse for leaving her alone! Let's pray that she is with villagers. Beatrice is with her, of course. We will know soon enough." With that, he marched out of the library.

As soon as he disappeared from sight, Matty clung to Gerald. They held on to each other as they walked to the kitchen in silence, neither believing the words of assurance she offered.

WHEN MARIELLE AND York reached the edge of the pond, York stopped and spent a few lazy moments soaking in the sun's sparkle on her auburn hair. Kidnapping was not his usual means of financial gain. In fact, his actions and reactions from the moment he saw her sleeping under the tree were out of character for him. His ability to stay in control had always been his protection, his survival and his success at his profession. Thieving from those who could afford to lose a bit of their wealth, he found justifiable, but kidnapping and its consequences, extremely unwise. Yet here he was with this bundle of fire. He had no idea what he would do with her, only that she caused his groin to ache with desire. On the other hand, leaving her in the woods for the wolves to find her was not a reasonable alternative.

"Please have the decency to leave me alone," Marielle demanded as she turned about and glared at her captive.

York smiled, hesitated, noting how her eyes changed color in the sunlight, more a misty green with a hint of brown flecks. "I bow to your wishes, Miss Henley. I'm just in awe of your beauty, even if your gown is rumpled and your hair in disarray. By the way, what is your given name?"

"My appearance or my name is irrelevant to this horrid situation. At least have the decency to respect my privacy."

"I must say, you are a bossy twitch of a woman. I'll wait on the path, but do not dally. I'm tired and still hungry." York patted his slim waist, turned and disappeared down the narrow path.

Left alone, Marielle knelt by pond, cupped a handful of the cold water and splashed her face and neck. The water felt refreshing and helped to snap her back into the reality of her predicament. She looked about her. The area beyond the pond was dense with trees and wild overgrowth presenting no apparent escape route. *The blasted tyrant was right*, she thought. How could she leave Bea and her pups? She couldn't fathom the plan her captives had for her, but she seemed relatively safe for the time being. Her innate sense that she was more valuable to them unharmed kept her from losing her composure completely.

I must somehow convince them of their foolhardy ideas and the danger they are creating for themselves. Perchance, I could offer them escape upon my return and a few pounds or a gelding to appease them. Her mind scrambled for ideas. Then her thoughts turned to York's description of her physical appearance. She tried, with little success, to comb through her hair with damp fingers and control the errant curls.

"What's taking you so long?" York called out impatiently. "Perhaps you need some assistance?"

"I shall be right along. Another moment,

please." Marielle refocused on her present reality, finished her ablutions and found her way to the main path. With a brusque nod to her captor, she passed him and headed toward the cottage.

York found himself enjoying the view of her slender ankles as she lifted her skirt to avoid the tall grasses and climbed the hilly path. *I am going to enjoy this adventure immensely*, he thought, as he followed close behind.

Braum appeared at the top of the ridge that led to the pond. "Thought I'd come and see if you'd be needin' some 'elp with the wench," he called out to York.

Marielle gave him a steely glance as she clutched her skirts more firmly and continued towards the cottage, keeping her distance from the gruff intruder.

"Everything's under control," York said grinning, "though I don't remember feeling so heated up on such a brisk April morning."

"I can see why, Yorkie." Braum watched as Marielle skirted by him.

"Yes, I may need to take a douse in the pond before this day is over," York snickered as the men walked side by side. They reached the cottage just as Marielle slammed the door closed behind her.

Once inside, Marielle noted how the older man, George, who poured each a cup of coffee, catered to the brothers, even calling York, lord. *How strange*, Marielle thought, as she returned to attend to Beatrice and her litter, refusing to join them at the table.

After serving the men, George came to her side

and bent down to offer her some bread and cheese. Her hunger overcame her stubbornness and she gratefully accepted.

As she ate, she watched out of the corner of her eye and strained to hear as her captors' plotted in low voices. She heard them speak of ransom and mention her father's name. Occasionally, their eyes would dart over in her direction. She noted that York spoke little, his words measured, controlled. Martin, like his brother, seemed reserved, thoughtful, while Braum often became blustery, his tone harsher, yet he quieted with just a look from the other two.

Marielle felt depleted, mind and body, from the entire ordeal. She wondered how they could sit and talk about her as if she were a profitable parcel. Her inability to do anything about her situation infuriated her, kept her rigid, her eyes, at times, glaring at her captors until she finally gave in to her body's need for rest.

Her fight against exhaustion had not gone unnoticed. York saw when she finally lost the battle. He stood quietly, went to her, reached down and whisked her up.

Her eyes snapped open. She tried to resist.

"Don't fight, my midnight miss," York whispered in her ear. "You won't be harmed and you need some rest."

"I need to go home," she murmured as he tried to push against his broad shoulders, but he held her too close. "I cannot sleep. I…"

Before she could say more, he'd carried her to the cot, released her, urged her to lie down.

Marielle felt the warm pillow beneath her head, the woolen blanket he placed over her. She wanted to protest, needed to stay alert, but the warmth of fireplace, the heat of York's body and her exhaustion took hold.

Watching her as her eyes closed in sleep, York motioned the men to join him on the porch and out of Marielle's hearing.

Braum hadn't missed York's expression after he'd tended to Marielle. "That girl, she's a prize all right, to be bartered for a 'efty price. Don't you get soft on her Yorkie," he muttered, eyeing his friend.

"Getting rock hard on her would be more to my liking."

"Aye, she's a lush piece of property I'd like to settle onto mi'self, but first we need to decide what she's worth."

York glared at his partner, surprised by the protectiveness he felt toward his captive.

"The two of you need to control your lustful thoughts," Martin said wearily. "She's most likely a virgin and a quick turn with her could cost us more in the long run. I suggest you both take a cold soak so we can settle down and decide what's to be done with her. I've become quite comfortable in this place."

"I agree and we've done enough talking for now," York replied abruptly, aware that Martin was the only one of the three whose head remained clear.

The two men, noting the dismissal in York's voice, nodded to each other and walked off to the barn to complete their chores.

Once the men were out of sight, York leaned against the porch railing and stared at the closed cottage door, thinking over Martin's words. His brother was right. They'd become comfortable here. The tiny cottage, hidden from passing travelers, was an escape from the squalid conditions they'd endured in London. Money saved through odd jobs, gambling luck and an occasional "transfer of wealth" from the London gentlemen and their ladies on the roads gave them a roof over their heads and kept them from the poverty of the streets.

The young lady, now asleep on his cot, was obviously well bred, her family name, well respected. He remembered the name. The Henley estate actually bordered the estate he'd grown up in, at least until… It seemed so long ago.

His thoughts wandered to the distant past, to a time when he and his brother roamed their father's estate, teased and frustrated maids and butlers. He thought of the many hours he sat with his tutors learning the classics, mathematics, history, Latin. He remembered the grand dinners and guests in furs and glistening jewels, drinking and laughing in the banquet rooms, while he and Martin would peer through the railing in the upper gallery. He grinned to himself as he pictured them crouching, giggling as they looked down at the ladies' hair piled high on their heads like melting sand castles and at the gentlemen's distorted faces, while they attempted to sport the fashionable monocles. He and his brother would imitate the men as they danced with the over adorned, buxom matrons.

York's thoughts went to his father. He closed his eyes. Why were all these memories surfacing now? He allowed them to come, remembered his father's affectionate laughter, his patience on their first hunting expedition together, his careful instruction.

Then, as was always the case, his thoughts turned to the night he could never forget—the night the uniformed officials marched into the grand hall, grabbed his father by the collar and dragged him from the house. York clenched the railing as his mind relived the horror. He remembered them kicking his father to the ground, shoving him into a large black carriage where a waiting guard slammed the door, his father disappearing from his sight.

He couldn't forget the officials' self-righteous sneers as they peered back at his mother, bent to the ground, shrieking in agony. She'd held out her arms in a pleading gesture for mercy as the ominous carriage drove away, disappearing into the fog-shrouded night, her cries piercing the darkness. He, just eleven at the time, stared down at the deep ruts carved into the gravel path by the carriage wheels, the only visible sign left behind that this had been reality and not a horrible dream. He remembered how he held back tears, while his younger brother squirmed into his mother's arms and wailed in fear.

His mind relived the surreal days that followed. Only hushed whispers broke the heavy silence that hung like death over the hollow halls of the elegant Blackstone estate. The ornate rooms once filled with the young boys' laughter, dinner bells and chatting visitors, were dark and dismal. Servants hustled about hurriedly packing a few necessary belongings for Lady Blackstone and her children who would soon be forced from their home. When the armed guards arrived, they searched clothing and baggage. York remembered how they pulled and tore at his mother's cloak, filling their pockets with jewels their mother had secretly stitched into the folds with the hope that their value would keep them from starvation.

Nights that followed were spent with friends who reached out cautiously and curiously, but as news of the charges against Lord Blackstone spread, few were prepared to help, fearing reprisal. With the aid of their dedicated servant, George, York's mother found work and with the sale of her wedding ring and a jeweled pendant which had gone unnoticed by the guards, she secured a small unheated flat in the dreariest part of London. How he remembered the musty smell as they carried their meager belongings into the empty rooms.

The image of his father after his release two years later captured his thoughts. Stripped of his title and lands and wasting away in prison, he was no longer the tall, handsome aristocrat. His face and body reflected the ravages of prison life. His tired eyes bled tears of shame and humiliation. He was a broken man, feeble, sickly and now shunned by the society that once extolled him. His health, undermined by the cold dampness, poor nutrition and disease-carrying vermin, could not be restored.

York clenched his teeth unconsciously holding

back waves of emotion as the vision of his mother appeared in his mind's eye, her body racked with sobs as she gathered her beloved husband into her arms and held him close. He'd stood apart, watched silently, as his mother washed his father's withered body with tenderness and love. He listened as his father, with the little strength he had left, murmured words of love in return.

He was too young to do anything but watch and keep close to his younger brother who'd been prone to sickness since birth. But he absorbed all that occurred, kept his powerful emotions at bay, while a deep-seated hatred for the man responsible grew within him. Days later, as he sat by his dying father's bedside he made a vow to someday avenge his father's dishonor and the sorrow his family endured.

After his father's death, times grew worse. His mother's daily trek to the workhouse left her tired and weak. She struggled to keep her boys safe and healthy, but before long her strength waned. Her two sons stayed by her bedside, waiting, hoping for a miracle, only to wrap their arms around her dying body as she took her last breath. York remembered pulling his younger brother out of his mother's lifeless arms and into his own.

Why was the past invading his thoughts? This woman has already become a menace, he grumbled to himself. Ignoring common sense, he gave in to the pain of his past, allowed memories he'd packed away to surface.

He recalled taking the few shillings his mother saved and managed to convince the local undertaker to bury his mother beside his father's grave. Without money or work to pay the rent on the flat, he packed warm clothing and a heavy blanket and dragged Martin into the streets to find shelter. He'd already seen his share of young waifs sleeping on doorsteps and begging for food or a shilling. Now they would join the ranks of the homeless and if it weren't for their chance meeting with Braum, also a homeless orphan, but older and street smart, they might never have survived.

York continued to stare at the closed door, pictured his captive sleeping on his cot. *While she was spoiled and pampered*, he thought, *my brother and I used whatever device necessary to survive*. Fortunately, as the years passed, they developed keen friendships with street-smart hoodlums, the skills to live satisfactorily and the strategies to outwit the law.

Finding the cottage created an opportunity to live more decently. One rainy night when they were dodging a wealthy landowner who found them stealing three of his fine horses, they discovered the isolated cottage nestled in this deep valley, surrounded by trees, brush and overgrown nettles and right on the outskirts of London. It belonged to an old couple struggling to make ends meet. The sickly man, suffering from a back injury and his wife, appreciated the help offered by the men who appeared at their door asking for shelter from the rain. Their stay lengthened as the couple befriended them.

The men fixed up the cottage so in need of repair. It became a quiet reprieve from odd jobs and the constant thieving. Soon they were taking care of the grounds, planting and hunting for food. All were content for a time. Within a year, however, the old man died and his wife left to stay with a sister in town. York was left in charge of the cottage and except for sending a small rent to the old woman, it became their home.

Yes, York thought, this was their home now. They'd found a measure of peace. Now it seemed this minx had stirred up the past, caused this restless fire within him.

She's a beauty and in kidnapping her, I've compromised her, perhaps ruined her in the eyes of society. What have I become – a thief, a rake of the worst kind, now a kidnapper? It hardly matters, except…my father.

York turned around, stared out at the fields before him.

No, his death destroyed any civility I might have claimed. His thoughts returned to his captive as he turned the door-handle to enter. *She'll be returned and for a pretty penny.*

Chapter Three

MARIELLE'S EYES FLEW open. She looked about, remembered York carrying her and her weakness at allowing it. The thoughts struck her briefly as she realized that little had changed. The men were sitting at the table just as they'd been before, though she sensed a change. The room was cooler, darker. The sun must be setting. How long had she slept?

York, Martin and Braum were bent over the table discussing their possibilities and concerns quietly, but the serious undertones of their dialogue could not be mistaken. Marielle thought it best to pretend she was still sleeping. Maybe she could learn their scheme and use it for her escape.

"Lord Henley will surely pay a handsome ransom for his daughter but it's a risky plan and I'm not convinced it's a wise one. If it works, we should be comfortable for a long while. If not, I'd prefer not to think of the consequences." Martin said shaking his head in concern. "I'd like to see her back with her father as soon as possible."

"I agree with Martin, York, but it's a shame we can't keep `er for a time," Braum mused. "She's pleasin' to the eyes with those long auburn locks and the rest of 'er causes mi' blood to 'eat up. I sure'd like to take a turn or two with the wench."

"This pretty package is no wench." York snapped. He didn't like the way Braum leered at her, not one bit. "We need to keep our mind on our goal."

Braum grimaced, but eventually joined in on the rest of the discussion. He was well aware of what York was capable of if someone defied him. When he first found York and his brother on the streets, they knew nothing of what was in store for them, but York learned fast and soon gained respect not only from Braum but also from the more ruthless and experienced hoodlums. He became a formidable opponent to fellow thieves who attempted to rob them of their night's profits or hone in on their territory. As he matured, he widened his horizons finding greater prosperity in highway robberies. York put enough fear into his victims to encourage their speedy relinquishment of valuables while allowing them to maintain their dignity. He found little resistance to his requests. Through the years the men shared a mutual camaraderie, but Braum also knew not to cross him and when to step back.

"We need to consider all angles if we're to take full advantage of this opportunity," York advised. "Then, we'll ask a handsome price. She deserves no less."

With a pause in their conversation, York turned his gaze to Marielle and caught her eyes flicker and close tightly. She was awake, he thought, the little twitch. He stood and walked casually over to the cot and bent down too close for Marielle's comfort.

"Perhaps I will find out right now if she desires

me," York crooned softly into her ear.

Opening her eyes wide, Marielle gathered herself for battle, until she saw York wink and step back.

"Have you been awake long, Miss Henley?"

"It's none of your concern and furthermore, you will not succeed with your foolish plan. My father has powerful connections. He is a man to be reckoned with. He'll not allow himself to be taken advantage of by petty thieves. You will be drawn and quartered if he has his way!"

"Ah, drawn and quartered? Petty thieves? Why, looking at our night's catch, I would say I've moved much beyond the level of petty thief. In fact, I would wager that your father will gladly open his coffers to have you returned safe and sound. Unless, of course, he finds you as hotheaded and difficult as I find your behavior. Perhaps I've done him a favor."

Marielle sucked in her breath and grew wide-eyed. A stab of apprehension silenced her. She recollected how her father disappeared more and more into his own pain since her mother's and sister's deaths leaving a shell of the man she'd once adored. Could she be just a burden or a reminder of what he'd lost? Would he carry out a prolonged search for her, or give up and dissolve into his drink? She looked away, lifted her chin, tried to hide the jolt of pain that threatened to weaken her resolve. Her quivering bottom lip, however, betrayed her.

York saw the cloud of sadness settle on her lovely face. "Now, now, my midnight miss, have I touched a tender chord?"

She turned, glared. "Most definitely not. I was only thinking how much I...I miss my father. You are cruel to..." Marielle could say no more. His look told her that she'd failed in her attempt to regain her composure.

"Have you noticed how often you leave a sentence unfinished? Are your thoughts as disconnected and irrational as your conversation?" York asked with a smirk. He much preferred the obstinate side of his feisty captive.

"Irrational? The conversation I've listened to in this room has been nothing but irrational and insane." Marielle snapped back as she sat up straighter, her back rigid, her lips pursed.

York smiled, pleased that he had succeeded in giving her back her dignity and control. "Perhaps you are correct. Time will tell if our insanity pays off."

He watched as she brushed her tangled curls from her face. He felt a pang of guilt for being the one to cause her such anxiety. He refrained from the impulse to touch her, feel the softness of her cheek, the silkiness of her skin, or to turn his thoughts into action. *Such a lovely face, he thought, lips red, moist and slightly swollen from her fit of anger.* His body reacted, causing him discomfort as he adjusted his position. He fingered an errant curl and brushed it from her eyes, gray green in the dim light.

Marielle's shoulders stiffened.

"Such silky curls, so soft," York whispered drawing closer.

She froze, not just from his alluring tone, but from her body's reaction towards his nearness. Her mind was drawing a curtain over her common sense. Afraid of her conflicting emotions, she pushed him away.

York pulled back. He felt the energy between them, but the magic melted as a shadow passed over them.

Braum moved closer. She didn't miss his condescending look or the knife in his hand as he turned toward York.

"A snip of a curl and a brief note will be an apt message to deliver. What do you say, York? The feel of one of those curly locks should 'elp Lord 'enley to digest the news that 'is pretty daughter is in unsavory 'ands." Braum reached out to grab one of Marielle's hands. "In fact, a few drops o' blood from a dainty finger will be more convincing. Meanwhile we can add polish to our plan."

Unaware of his protective action, York twisted around and grabbed the knife, brushing Braum aside.

"Be damned, York, keep your 'ead on straight, if the prize is to be won. She's bait and booty. That's it. If you want 'er for your pleasure, it's a shame we can't all share in the prize. But, as you said, we need to secure our future." Braum turned and glared at Marielle. "Don't forget that it's people like 'er, who 'ave been spared the 'ard life, who 'ave treated us like dogs to be spat on!"

York turned, slanting his eyes toward Braum. "Enough. I fully understand our mission and I know exactly what we will achieve. It isn't necessary for us to act like the dogs they think we are. You must remember we get nothing if she is harmed." He paused, looked down at Marielle, considered his partner's words, reached down and held one long, careless curl and sliced through it. Ignoring the stunned look on Marielle's face, he turned to Braum. "Use a drop of blood from the mutt."

"You monster!" Marielle screamed as she jumped up to run to Beatrice.

York held her back firmly with one arm.

"Please! Do not touch my pet, nor add more to the suffering my father has already endured." She pushed against his arm, dived under, rushed to her pet's side while continuing her tirade. "Furthermore, Richard, my betrothed, will stop at nothing to find me. His father, Lord Craymore, will spare no expense to hunt you down like dogs!"

Marielle paused, suddenly aware of the suffocating silence in the room.

Braum and Martin stood, their eyes glued to her face, both waiting for York's reaction.

York's face became a cold, hard mask. His fists clenched to his sides. Breaking the silence, he slammed one fist down on the table as he walked slowly towards her.

She could see the smoldering fury burning in his eyes. Her body cringed.

Reaching down, he grabbed her by the shoulders, lifted her towards him, his face hardened to stone. He held her tightly in his grip, hurting her. He remained unmoving, clutching her shoulders as his mind replayed the name

Craymore. He learned long ago the importance of staying in control, to plan carefully, stay clearheaded, never to allow anyone to see his ravaged insides. Now, hearing the name he hated more than the evil he found packaged in the cut throats he dealt on the streets, caused him to nearly lose the self-control he'd mastered. His mind raced. *Could this be the moment I have been waiting for?* His lips barely moved as he loosened his hold, slowly lowering her to the floor.

Marielle felt the ground beneath her, his arms still holding her rigid form.

He whispered, "You are betrothed to Craymore's son?"

She nodded, unable to mouth a word of assent.

Yes, the time has finally come, York thought, as his breath caught and then relaxed. Finally, he would taste the sweetness of revenge. Gaining mastery over his emotions, he let go of Marielle and turned his back to her.

Stunned by his reaction, she sank down onto the rug near the fireplace, near Beatrice and her pups, comforting herself in the warmth they offered.

York pulled out a chair and straddled it, glared at his captive before addressing her in a tightly controlled voice. "Craymore's son. His firstborn and heir?"

"Yes," Marielle answered a touch of haughty indignation in her feeble utterance. "My father…it's been arranged since I was fourteen." Marielle sat up straighter, returned his glare. "Why am I telling you this? He will surely go to any lengths to find me. You must see the folly of your plan. Return me to where you first found me and I'll not whisper a word of what has transpired."

Before she could breathe a sigh and continue, York rose from his seat, moved with one powerful stride to the fireplace, reached down and prepared to grab her by the throat.

Marielle's breath caught.

York knew he'd better leave…fast. He turned abruptly and without a word, walked out the cottage door.

Braum and Martin, both watching the drama unfold, followed silently.

Marielle, alone at last, pressed her cheeks against Bea's warm coat in disbelief and despair. She couldn't mistake York's reaction to her words. His rage could hardly be concealed. She stood and looked out the window. The men were not in sight, only the darkening sky, the open land, the trees, the distant hills. She reached for the door, locked. She rattled it, cursed at it, knowing an attempt at escape was fruitless. She looked around the room. Perhaps a weapon could be found, nothing, but a kitchen knife. She held it, thought of her revenge, slipped it under the cot mattress.

York and Martin, with George following behind, returned hours later without Braum. They found Marielle sitting on the cot, wrapped in the woolen blanket. The fire had died, leaving only glowing coals. Her face revealed her discomfort, her anger.

"We've left the lady too long," Martin acknowledged, giving Marielle a sympathetic nod and noting the depleted wood stack near the fireplace. Without a word, he left to retrieve more logs while George prepared supper.

York glanced briefly at Marielle before sitting at the table. Braum had been sent off to meet with Jasper Griggs, an unsavory but loyal conspirator they'd had occasion to work within the past. For the right price, Griggs could be trusted to deliver a message to Lord Henley demanding a price for her return, but Henley's daughter had much more to offer than a ransom. *The game shall begin*, thought York.

He stood at Martin's return and walked to the fireplace to stoke the dying embers as his brother restocked the woodpile. Soon the fire blazed and the smell of beef stew filled the air. Both men sat in silence, barely touching the food George set before them. There was little left to be said. The waiting had begun.

Marielle refused to leave the cot, reluctantly accepting a dish from George. She picked at the meal, still attempting to grasp the change in York's demeanor since she'd revealed her relationship with Richard.

After the meal, York walked out to the porch. He stood, arms held snug against his chest, staring at the moon's light that wrapped around the pond. His somber mood was reflected in the dark muted tones of night, in the ripple of the water stirred by the wind.

He knew Braum wouldn't return for hours from his errand. If he'd made contact with Griggs, he'd probably stay for a time in the city to entertain himself at Sherry's Place.

With the land walled in darkness, York went inside, saw that Marielle had given up the stubborn pose she'd held since dinner. Now curled up on the cot, she'd fallen asleep. He found a bottle of whiskey, poured himself a glass and settled into one of the chairs by the fire. Martin, wise enough to realize York needed time alone, left to help George with chores in the stable.

She should wake with a healthy appetite, York thought, having noted that she barely touched her supper. The firelight dramatized her delicate features and enhanced the reddish highlights in her hair. *She's damned attractive*, York mused and not scrawny either, tall, shapely and delightfully strong-willed. He enjoyed their confrontations, her spunk and even her chatter, not the silence that pervaded the cottage since his new found revelation.

It had been a long time since he'd been with an innocent. Clarisse, who worked at Sherry's Place, was available to him whenever he returned to London. She'd come to know him on the streets before she took up the profession and encouraged York's visits, admirably taking care of his needs. York treated Clarisse like a lady and she, in return, doted on him as she would one of the lords. She would easily brush another aside when York arrived and he often helped to remove a customer who didn't follow the rules of the house. The arrangement worked well for both of them.

Clarisse, however, was far from his mind as he gazed lustfully at Marielle. The irony of the situation, York mused, Craymore's future daughter-in-law, here, stirring up all the ghosts of the past. Finally, he would face his demons and put them to rest.

Tonight the demons reared up. The vision of his father deteriorated like a crumbling statue haunted him. The memories of his beautiful mother scraping together pennies by doing others' dirty work, even begging to be able to feed her children until her face became drawn and her body weakened from her own hunger, still caused nightmares. He remembered her tears as she bundled young Martin up in her worn cloak during one of his coughing spells, holding him tightly to her breast, praying that the dampness that permeated their cold flat would not be absorbed into his frail body. Her prayers never ceased, but eventually she lost her own battle, dying of pneumonia just before Martin's eleventh birthday. He thought of her final prayer. Please Lord, take pity on my beloved sons. Meaningless, York thought, just like so many other prayers his mother uttered during those years. She died. They survived, but without a prayer. His faith died with his mother's last breath.

After the loss of his parents, finding warm shelter or a scrap of food was close to impossible until the day he stole a loaf of bread and two apples from a street vendor. Racing away, he stumbled and would have been accosted if he hadn't knocked over another vendor's table distracting his pursuers. He dodged into an alley where Martin waited, not knowing that Braum, a stranger to them at the time, was on his trail. York's first reaction when the intruder came upon them was to shield Martin and prepare to fight. Unexpectedly, he heard stout laughter as the older boy crouched down and stared at the two. York, then only a boy of fourteen, attempted to swing at him. Braum grabbed his arm and told him to save his strength for when it was needed. York smiled at the memory. From then on the three became inseparable. Braum taught them where to bed for the night, obtain food and how to pick pockets with finesse. Most importantly he taught them how to survive the streets.

Despite their actions necessary for survival, neither York nor Martin could completely wipe away the tenets taught in their noble childhood left behind, their mother's wisdom, or their father's guidance. The contradictions tore at their souls, while, at the same time, they accepted their new way of life. They'd beaten the streets, but York never overcame his obsession for revenge.

The whiskey eased his tension. He had no wish to harm Marielle but with the news of her betrothal to the son of Ward Craymore, the man who destroyed his family, she'd become his enemy, or at least his pawn. He stared over at the cot, noted the position in which she slept. Her bodice had loosened revealing a glimpse of lush breasts now highlighted by the firelight. In her fetal position, each deep breath caused the creamy mounds to swell. The thought of pulling at the ties that kept them bound brought an aching to his loins.

Perhaps I'll take her for my own after the matter is

settled. It seems fitting for me to spoil her for young Craymore. Everything that is meant to be his someday should be mine. A chill went through him and not just from excitement and expectancy.

The fire was going out. He rose to his feet to attend to the dying embers. When the fire glowed once again, he walked over to Marielle, drew the blanket over her and sat watching her until his eyes grew heavy. Drawn by her warmth, he stretched out beside her and, before long, fell asleep.

When Martin returned an hour later, he took in the sight and withdrew himself quietly, deciding it would be better to spend the night in the barn.

SHE'D LOST HER *way in a maze of trees until she reached a cave. The opening was small, but she fit in perfectly and found safety and comfort.* As sunlight seeped in through the cottage windows, Marielle began to stir. She snuggled deeper into the cave, but the morning light pulled her from her dream. The reality of the moment hit like a lightning bolt. She tried to lift her body, but she was trapped beneath York's arm draped across her middle, his chin resting on her shoulder. She tried to wriggle free which made matters only worse.

York, still in a heavy sleep, moved closer, draping a powerful leg over her own. She could smell his manly scent, his potent presence. *Heaven's angels, deliver me*, she pleaded silently. Slowly, carefully, she tried to lift York's muscular arm, only to have him snuggle closer. She tried turning towards him, hoping to wriggle out of his grasp, inch her way to the foot of the bed and onto the floor. This made matters only worse.

York's eyes opened slowly. He yawned, stretched, turned, found himself nose to nose with his captive. It took him only a moment to recall the previous night, to shake off sleep. He said nothing, waited, not wanting to move away.

His searching eyes startled her, captivated her. A mixture of shock and curiosity captured her senses. His eyes, however, told her that he too found the situation disarming.

York lifted his arm, drew it gently, caressingly, across her breast, touched his finger to her parted lips.

"You are beautiful in the morning, so very beautiful," his voice a soothing whisper before he brought his mouth down to hers.

The kiss, soft, tender, his lips barely brushing her own caused Marielle to push away conscious thought. He deepened the kiss and her body responded, tingled, vibrating deep into her womanly core.

Slowly, he parted her lips with his tongue, urged its way in to touch hers. York felt her submission, drew closer, his kiss becoming more demanding. His free hand reached to cup her breast, felt her nipple harden. He circled it softly, stroked, moved to capture the fullness of the other.

Her body shuddered, pleasure gripping her. She opened to each new sensation, then, as quickly, her mind woke from the brief touch of heaven to the reality of the situation.

York felt her body stiffen. He hesitated, drew back slowly, then wrapped his arms loosely about her, allowing his own body to cool down.

She tried to move away but found herself caught under the blanket he still held down with his body.

Rising on one elbow, he stared down into her face, saw her bottom lip tremble. The urge to comfort her surprised him. He reached for her, but she pulled back. He could see the confusion in her eyes, then fear. He smiled down at her, spoke softly. "I am accustomed to sleeping here. I must have... I assure you I was a complete gentleman." He hesitated, "At least, I think I was."

"This morning you proved otherwise," Marielle's voice disguising the turmoil she felt.

"You didn't seem to mind my advances. In fact, I'd say that you were as entranced as I," York chortled.

"I was caught unaware. My opinion of you has not changed in the least."

"Not even in the slightest?" York touched her cheek, drawing his palm slowly down to her neck, her shoulder, brushing her hair aside before removing his hand. Marielle shivered at his touch, drew away. "You took advantage. I detest you even more. Now, please, allow me to get up."

"Ah, yes, this is a scandalous situation. Your fiancé would be outraged. He would quite possibly rethink his commitment if he saw the fire of desire in your eyes that I saw only moments ago."

Marielle, touched, unwillingly, by the truth of his words, lunged at him, pushing him away with all the force she could muster.

He barely moved. A lazy smile crossed his face

as he lifted himself from the bed, his eyes still transfixed upon her, his body hovering over hers as he reached down to gently stroke her chin.

She didn't miss his tender gaze, the heat of his touch, then, as quickly, she watched as the muscles in his face became rigid and he straightened, stood to his full height and turned from her, walked away.

Marielle stared numbly at this paradox of a man. He was a tyrant, but despite the reality of the situation, she sensed decency and she couldn't deny her response to his closeness, his touch. She had to know more...

"York?"

He turned, surprised. "That's the first time you've spoken my name." He stared, tried to read the look in her eyes, lost the struggle to calm his emotions. In one quick stride, he stood over her, reached down, lifted her in his arms, kissed her roughly, hungrily.

Marielle knew she should resist. Instead, she clung to him, erased intruding thoughts, allowed herself to be swept up into his arms.

When the kiss ended, York held her close, said nothing. Using every bit of constraint within him, he let her go. Now was not the time to lose control. He felt, believed, that her desire for him was almost as strong as his own, despite her innocence and he had no doubt that she was an innocent. A smile played on his lips. "You haven't told me your name."

She hesitated. "Marielle."

"As lovely as you are."

He planted a tender kiss on her forehead. "Forgive me, my sweet Marielle, for what I must do." Forcing himself to control the urges of his body and the throbbing in his groin, he refocused his mind towards his goal. He turned his back to her, leaving her speechless.

The sound of horses commanded their attention. Minutes later Martin entered followed by Braum. York eyed the two men. Without a word, York knew the message had been delivered. Fully dressed from the night before, York grabbed a towel and headed out towards the pond for a cold swim.

Chapter Four

"It won't be long now, missy. You'll be out of our 'ands and we'll be into a 'efty sum."

Marielle glared at Braum wanting to spit into his gloating face. Instead she chose to ignore him. She had too much to think about. Martin, who remained silent, made coffee, while Braum filled him in on his short escapade to London the night before.

An hour passed before York's return. He barely made it through the door when Marielle demanded time alone. She drew Bea to her side, leaving the pups wriggling alone in their bed, skirted around York and walked out, slamming the door behind her, not missing a careless comment from Braum or another from York telling him to let her be.

While Bea ran on ahead Marielle quickened her steps to the pond, her thoughts a mass of confusion. *He'd been there, with me, through the night. What audacity to take advantage of my exhaustion! But, I allowed him to kiss me. Worse, I enjoyed it!* She slowed, a sinking feeling rose in her chest. *What am I to do?*

Richard had kissed her, more than once. They were pleasant enough, but his kisses had never ignited the passion she felt in York's embrace. She stopped, picked a wild flower along the path, twirled it in her hands, touched it to her face and breathed in its scent. Her body stirred with the memories of York's touch, still felt the warmth of his lips on hers. She couldn't deny her attraction to him or the glow she felt from the first truly womanly experience that went beyond her mind but simmered in her body.

When she reached the pond, she had a sudden impulse to bathe, to wash away the shame of her impulsive behavior. She removed her dress and petticoats and with only her thin undergarments waded into the pond. Despite the shiver that went through her, she felt relief. She swam beneath the water reveling in the numbness and the mindless moments of total oblivion, surfacing only long enough to catch her breath. Time escaped her, only the soothing freshness of the cold water freed her from the reality of her predicament.

A loud splash brought her back to reality. A strong arm grabbed her about the waist, pulled her to the surface and dragged her to shore. She could hear Bea barking as York laid her down on the grassy slope. She looked up into his face and shrieked.

"You!" She pounded on his chest, only to have him draw her more tightly to him warming her shivering body.

"My God, I thought you were drowning," York spat out. Your hound ran back to the house without you."

"Oh, heavens, poor Bea. I forgot. I wasn't thinking, but I certainly was not drowning. My father taught me how to swim as a child. I did not need to be saved!" Marielle's voice shook, her lips quivering from the cold. "I must get out of here. I will plead with my father. He'll give you whatever you want. You can just go away and leave me alone!"

"You must stay until the time is right," York said coldly.

"Why? So you can drain what life my father still has left in him?" Marielle words seethed from her shivering lips. She could no longer contain the turmoil within her or her own emotions that betrayed her. "You have no understanding of a family bond. I can only imagine what my father must be going through right now. He's already lost my mother, my sister... How could you possibly understand?"

"Perhaps I understand more than you think." He had no desire to tell her of his own losses, that he'd been there too, felt the loneliness and emptiness when a family's torn by death and separation.

"Are you so insensitive?" Marielle continued, ignoring his response. "My father has never stopped mourning. He was unable to go on, unable to see me..." She stopped. *What am I saying? I am being undone.* "What kind of a man are you? Were you reared by beasts? Was your own father as cruel? Have you no understanding of what you are doing to my family, my fiancé?'

"Stop!" York barked, clenching her arms so tightly she could barely breathe.

"Let me go! Can't you see that you're hurting me?"

York loosened his hold, but hardened his heart, a more natural state, a state he'd found to be his salvation. Through clenched teeth, he whispered slowly, gruffly, in a measured tone. "If you care at all about your safety, you must never say a word against my father. Do you understand?"

"I...I'm s-orry. I did not mean to..." Marielle felt his simmering rage, shivered in fear. "I must leave this place!"

York wrapped his arms around her, held her close. She didn't resist. He believed despite the way they'd come together, or his own treachery at taking her away from her home, that they both wanted more. He knew he'd overreacted to her words, frightened her. But, she'd responded to his touch when she awoke in his arms. Now, he wanted to lay her down, take her, set her on fire, feel her need of him too, but the mention of the Craymore name... She had unknowingly opened a wound he'd spent years covering up.

As a measure of calm returned, he broke the silence. "I'd like to go home too, my true home. I desire to walk the lands my father and I walked together and touch the rich mahogany banister that Martin and I slid down when we were children, much to my mother's chagrin." He smiled as the old images came to mind, then his body stiffened. Why was he telling her this? He'd been careful never to reveal his vulnerability to another nor allow himself the luxury of sentimentality.

The air seemed colder between them. Marielle looked into his eyes, saw a cloud of pain pass through, then anger. She kept silent, waited to hear more.

"But your damned future father-in-law made that impossible and I will correct the injustice. He'll suffer just as my family has done. You've become the key to correcting a grievous wrong and I'll let nothing stand in my way until I've avenged that wrong. Regretfully, you've become the catalyst to reach my goal, but I will reach it. Craymore is going to suffer for his evil deeds."

"What are you saying? Lord Craymore has been our neighbor and a respected member of the *ton* for many years. How could someone like you...?

"Why would a scoundrel like me have any connection with a lord and gentleman such as Craymore? A man held in such high esteem by the king and the courts?"

"I didn't mean it quite that way. I mean...you're not at all common. Actually, you're quite a contradiction. You can be brutish and yet your language and even your bearing is more like that of a nobleman. I don't understand any of this, or you."

"You might say I've lived a double life. My earlier life was very different from my life on the streets. Quite contradictory, I must admit," York grimaced at his admission.

"One minute, your behavior is demonic, the next considerate, almost tenderhearted."

York loosened his grip and sat down on the bank facing her, grinning at her choice of words. "Tenderhearted? Hmn, I must be more careful to protect my sinister image. I assure you, I can be quite sinister." He reached out, grasped her hands in his.

Bea, seeing a place in which to settle, crawled between them. The friction between them turned to laughter as Bea's bottom wriggled into the comfortable spot.

York stared at Marielle, at her moist lips. His eyes slid down over her body. Her damp chemise clung to her, outlining her full breasts, her nipples lifting upward beneath the thin gauze.

Marielle followed his eyes, gasped, grabbed Bea to cover herself.

York, a wide unabashed grin settling on his handsome face and acutely aware of his own arousal, stood, looked about, found her garments and tossed them to her.

"I'll take Bea back to her pups and give you time to make yourself presentable."

Marielle pushed Bea swiftly towards him and scrambled to her feet holding her garments clumsily against her. As she dressed, she could hear his laughter fading in the distance. "Damn him to hell," she muttered, as she attempted to swirl her wet, tangled hair into a chignon and straighten her damp and wrinkled garments.

Meanwhile, her mind replayed York's words concerning Lord Craymore, his father and her role. What could her future father-in-law have done to his family? Yet, she could not dismiss his admissions or ignore the disturbing feelings he aroused in her. Worse, she realized she didn't want to.

When Marielle entered the cottage, the men

were seated around the table again in deep conversation. Martin and Braum looked warily at Marielle and then at York.

"Don't be distracted by her presence," York said calmly. "She's as much a part of this as we are. We may not have her cooperation, but we do have her and that's all we need for now." The other men nodded in agreement.

"Griggs should reach 'enley by noon tomorrow. If 'e agrees to our conditions the money will be in our 'ands in no time," Braum said confidently. "We'll leave a message about where they can find 'er after we're on the road. Are you agreein' with me, York? Unless, of course, you've changed your mind and 'ave decided to keep 'er. I do think she's taken a fancy to you."

Before Marielle, who'd taken a seat by the fireplace, could protest, York intervened.

"I've other plans. After we've collected the ransom, prepare to leave. I'll meet up with both of you eventually. The lady will come with me."

Martin glared at York. "I know what you're thinking. It's too dangerous. You must give up this obsession. If Henley agrees to our demands and no doubt he will if he cares for his daughter, we have a chance to begin again and enough money to live in comfort." He stopped to look over at Marielle before turning his attention back to York. "Henley can easily afford to lose a bit of his wealth and we'll have the opportunity to put the stench of the streets behind us for good."

"And justice will not be served," York growled. "This opportunity won't come again. I'll meet you at the destination we've discussed as soon as my business is settled."

Martin slammed his fist on the table. "Your business, as you put it, is mine also! If it must be done, we'll do it together." He leaned down and stared into his older brother's eyes. "I may not have your deep need to recapture what we've lost, but you're my brother. I'll not let you meet your demons alone."

Marielle watched in awe as the two brothers argued. More questions gathered in her mind. If York was telling the truth, how could he possibly recover his family's loss? How would she fit into this? Curiosity began to replace her indignation.

Before she could attempt a question, Martin slammed out the door. Braum and York sat in silence until they heard him ride away.

"Damn!" York rose to go after him, but Braum grabbed hold of his arm.

"'E'll be okay, York. Let 'im vent some steam."

"Hell! Who knows what foolhardy thoughts he has in his head? I'm going after him."

As York headed for the door, Braum cursed under his breath and followed him. Marielle heard their horses gallop away. She sat staring at the closed door, stunned and alone, with nowhere to go.

Chapter Five

MARIELLE PACED, FEELING useless, neither able to escape nor take part in the mystery that now captured her thoughts. She recalled how York's facial features hardened at the mention of the Craymore name. Admittedly, rumors surrounding Lord Craymore were far from flattering. Her own father grimaced whenever he had to entertain him and the few times she'd conversed with Richard's father, he flattered, offered polite conversation, but she felt a discomfort in his presence.

When her thoughts turned to York, different feelings intruded causing her body to shudder, a pleasurable sensation, maddening! *What was she to do*, she wondered. Her attraction to York was insane, but undeniable and she had to admit that she'd begun to believe his story. Gerald and Matty often warned her that her rebellious nature would be her undoing. Now she wanted to toss aside all propriety. She wanted more of this man who muddled her senses.

Time passed slowly. Frustrated and bored, she walked over to the fireplace to check on Beatrice and her pups. She added a log to the fire, discovered a few books on a shelf, picked one, sat and read for a time until Beatrice began nuzzling against her, wagging her tail. Marielle smiled. Bea needed a walk and she did too.

It was dark when the men returned. All were in a somber mood except for George who started preparing a meal. After dinner George and Braum cleaned up and left for the barn. Martin and York removed to the porch.

Her anger flared as she peered out the window and saw the two brothers talking. She still knew nothing of what was going on and she couldn't stand one more minute of it. She jerked open the door, crashing into York.

"And where are you going in such a huff?" York questioned, catching her in his arms.

Marielle's words caught in her throat, her hands pressed into him, while his arms went instantly about her waist. She gathered her wits, pushed against his chest to back away.

"I want to hear what you're planning! I have every right to know what's going to happen to me."

"Why don't we shut the door before we let in the cold air." York urged Marielle back, closed the door behind him and loosened his hold, slightly.

Marielle looked up, glared into his eyes, stood rigid, unmoving. She didn't want to be alone, but she also didn't want to be alone with him and right now he was much too close. "You haven't answered my question and..." she hesitated, noticeably uncomfortable. Where's your brother? Will he be returning?"

"Which question would you like me to answer first?" York questioned, a gleam in his eyes. "Are you more concerned with what we're planning to do with you, or being alone with me tonight?"

"I am not afraid of you," she said, her voice betraying her. "I know that I am much too valuable to you to be harmed."

"You're quite right, but could there be other reasons for your discomfort in my presence?" York still held her, now at arm's length. "Do you know that the light of the fire enhances your beauty and your hair? I much prefer it when it falls over your shoulders." He pulled at her chignon, causing her hair to fall recklessly to her shoulders.

"How dare you take such liberty?" Marielle pushed her hair back, stepped out of his reach. York stepped closer, reached for her.

With the cot just behind her, Marielle was trapped. She pursed her lips and crossed her arms. "Do you mean to take advantage of me?"

"Only if it's what you desire." York smiled mischievously, lifted her chin, before lowering his head to gently capture her lips.

Marielle knew she should push him away, lifted her arms to his chest to do so, felt the gentleness of his kiss, tasted, wrapped her arms about his shoulders and returned his kiss.

York drew her down onto the cot, gathered her to him, easing her mouth open to receive his tongue. Her breath caught, her body responding instinctively.

York, enticed by her response, deepened the kiss, felt the firmness of her breasts against his chest, caressed, slowly easing her bodice down, lightened his kiss, moving his lips down her neck as he savored her scent, moved lower, found the small brown nubs, laved them, kissed, fondled.

Marielle shuddered, dug her fingers into his back, while her body surrendered.

He lifted his head, captured her lips again, as his hands moved down her body, relishing in the touch of her. He lifted her skirt slowly while his kisses became more urgent.

Startled, his touch too new, his effect on her too powerful, she tensed.

York felt the change, forced his mind back. *She's a virgin. What the hell am I doing?* He drew his hands back too abruptly, pulled her skirt down. Still holding her, he forced restraint.

Taking the younger Craymore's betrothed had its temptations, but it was more. His desire for Marielle went beyond a mere victory. She fascinated him more than any woman he'd ever met. He enjoyed her spunk, admired her courage, her beauty. His feelings were going deeper, too fast and this was not at all wise. He stared into her eyes, saw her confusion, loosened his hold and lay back on the pillow, one arm above his head.

Marielle felt suddenly embarrassed, her thoughts muddled. *Does he find me unattractive*, she wondered. Perhaps she'd been clumsy in her kisses.

York rose slowly, refused to look at her. He wanted her, but it wasn't the right time. He sat on the edge of the cot, his back to her.

Marielle twisted away, adjusted her clothing, her body still reacting to his touch, her mind in turmoil.

York broke the silence between them. "I didn't

answer your earlier question. By tomorrow evening, I should have some answers for you."

Marielle, shaken by his rejection but unwilling to let him see her hurt, gathered her wits, tried to ignore what just passed between them. Anger replaced her insecurity. "I don't want to spend one more day here."

"I thought you were beginning to enjoy my company." He smiled, knew he was goading her. She had gotten under his skin and he had other things to think about.

"You are truly ruthless."

"No, but I am determined, my sweet Marielle." He touched her cheek, softened his expression, wanted to say more. Instead, he turned and left the cottage. Marielle, more confused than ever, stared numbly after him.

It was early morning before anyone returned. George prepared breakfast while the men went about their chores. York said little during the meal and all could feel the tension in the air. Marielle chose silence, knowing it was a waste of time to question them. Keeping a watchful eye on her kidnappers and attending to the pups consumed her time.

Martin walked over to check the fire, reaching down to pet Beatrice and laughing at her squirmy little pups that were falling all over themselves. His attention and gentle manner towards Bea and her pups had not gone unnoticed. Bea, without even a growl, allowed him to pick up some of her tiny ones.

Marielle was warming up to York's younger brother. She noticed that he seemed uncomfortable with York's plan. Whatever it was, she was still in the dark. As he added more wood to the fire, she thought, he is almost as handsome as York, the strong chiseled jaw, high cheekbones, the mass of dark hair, his eyes a misty gray. He's lankier, his manner more congenial, especially when York and Braum are not present. She noticed that he tended to step back until it was his time to take part. She sensed no weakness about him. At times he demonstrated a patient wisdom, his dialogue with the other two marked not by a conciliatory manner, but more as a mediator.

Even Braum whom she feared most had leaned his greater bulk down to her pets, snuggled his ruddy face and bristly red whiskers against Bea's fur and spoke tender words to the pups. He showed a special admiration for the runt of the litter, talked about keeping the "wee one" for his own. Marielle bristled at his words, ready to do battle, but held back.

York noted her reaction. Waiting until Braum left the cottage, he sat near her and told her a little about his friend's background. Braum believed his mother had been forced into prostitution because she was without a husband to give her protection and financial support. His father, a Scottish sailor, had been around for only a short time before deserting her. When Braum was old enough to realize that he was in the way of his mother's "profession", he left and took to the streets. With a growing boy around, she couldn't deny her age and her customers were disapproving. He grew up despising the wealthy, powerful nobles who used and tossed aside women like his mother.

York's explanation helped Marielle curb her reactions to his rough mannerisms and surly behavior. At times she even felt compassion for her captors. Like the animals of the woods, they were forced to survive in whatever way they found necessary.

AFTER LUNCH THE men left the cottage saying only that they'd be back after dark. Marielle watched as they rode away and disappeared from sight. Alone again, she paced for a time before resigning herself to having nothing to do but wait. If only she knew what was going on.

She sat on the porch until she became chilled, sat by the fire and read for a time, even napped restlessly, her mind unable to stop even in sleep until she heard Bea whimpering. "Oh, Bea, I haven't forgotten you." As she prepared to take her for a walk, she heard a soft knock at the door.

Old George, as he was affectionately called by the men, knocked again before opening the door slightly. "Ah, you're up and about lass. He bent down with some difficulty to scratch Beatrice's head. "What do you say we take her out for a bit of a run? Ha, but she'll be do the runnin' for sure."

"I would enjoy the company and I could use some fresh air, Marielle said, giving the older man a smile, while considering the opportunity to obtain information while the others were away.

George held the door opened for her while Bea

ran out, her tail wagging in delight. They followed the path to the pond, Bea running happily at their side or circling them playfully. George laughed jovially at the dog's antics, while Marielle pondered how she might approach her topic. She wanted to learn more about York but didn't want to seem too curious. Straightening the sash on her dress, she asked casually, "I wonder when the others will return?"

"They're probably off to London to let off some steam. They'll return soon enough."

Marielle wondered where they spent their time and with whom, especially York. "I am more interested in knowing when I will return home," she responded coolly, watching his reaction.

"Aye, missy, I do pity your situation being cooped up against your will, but I've lived many years around the boys. They're good men albeit they take part in some businesses I disapprove of and they cause a bit of havoc here and there. When they brought you here, I thought this time they'd finally crossed the line, but you'll be brought home safe and sound, I'm certain." George nodded with assurance. "York won't let any harm come to you. All will be well, lass. I pity your father, though. They're causing him some heartache. Not right, but he'll be with you soon."

Marielle remained silent, weighing his words. Reaching the pond, she knelt and dipped her hand into the cold water. She hesitated before making the decision to simply plunge into her topic. His response might be as chilling as the water, but she had nothing to lose. "Is it true that Lord Craymore is involved in the demise of York's family? I must admit I do find it difficult to believe such an outrageous story."

"It's true all right. I worked for Lord Blackstone, tended the horses and drove him about. A fine man he was, a true aristocrat who treated his servants with respect."

"And Lord Craymore?"

"Craymore, now he was of a different sort. Believed himself to be an aristocrat, but was more a braggart if you know what I mean, always going on about his bravery in the war and such. He was a mean one too," George grimaced, shaking his head. "Always had an eye for Lady Blackstone, hoped to be the one to marry her, but she chose Lord Blackstone. My lord and lady, ah, a love match, for sure and a wonderful mother to those boys. Craymore never gave up tryin' to steal her away, even after she became Lady Blackstone. Treated his new wife pitiful, but she gave him a son that he boasted about every chance he got."

"Richard, my betrothed."

"Oh, forgive me, lass. I shouldn't be talking like this about your future family."

"Please, go on. I've heard rumors of Lord Craymore's mistreatment of his family. You'll not shock me."

"Rumors be true, miss. I knew his servants well and the stories were always the same. He was a tyrant. Craymore's wife had another wee one, a little girl, but he had no interest in a daughter. He ignored his wife, kept her cooped up most of the time and seldom mentioned his daughter's name.

Gossip was he named her after some Italian mistress."

"Her name is Alaina," Marielle interrupted. "We were friends as children, though I've seen very little of her over the past few years."

"I heard many a story of what went on in his household, being quite friendly with one of the chambermaids. Never married myself, but I had some fun in those days, when I wasn't servin' my master, of course."

Marielle gave him a smile, encouraging him to go on.

"News was the more Lady Blackstone spurned Craymore, the worse he treated his own wife. He wasn't accustomed to losing. When he finally accepted that Blackstone's wife despised him, he vowed to get even and that he did. Being friendly with his staff, as I told you," he cleared his throat, grinned knowingly, "I picked up assorted tales and tidbits. The two men fought in the war together. I heard that Craymore was none too happy when Lord Blackstone was handsomely rewarded by King George for his honorable service."

As far as what took place to cause the loss of my lordship's estate, you'll need to ask York. I never understood how it all happened, only that Craymore succeeded in involving the crown in his devious plot. York doesn't like talking about it and it's not my place to ask."

"It must have been very difficult for you." Marielle patted his arm hoping he would continue.

"Not as difficult as it was for York and his family. My heart breaks that I wasn't there for them. Their mother, she had it hard, what with their father in prison and she being disgraced and having to make a living for her and the boys."

Marielle repressed her shocked reaction to his words. His father imprisoned? Even with the bits and pieces of the story, her mind created a picture of their wretched lives.

George seemed to have forgotten that she was there. He stared out at the water and continued, regret now revealed in his voice and countenance. "I was supporting a sister then and had no choice but to find other employment. My new employer, Mr. Gettins, traveled for business. I was on a trip with him when the boys' mother died. When I finally had a free day, I went to visit only to find their flat empty and the boys gone. I tried to find them, but they'd been swallowed up by the streets. Eventually, I returned to Ireland when Mr. Gettins decided to seek his fortune in America. My sister was getting on in years and it was time for a visit."

Marielle cleared her throat and coughed, hoping to refocus him back to what he knew of York's life. The men might be back at any time.

George continued. "I stayed a time with my sister in Dublin until she passed on, then decided to return to London to find work.

"When I arrived, I asked around for news of the boys. I feared all manner of harm had come to them. No matter where I set my body down, in a park or at a pub, my eyes just naturally took in all the faces hoping I'd find a familiar one."

"And you did find them."

"As Irish luck would have it, after I had been

back about a month, a group of players came into town. I was sitting by the Thames, enjoying the music and gaiety. I see this young man, the picture of my master Lord Blackstone, when he was in his prime of course, leaning against a post laughing loudly at a monkey that had taken off into the crowd. I knew this lad had to be York. Sure enough beside him was a skinnier version of himself, Martin. I was never so happy in my entire life.

"We never parted after that, but those years they spent before I met up with them again, well, you'll have to ask York. I am not obliged to say any more. They were forced to be tough and take advantage of opportunity, but as I said they're good men. I'll stake my life on that. Whatever happens, York will not compromise your safety." He looked over at Marielle, a smile spreading on his face. "If I'm not mistaken, I'd say he has a soft spot for you, lass."

Marielle had no chance to respond. A galloping horse could be heard in the distance. They hurried back towards the cottage, Beatrice chasing after them.

York had returned…alone. Something was wrong. As he swung down from the horse, he took no time to tether his mount. He leaped up the steps and into the cottage, not seeing Marielle or George approaching from behind.

While George took the overheated horse back to the stable to wipe him down, Marielle called Bea to her and rushed onto the porch. Rather than enter, she watched through the window, her heart pounding.

York stood by the fireplace, his back to her. She watched as he reached for a glass, filled it half full of whiskey, took a gulp and smashed it against the stone of the fireplace, just missing the pups nestled in the corner. Marielle rushed into the cottage.

"Heavens, be careful! The pups could have been harmed!"

"To hell with the damn mutts," York snarled barely looking at her. "They've got Martin." York kicked a large piece of glass into the fire before leaning his head against the mantle.

Marielle reached out to him, only to have him shrug away from her touch.

"Who has him? I don't understand."

Emotionally drained, York sat down heavily at the table, his hand brushing through his damp, windswept hair.

Marielle sat down across from him waiting silently until, she hoped, he'd be ready to talk to her.

York looked up at her, his face drawn, but hardened. "Braum and I went to meet our contact to collect your ransom and deliver a new message for your release."

Marielle brushed aside a surge of anger at his nonchalance at her situation and held back a retort she would have easily uttered if she did not feel his suppressed rage. "Martin waited with the horses. Your illustrious suitor followed Griggs, our messenger, back to the designated meeting spot. He and his men were waiting for us."

"Had Griggs gone to my father for payment?" Marielle closed her eyes, imaging her father's reaction.

"Where else? We had to carry through with our original plan."

"Then Richard created a plan to rescue me, to find out where I'd been taken?"

"Yes, he is an admirable opponent and concerned about your welfare, or perhaps his own future plans," York admitted. "They roughed up Griggs enough to get a description and find out what he could about us. Griggs was able to tell us this much before we were attacked. Braum and I had little problem handling those fumbling idiots. However, Richard signaled his men to grab Martin and they took off with him. Your Richard stayed behind, held a gun to my throat when I tried to pull him from his horse."

Marielle gasped, imagining the scene.

He threatened to hang Martin if you were not returned by noon tomorrow. Braum managed to grab a horse, followed them. He'll not rest until he catches up with them or finds out where they've taken my brother."

York lifted his head and stared darkly at Marielle. "You should be proud of your fiancé. He has some wits about him, but if he wants you returned, he'll think twice about harming Martin." Twisting out of his seat, York turned from her, stood and walked toward the fireplace, slumped down into the battered, cushioned chair and stared blankly into the fire.

"Your brother would not be in this predicament if you had not kidnapped me in the first place," Marielle responded acidly. Standing directly in front of him, she looked into his stormy eyes. "Return me to my father and I'll plead for your brother's release. I'm sure his safety means more to you than your impossible plan to right your perception of old injustices."

York stared at her, his response cold, abrupt. "I don't need advice from a spoiled, pampered child who's been catered to her entire life. You have known nothing but luxury despite your family losses. While your father, most likely, went off fox hunting with that monster, Craymore, my father rotted in prison." Marielle stepped further back, feeling the heat of York's smoldering rage surface.

"Let me tell you about your future father-in-law who's lived comfortably in the Blackstone estate for the past seventeen years," York snarled. "You, my sweet, would have been too young to remember, but your father would know. Had he never mentioned my father, the honorable Lord Blackstone?"

Marielle searched her mind. "I do remember threads of conversation between my mother and father. It was so long ago. He'd been a neighbor, had sons..."

"Yes, the tyrant you see before you happens to be his heir. Is that shock or disbelief I see in your eyes? You see, I was just eleven when the king stripped my father of his title, threw him into prison and tossed our family into the streets."

"And Craymore was involved in the arrest?"

"Craymore convinced him that my father, a collector of rare manuscripts, used his hobby to commit treachery. King George had previously honored my father for his bravery in war, but he was in one of his bouts of insanity. Craymore took advantage of the situation. He forged papers which proved falsely that my father had been sending traitorous messages back and forth between France and England, hidden in his books and meant for French loyalists and traitors to the crown.

"The evidence could not be disproved?" Marielle questioned, having settled in the opposite chair.

"My father was an avid collector, had friends all over Europe who shared his love of antiquities, especially rare books and ancient manuscripts. His priceless collection disappeared from his library, but one of the books was conveniently found in the hands of a French spy. My father's seal found in the book was enough to discredit him, but not enough to hang him for high treason. No secret messages were found, but Craymore indicated there must have been a warning given and the evidence probably thrown overboard." York paused, stared into the fire.

"The king believed him without other proof, despite your father's reputation?"

"When the authorities discovered that my father's entire collection had been reported stolen, Craymore spread rumors that my father must have destroyed evidence to save himself. The charges couldn't be proven without stronger evidence, but it was enough to cause the king and his ministers to seriously question my father's loyalty to England. The king praised Craymore for his loyalty, ordered my father imprisoned, his possessions confiscated and his estate placed in Craymore's hands."

"Your family was forced to leave?" Marielle reached out to him.

York, not wanting her sympathy, shrugged off her touch. "Thrown out would be a better description. We were destitute, my father taken away. When my father was finally released several months later, the vermin-infested conditions had destroyed him."

Marielle saw the pain cross York's face before he covered it with anger.

"Craymore didn't have the initiative or the intelligence to create his own success. He fed on the success of others." York turned to her, his eyes narrowed. "Don't be surprised if his desire for his son to marry you does not have strings attached. He most likely has his eyes on your father's estate."

"Are you insinuating that his only interest in me is my father's land?" Marielle face reddened in anger.

"It has been done for hundreds of years."

Marielle ignored his sarcasm. "If your father had earned the respect of the king and courts, could he not fight to clear his name, perhaps through members of Parliament?"

"Once cast out of the courts by the king, do you think London's elite would want to admit any allegiance to a possible traitor to the crown? He sought those he once called friends to help him in his defense, but they treated him like a leper. By then the king was in and out of London to recuperate from his lapses into insanity. My father's plight was the least of his worries."

Marielle knew about the King George III's illness. His strange behavior was well documented. "Are you absolutely certain that Craymore devised this scheme?"

"There is no doubt." York glared angrily. "In desperation, my own mother went to Craymore without my father's knowledge to plead for him. He had the audacity to urge my mother to become his mistress, offering to pay for her children's care if she'd agree. My mother spat in his face. Craymore had his servants remove her bodily from the estate. She returned home bruised, shaken and defeated. My father, being held by the authorities, could not retaliate. With all his holdings confiscated, there was no money to fight for his freedom. He was imprisoned, forgotten." The anger in York's voice subsided. He grew silent.

Marielle stared into his eyes, stormy harbors of vengeance and grief, before he turned from her. Her eyes followed him as he stood and walked out the cottage door, leaving her with her thoughts.

MARIELLE, OVERWHELMED BY all that she'd heard sat on the cot, wrapped in her servant's cloak. Could York be telling the truth? Was she under some spell blinding her to reality? Her life had been settled, although she had to admit to herself, it wasn't a freely chosen future. Would she be able to take the name of Craymore after hearing York's story, if Richard still wanted her? Did she feel impelled to accept the betrothal as custom, believing that it was her destiny? She'd believed her love for Richard would grow. In time, there would be children and she wouldn't be alone. Yet, York ignited feelings she'd never felt before.

She stared at the fire that was slowly dying out and at Beatrice and the pups resting comfortably near the hearth. *Have I ever really thought that another life, a happier one might be possible?* she questioned as her past and present paraded through her mind. She hadn't realized until now what little freedom she'd had to choose her own destiny. This mysterious, complicated man somehow gave her a sense of herself she'd not known existed.

Emotionally drained, she dozed for a short time, her mind unconsciously piecing together her scattered thoughts. When she awoke, she knew what she wanted to do. It came, peacefully, from the center of her being. She stood up and walked over to the fire, added a couple of logs and stoked it until she heard movement behind her.

She turned to see York staring at her.

She walked over to him, reached out for his hand. "I don't know how, but I want to help you." She paused, stared into his eyes. "Tell me what I can do."

Before Marielle could speak another word, he reached for her and swept her into his arms, crushing her to him. His lips found hers. She clung to him, her old life swirling around her, disappearing, as she felt herself drawn into a place she could never have dreamed existed.

The storm surrounded them, but the strength of their need held all turmoil at bay. One kiss followed another, neither saying a word nor wanting to break the spell until York released his lips from hers, gathered her close, her head resting on his shoulder.

Marielle was the first to speak. "I don't know what has brought us to this moment or where it will take us, but I understand your need to right the wrongs that have destroyed your family. We must find a way to bring Martin back safely."

As she spoke, the hardness that protected York's heart betrayed him. His captive had captivated him. He knew she touched something inside of him that he'd shut down long ago. He framed her face with his hands, questioned his own sanity before kissing her again, spreading kisses across her cheek, down the silky softness of her neck to her breast, pushing the fabric aside, wanting more and more of her.

He felt her surrender, knew she wanted him too. He drew her over to the cot, wanting to lay her down, pull away every inch of fabric until she lay naked before him.

"Marielle, I must leave. If I don't..."

She sat on the cot, drew him down to her until they were wrapped in each other's arms. How could she explain the feelings leading her on? She couldn't. Her body felt on fire, his heat melding with her own. She wanted him, more than anything she ever wanted in her life.

She urged him on, not knowing what to expect and not caring about the consequences, wanting only to dissolve into this man who'd brought her alive with his touch.

"Marielle." He whispered her name, barely

able to hold back. "Do you understand where this is going?"

She wanted to silence him, silence the warning voice within her. As crazy as it seemed, she trusted him. She didn't want him to let her go. She reached up, gently drew her curved palm along the sides of his face, reached behind him to the curls at the nape of his neck, played, her eyes never leaving his. She saw gentleness in his eyes and a hunger that matched her own.

He remained still while she brushed his lips with her own. Their need for each other consumed them. There was no turning back.

Later, both sated and exhausted, they slept in each other's arms through the night.

YORK WAS THE first to awake as the sun spilled through the window. Marielle still slept soundly, curled in his arms.

Her warm body, her scent caused his own to ache with need, but his mind adjusted to the reality of what he'd done. He'd kidnapped her and he accepted that transgression. But this…

He'd gone too far. He had taken her innocence, when he had nothing to give in return.

Chapter Six

WARD CRAYMORE SCOWLED as he watched Lord Henley wipe his damp forehead with his handkerchief. If it wasn't for his desire to have Henley secured in his back pocket and Marielle married off to Richard, he would've ignored his neighbor's request to search all avenues for clues to Marielle's whereabouts.

She isn't good enough for my son, the way she prances around her father's estate, coming home with mud up to her ankles, Craymore thought, as he waited for Henley to stop his pacing. *It'll take a firm hand on Richard's part to bring her under control.* He believed that after the marriage, the Henley Estate would come easily under Richard's expert supervision. Secure in his holdings, his son would be free to keep a mistress for his pleasure, while Marielle spent her hours engrossed in needlework preparing for their future heir.

With the ransom note in hand, he felt certain that Marielle would be returned, though, no doubt, with a sullied reputation. Henley may need to offer a bit more in her dowry, Craymore decided, as he listened with irritation to her father's continued mutterings.

"Lionel, this pacing and groaning will not bring your daughter back. I promise you my son and his men will not fail—the kidnappers were foolish to use Griggs as their messenger," Craymore jeered.

"You know the man?" Lord Henley stopped abruptly, visibly shocked.

"I've had no business with him myself, of course," Lord Craymore answered hiding a snide grin, "but I've often heard his name come up in the clubs. You know how gentlemen go on when they're in their cups. Someone might need to rid themselves, discreetly, of some pregnant whore or have another trivial matter resolved. Griggs has been often used to, let us say, correct an embarrassing situation."

"Despicable!" Henley spit the word out as he reached for the brandy decanter. "Why the likes of him standing there in my parlor gap-toothed, smelling of stale whiskey and looking as if he'd just come out of the bogs was horrifying enough, but then to realize that he carried a message about my daughter. What kind of animals could have taken her and what have they done with her?" Lord Henley bowed his head, his voice lowered just above a whisper. "I am afraid to think of it."

"It's of no help to imagine all sorts of evils. I, too, as you know, am deeply distressed. Marielle is to be my daughter-in-law. The thought of her with someone other than my son...well...we just cannot fear the worst," Craymore paused, then looked up wearing a sorrowful expression, which hid his satisfaction when he saw Henley's face. He'd succeeded in adding to his distress.

He continued, "We must trust that my son will

find the kidnappers. Griggs has the gold to deliver. I hated to ask for your geldings as security for payment, but I am first a businessman you know. It's always been my policy to keep a store of gold handy, although I've not let it be known until now, what with the issues in parliament over the gold standard. It might raise some eyebrows, but I do like to be prepared for an emergency."

"I appreciate your help." Henley's sarcasm was not missed by Craymore.

"I'm glad to be of assistance. If we'd waited until you reached your banker, why who knows what would have happened in the meantime?"

Lord Henley chose not to respond, knew when he signed the papers that regardless of the outcome or of repayment, his prize geldings would be lost to him. He was well aware of Craymore's shrewdness, had heard enough rumors about underhanded dealings. He still remembered the rumors surrounding Lord Blackstone's demise. Many were suspicious of Craymore's involvement. Henley liked his previous neighbor, respected him, much preferred him to this man who'd been gifted Blackstone's estate.

He maintained a guarded friendship with Craymore over the years, especially since they agreed upon the betrothal shortly after his own wife's death. Having never fully recovered from the loss of both his wife and Marielle's older sister Katherine to consumption, he wanted Marielle protected if anything should happen to him. Craymore's idea of the betrothal seemed like the best idea at the time. Richard, after all, seemed to be a fine young man and Marielle's future was one less thing to worry about.

Now, the guilt that he felt for the years he'd spent mourning his loss and avoiding Marielle, surfaced unmercifully. Even when he thought of her hopping over the rocks in the brook or running with her pet Beatrice, she was endowed with the regal grace and the delicate beauty of his dear wife. He still found it painful remembering how his wife refused to leave young Katherine's bedside until her own health was lost. They'd died only a few weeks apart and now he might lose Marielle without the opportunity to ask for her forgiveness. No, nothing mattered but finding her. He was thankful that Craymore's son showed genuine affection for Marielle and believed that he'd use every possible avenue to find her.

Both men were deep in their own thoughts when Gerald rushed into the room.

"Your Lordship, Master Richard has returned!" Gerald stammered anxiously, forgetting formality. Realizing his blunder, he stepped aside as the two men hurriedly brushed by him.

RICHARD DISMOUNTED, WHILE one of Craymore's men pulled Martin, bound and gagged, off another horse. Martin struggled to free himself, but another rider reared his horse over to him and knocked him down. As he lifted himself from the ground, two of the men laughed, kicking him unmercifully.

"Leave him," Richard ordered as he looked down at Martin buckling over in pain "We'll beat the truth out of him soon enough."

As Richard approached the steps, Lord Henley rushed to meet him. "Tell me, where is my daughter? Has she been harmed?" He grabbed Richard's coat, only to have Lord Craymore pull him away.

"My son will give us the news soon enough." Craymore took control and ordered Simon, one of the riders, to take the prisoner to the stables, bind him and stand guard. He patted his son's broad shoulders, so much like his own and beamed at him. "Nice work, son."

He turned to Lord Henley. "I suspect our prisoner will lead us to Marielle, unless my son has other news for us. Richard?"

"Since the tyrant hasn't had the chance to get his hands on the money or return to his den of thieves, I suspect she's still alive," Richard answered, as he followed his father up the mansion steps.

Once inside, they followed Henley to his study. Gerald served them drinks and stood silently in the corner, hoping for word of Marielle.

Craymore glared at him disdainfully, waiting for him to leave.

Lord Henley noted the exchange. "Gerald has been my daughter's protector since she was a small child and especially since my wife's passing. He may stay and listen to whatever you have to say." He turned to Richard. "Now please, I beg you, tell us what has happened and what you know of Marielle's whereabouts."

York and Braum sat at the table devising their

plan. Braum had returned after following Richard's men back to the Henley estate. He noted where the guards were placed before bringing York the news. York, forcing himself not to jump on his stallion immediately to save his brother, listened to Braum's description of the situation and the setup of the grounds. Marielle stood behind York, her hand resting on his shoulder.

Braum harbored doubts about Marielle's new allegiance to his friend, but there was no time to argue the point. Martin's life was at stake. He wanted to gather a group of his trusty friends from London and storm the place, demand Martin's return and dump Marielle in their laps. Their scheme had gone awry and it was time to get out of the mess before it was too late. He was surprised and angered that York did not agree with his logic. In Braum's estimation, every minute wasted brought Martin closer to the grave.

"York, we can ride into London, gather the men and be at the 'enley estate by daybreak. They'll be forced to free Martin or suffer the consequences. 'is men will be no match for the blokes we'll 'ave on our side. We'll deliver 'er back to her father. To 'ell with the bloody gold! She'd never be able to lead them back 'ere and we'll be done with the matter."

Marielle stared scornfully at Braum, despite the knowledge that she knew he was right. She missed Matty, Gerald, even her father and she had much to say to him. She also knew that going home meant she might never see York again, but she had no choice.

When Braum finished his tirade, she interrupted. "York, I need only to speak to my father. Trust that I will let no harm come to your brother. Violence will only make matters worse. Please protect yourself by leaving the matter of your brother's safety to me."

York twisted in his chair to face her. "You have not yet conceived, Marielle, what Craymore is capable of doing. You are his son's betrothed. Your kidnapping is a humiliation to him."

"I can persuade my father to release Martin. I'm sure of it."

"Even if you have the power of persuasion over your father, Craymore won't let Martin walk away unscathed. God forbid he finds out who he's captured."

"Please..." Marielle stopped, saw the look on York's face, knew nothing she could say would change his mind."

York stood, brushed her aside, before giving his orders.

"Marielle, prepare to leave. Braum, gather the hound and her pups. We'll not need more men. Marielle won't be released until Martin is safe and on his way home."

Braum moved quickly, emptying a potato sack and filling it with the whining pups. Before Marielle could protest, he tied a rope to Bea's neck, pulled her out the door and settled her and the sack of pups securely in a large satchel attached to the side of his horse. Meanwhile George met them with Martin's horse saddled and ready.

Marielle knew her animals were an

inconvenience, yet, they did not leave them behind. *They created this mess*, Marielle thought. *Why should I feel gratitude?* But she'd come to be part of their lives, know their stories and see them as human beings. She could never have imagined finding herself in this predicament and had never felt such turmoil. She took one last look at the cottage before accepting York's arm as he lifted her onto the saddle of Martin's horse, this time, to be taken home.

They rode quietly in the darkness. York remained silent while his mind continued to strategize. *Saving Martin came first. Returning Marielle was a necessity. After all, she was concerned about her father. Suddenly this mattered to him, her feelings and her needs. Blast! He had trapped himself anew. This time by a beautiful woman whose innocence reached into his soul and invaded the protective wall he'd firmly built against feelings.*

Feelings brought about only weakness and now he felt guilt. He needed to focus on his goal and use every ounce of strength he possessed to master this situation. He must bring Martin to safety, but then what? He couldn't turn back from his mission. His feelings for Marielle were just that, feelings. Feelings could be harnessed and controlled. Eventually they would diminish or at least be kept at bay, but he'd made her his own. *He couldn't think of that now. Another day, another time...*

Marielle could hear the fast pounding of York's heart beneath his coat. How different she felt from the last time they'd ridden together. This time she dreaded saying goodbye. Darkness swallowed up the daylight as they rode on. In Marielle's estimation, four or more hours passed before York called out to Braum and the horses were being led off the path.

"Where are we?" Marielle asked, her voice barely above a whisper.

York wrapped his arm more snugly about her, lifted her chin and spoke softly, his lips close to hers. "Where we first met, my midnight miss." He pulled up the reins and dismounted, reaching up for Marielle. "You must stay here with your animals. Take this once again for protection." He handed her Gerald's scabbard. "By the way, the knife you hid under the cot is still there. I'm glad you never had to use it."

Marielle looked up surprised, smiled, then stopped, pleaded. "York, let me ride the rest of the way with you. I can help."

"And what would you do with your pets? I'm sorry to have to leave you here where this journey began, but I want you safely away from the estate until my brother is freed. Tell me, who on the estate would know where to find you?"

Marielle stifled her frustration. "My servant Gerald, he and his wife sleep in a small room off the kitchen…" Marielle held his gaze. "When will I see you again?"

"Time will tell, but I will find it hard to stay away from you. I may have to kidnap you again," he whispered as he brushed her forehead with a kiss. "Take care, Marielle. We must go."

"York," Marielle reached out to him. "Please, before you go, let me at least tell you the best way to get to the stable unnoticed."

In the next few minutes, Marielle explained the areas with the most cover and how to slip into the kitchen area where Gerald and Matty slept. When she finished, she reached up, wrapped her arms about him and kissed him without regard to Braum's presence.

York held her for a moment, released her. "We must be on our way." Before riding off, he pulled out a small revolver secured to the side of his saddle and handed it to her. "Keep this for added protection and use it if necessary."

Without another word, he rode off, with Braum close behind.

Marielle stared into the darkness, fearful for what was to come. When she finally accepted that York was gone, possibly forever, she curled up against the old tree, gathering Bea to her, while loosening the canvas sack that held her litter. When they were settled, she wrapped herself tightly in Gerald's cloak.

She thought about coming home to Gerald and Matty — she'd been so worried about them and how they must be fearing for her safety — but her mind kept returning to York's situation. Her anger at her inability to participate grew.

Why wouldn't he let her intervene? She wanted to help. Instead, she was sitting under a tree totally helpless. She thought of leaving Bea and her pups and trying to find her way back to the estate, but in the darkness she knew it would be difficult and if she left them what would become of them? She was right back in her original predicament.

Damn him!

York and Braum's experience on the streets made it easy for them to slip onto the grounds of the Henley mansion. Marielle's descriptions that included natural hiding places among the shrubbery created good cover. Once the stable came into view, they found it unguarded.

Something wasn't right.

They dismounted, moved closer to the stable and peered through the windows but met only darkness. While Braum stayed with the horses, York moved to the rear entrance, found it unlocked and unguarded. Once his eyes became attuned to the darkness, he entered and moved from stall to stall.

Braum became impatient, tied the horses to a tree and slipped in. His knife gleamed at his side. His pistol in his hand he waited for an attack but none came.

York appeared beside him, cursed. "Where the hell is he?"

What do ya think is goin' on?" Braum muttered.

"I don't know." York's voice low, chilling. "We'll not leave until we find out."

Braum followed as York made his way to the kitchen area. He found the door to the servants' quarters easily, just as Marielle described. Once inside, they moved cautiously to the small bedroom. Braum guarded the door while York entered.

He walked silently to the bedside of the sleeping servants. One hand came down quickly covering the cook's mouth, the other pointed the edge of a dagger to Gerald's throat.

Matty woke in horror, her eyes opened wide, her free arm reaching to her sleeping husband.

"I warn you," York whispered, "don't make a sound, madam, or I'll cut your husband's throat." He hesitated before slowly removing his hand from her mouth.

Her stunned expression turned to a fearful plea as she clutched her husband's arm.

Gerald woke suddenly, stared into the eyes of the intruder whose menacing look could be seen in the sliver of moonlight that slipped through the window.

Then he saw the knife and his eyes widened. He grabbed for his wife's hand. Both remained speechless.

York felt their fear, lowered the knife.

"Listen carefully," he whispered gruffly. "Neither of you will be harmed if you give me the answers I need. Miss Henley seems to have a great deal of faith in your discretion."

"Marielle?" Gerald choked out, his voice barely audible. "She's safe?"

"She's doing quite well. No harm has come to her, yet. But, if you want her back alive, tell me what they've done with my brother."

"Your *brother*?"

York drew the dagger closer to the old man's throat. "Do not waste my time! He was brought here, dragged into the stable. Where have they taken him?" York hissed at the servant as he crouched down closer, his eyes blazing coals in the dimly lit room.

Gerald whispered hoarsely. "He was brought here hours ago. Lord Craymore convinced Master Henley that he'd be more secure on his own estate until…until Marielle's return. Please, sir. We want only to have Marielle home safely. Master Henley will pay generously."

"I don't want his money," York growled. Losing patience, he began to trace the knife along Gerald's neck.

"Matty could not hold her tongue any longer. "What *do* you want then?"

"You'll know soon enough," York muttered, as he stood to his full height and held the knife above their heads, the point directed towards Gerald's throat.

"If my brother is safe, Marielle will be returned, but if any harm has come to him at the hands of that bastard, Craymore, you'll never see her again."

"Please, sir," Gerald pleaded, "Let me speak to Master Henley. He will…"

"You'll speak to no one tonight, do you understand?" York brought the dagger down drawing it closer to Matty's face. "Go back to sleep. Your silence will keep Marielle alive. If all goes well, you'll find her tomorrow right where you left her."

York withdrew the knife and left as swiftly as he'd entered. Within minutes he and Braum were headed toward the only place that York had ever called home.

The Craymore estate.

Chapter Seven

STILL BOUND AND gagged, Martin kicked one of his captor's in the shins, after being pulled off his horse.

"You piece of scum," the man snapped, cursing as he stumbled. You'll be sorry you were ever born when Craymore finishes with you."

"Craymore is lower than scum," Martin managed to spit out through the loosened gag.

"Shut him up," one of the men yelled out as he opened the stable doors.

The men jeered as they pulled Martin by a rope towards the stable, beating any defiance out of him. When he fell to the ground, he turned his head and spied a young woman peering out from her hiding place behind the vine-covered arbor.

His eyes bore into hers just long enough for her to see him wince in pain after one of her father's brawny footman jabbed him in the side.

Standing in the shadows, spellbound by the drama, she felt pity for the man, regardless of his deed. Few dared to incur her father's wrath.

Later, standing unnoticed outside her father's study, Alaina listened as her father and brother recounted the events of the day. The prisoner was somehow involved in Marielle's kidnapping and they seemed confident that their captive would lead them to her or suffer painful consequences. She had no doubt of that. Lord Henley's daughter was much too valuable to both to them.

Having heard enough, she went up to bed, but sleep eluded her. She wondered about the man. He didn't look evil, but she knew that evil masked itself well. Alaina remembered her father's concern that the prisoner's partners in crime would be searching for him. He'd ordered guards to be posted around the boundaries of the estate and others to take shifts. He wanted nothing to alter his plan to interrogate the prisoner.

She knew he looked forward to the encounter, relished the thought of the captive lying awake through the night fearing for his life. By morning, he'd be well primed for their meeting, her father had gloated. Meanwhile, her brother Richard and other servants would be combing the area for others.

Kept in seclusion on the estate for most of her life, she could easily slip out of sight or hide in the shadows without anyone missing her. Even as a small child, she felt invisible in the presence of her father. He saw only Richard, his heir and only son. She was an inconvenience. He showed no respect for women and now as she prepared for her debut into society, she'd become an expense. Only if she found a wealthy and pliable suitor, acceptable to her father, would she be of some value to him.

She was a game piece, like Marielle, to be moved at the appropriate time for her father's purpose and in his favor. She wished that she could have warned Marielle, urged her to refuse her brother's marriage proposal, but she had no opportunity.

She and Marielle once played together as children whenever their mothers were able to visit with each other. They even promised to be friends forever, as little girls often do. But after Marielle's mother's and sister's deaths, the visits stopped. Only on special occasions, a celebration at court, or a holiday ball, would they see one another where they exchanged pleasantries. If she'd tried to warn Marielle of her father's motives, she'd probably not be believed and she feared the consequences, not so much for herself, but for her sickly mother.

Through the years, Lady Craymore received the brunt of her husband's dark moods and displeasure. She taught her daughter to stay out of his way at a young age. Alaina, however, unbeknownst to her father who thought her to be a bit stupid because of her silence in his presence, was extremely astute and wise beyond her years. She was very aware of the goings-on. Her father's affairs were no secret to her.

Nothing escaped her notice, including any change in her father's moods. Only her loyalty to her mother, who for the past year had been bedridden, kept her in obedience to what was expected of her. Someday her opportunity would come to escape her father's tyranny.

Alaina's thoughts dwelled on the prisoner. Her curiosity and her own restlessness became too much. She dressed, wrapped a cape around her shoulders and slipped soundlessly out of the house.

The side entrance to the stable, partially hidden by an overgrowth of clinging vines gave Alaina easy access. The two men posted at the front entrance were passed out from too much rum, just as she expected. She stepped cautiously past the horse stalls, her lantern casting golden halos along the straw-covered floor guiding her steps.

MARTIN, HANDS AND feet bound, pressed his body into the corner of the stall, his senses alert. Someone was coming near, but the wooden partitions surrounding him made it impossible for him to see. His years on the street gave him keen instincts and though he hadn't heard a sound, he felt movement and a change in the atmosphere. Someone was coming closer and he was helpless to defend himself.

Damn, he thought, *I've made a mess of things*.

He caught a flicker of light, felt slipper-soft movements, a very subtle swishing. A petticoat? *Impossible*, he thought. He lifted his arms bound together and slowly, carefully, reached his fingers through a wooden slat, until they grazed whisper-thin material. A soft blush of light filtered through.

Grasping what he could, he began to pull at the light fabric, until…

"Oh!" Alaina gasped when she felt something tug at her gown.

"Shh…don't scream."

Alaina stood still, rooted to the spot.

"Tell me who you are," Martin whispered. "I feel as if I know a great deal about you already."

"What are you talking about?" Alaina blurted

out in a strained whisper.

"I know that you move with a genteel grace, featherlight on your feet, like a dancer. Your gown is soft and you smell of lavender."

Alaina was stunned. This was not what she expected.

Without a second thought, she stepped up onto one of the slats to peer into the stall. Their eyes met and held. She saw the surprise in his eyes and a hint of a smile. Dried blood streaked his face — an attractive face, even bruised and bleeding, she thought. His bloody shirt gave evidence of a whipping.

She stared open-mouthed, the light shaking in her hand.

"Would you mind setting that lantern down before it lights up the place with more than a fiery wick?"

In the light, he could see her soft brown eyes, her creamy complexion. Dark curls secured by a red ribbon framed a sweet and very lovely face. His smile widened.

"The Lord is merciful. He has sent me an angel."

Her common sense fled. She smiled back before regaining control over her thoughts. "You are the one who kidnapped Lord Henley's daughter?" She hesitated, finding it difficult to believe that this man, with the boyish grin and tired eyes, could be a criminal. "How could you do such a thing?"

"So quick to believe that I am a scoundrel? You give me no chance to defend my honor. I assume that you are some relation to the brutes who whipped me and left me here to await interrogation?"

Alaina absorbed his words. Could he be innocent of the charges? In their haste could they have captured and beaten the wrong man?

"Would you at least tell me your name?" He stared up at her waiting for a response.

She turned her eyes away from him.

He could understand her distrust and nervousness, but she was one brave young lady to come in the middle of the night and talk to an alleged kidnapper.

"Alaina... My father is Lord Craymore, my brother Richard is Marielle's betrothed."

"A beautiful name, it suits you." He made no comment at the mention of the Craymore name.

"I appreciate the compliment. However, I'd much prefer that you tell me of your involvement."

"How kind of you to ask," Martin said ruefully. The pain in his side throbbed. His attempts earlier to extend his arms toward the wooden slats had caused the bleeding to start again.

"I took no part in Marielle's kidnapping, but I have some responsibility in not returning her to her father. In fact, I have much enjoyed getting to know her. She is a lovely, young woman, sensitive and compassionate. Why the way she hovers over her dog and its new brood is quite touching."

Alaina was shocked by his intimate knowledge of her, even more surprised at a tinge of jealousy that crept in. It sounded as if she was more of a guest than a hostage.

"You may not be aware that her hound birthed

and has five delightful pups," Martin added.

"Marielle and I have not been in close contact for years. My father prefers that I stay close to home. My mother needs extra care. I was not aware that she expected a litter, her pet, I mean."

Alaina realized her response was clumsy, but Martin just grinned. She felt strangely awkward, her eyes focusing on a harness hanging from a distant post.

Suddenly Martin moaned as pain ripped through his side.

"What is it?"

"My side, it's raw."

"Why, you're still bleeding. You must add pressure to the wound."

"Difficult to do with my body tied in knots." Martin began to see a possibility of escape. "If this rope holding me to the wall could be loosened, my arms and legs would still be bound and I could at least lie against the wound. I might even get some rest."

An uncomfortable silence followed.

Before Martin could attempt any more persuasion, her mind jolted and guessed his ploy.

"Do you take me for a fool?"

She'd begun to realize her mistake in coming to the stable and conversing with a stranger, one charged with kidnapping. What could she have been thinking? She'd watched both her father and brother manipulate others with sympathetic words and kind gestures meant only to reach their selfish ends. She should leave before she became too entangled in his words. He was already having an unusual impact on her.

"Morning will come soon enough," Alaina said acidly. "I see that the bloodstain has grown only slightly. I'm sure you'll live and tomorrow we shall find out what you have done to Marielle."

"I told you, Marielle is safe."

"Why should I believe you? I don't know if she is even alive or if she hasn't been ruined."

Martin saw her face transform from curiosity to mistrust, knew he'd lost the opportunity to obtain her help.

"You my dear lavender lady have an imagination," he said, giving her a devilish smile and hoping to melt the shell she'd slipped into. "I give my word. Marielle is unharmed and her pets are quite comfortable."

"Your word… I'm to believe the words of a common criminal?"

Martin attempted to adjust his position. "I'm telling you the truth but, no, I don't expect you to believe the words of a common criminal. I doubt your father will believe me either."

He stopped short. The clamor of horses' hooves could be heard in the distance.

Alaina froze. "I must leave. If my father sees me…"

Martin watched as her face paled, dread replacing the anger.

"Why such fear of your father? Has he shown you cruelty too?" He could see the truth in her eyes. "I'm sorry."

Alaina stared, surprised by his perception and, even more, that he seemed genuinely sorry.

"They're coming!" She could hear the sound coming closer. "I must leave!" She stepped down quickly, the lantern shaking in her hand.

When she reached the side door, she doused the light and slipped out. Men's voices could be heard much too close to the path from which she'd come. Pressed against the side of the building, she inched her way in the opposite direction, hoping the darkness would shield her. Just as she turned the corner, her brother grabbed her arm.

"What are you doing here?" Richard growled.

"Please, you're hurting me. I couldn't sleep. I only wanted to see what was going on. I did no harm."

"Your curiosity has reached its limits. Get back to your room before Father finds you." He let go of her arm, pushed her away, cursing as she fled.

Once his anger subsided at his sister's foolishness, Richard directed his men to take some rest after admonishing the stable guards for their negligence. Fortunately for them, they too had heard the sound of horses' hooves and were at least awake.

Richard checked the prisoner and finding him asleep returned to the house.

Back in her room, Alaina sat on her bed, her knees drawn to her chest, her thoughts on the stranger. She hadn't asked his name. Why should it matter? He most probably was guilty.

THIS IS NO time to sleep, brother. That pretty little thing must have worn you out,"

"York? Is that you?"

"Hell, who else do you think it is? I thought your visitors would never leave. I've been here for close to an hour waiting for you to stop socializing," York chided as he cut through the ropes that secured his brother's back. Entering the stall, he cut the remaining rope away from Martin's arms and legs.

"Where in God's name have you been and what took you so damn long?" Martin said as he rubbed his wrists together, raw from rope burns.

"Your lady friend lit the way for me while you were getting to know her — a little too well I might add. I've been resting on those red velvet cushions in that carriage back there and listening to you make a fool of yourself. I figured she'd leave soon enough and we could get moving, when who comes along but Master Richard with his ruffled shirt, his fancy riding pants and a whip in his hand, checking to see if you were behaving yourself. I guess you were no challenge once he thought you were asleep."

"I heard him. I'm sure I looked quite dead to the world."

"Smart move, brother, but I can still sneak up on you unnoticed." York smiled as he brushed straw from Martin's back. "Master Richard may look fancy and act cocky, but he doesn't realize we've had the best training of all, thanks to his father. Slipping by his men is easier than stealing a wallet from an old drunk. How are you feeling? You look like hell."

"I've felt worse, though I can't remember when."

"We'll get you all fixed up once we get back to the cottage. Now let's pick out a couple of these pretty geldings in here, get rid of those two rummies who are supposed to be guarding you and get out of here."

"Sounds good to me. Where's Braum?"

"He's waiting under the old bridge near that brook we used to fish in, remember?" York questioned as he unlatched one of the stalls, while Martin did the same.

"I don't remember catching many fish, but I do remember you pushing me in too many times to count."

"Taught you how to swim, didn't I?" York whispered, grinning at the memory. "The damn fools guarding the estate have no idea how well I know this land. I'll bet you haven't forgotten your way around either."

"Can't say I've had much chance to look around."

"Perhaps another day. Now let's get this over with. We'll leave by the front doors, after we take care of those drunken idiots who are supposed to be guarding you."

The guards, sprawled on the ground near the entrance, never knew what hit them. York and Martin mounted the geldings and side by side, giving each other a nod, slapped the horses into a gallop, raced through the open doors and were on their way.

Craymore's men positioned about the estate were caught off guard. With their lord's son gone to bed, it seemed safe enough to catch a bit of sleep.

Dazed and shaken, they ran to the large bell to alert everyone, while fearing Lord Craymore's wrath.

York and Martin turned off the main path which led to the brook and sidled down the rutted path carved by an underground spring. They could hear the gong of the warning bell in the distance, but no one saw them turn off the path. In no time they reached the bridge.

Braum heard the horses approach. When his partners came into view, he let out a sigh of relief. "I was about to come after you. What took you so long?"

"No time for explanations now. Let's get out of here. Martin needs some tending." Wasting no time, the men switched to their own horses, sending the geldings on their way. They rode across the brook and through the thicket on the other side. Stopping at a safe distance from the main estate grounds, York ordered Braum and Martin to head back to the cottage. He was going back for Marielle.

"Are you crazy? Let's get the 'ell out of 'ere," Braum shouted angrily. "We've saved our skins. We don't need any more trouble. I don't want to 'ave to go searchin' for you next."

"I'll be back before you know it. Now get out of here before you're followed. Martin needs some bandaging up and a good night's rest."

Without another word, York took off in the direction of the Henley estate. He wanted to be sure Marielle was safe.

The men, reluctantly, headed for home.

MARIELLE SAT STARING out into the darkness. Unable to sleep, the hours crawled. It would be morning soon when she could find her way back on her own. She'd carry the pups now that Bea was able to follow along.

Unlike the night that York found her, this night the moon hid its face. Only its eerie pallor hung like a ghostly gray shroud creating nightmarish silhouettes. Night sounds seemed amplified. In her anxiety and fear as she wondered what might be happening while she waited, feeling useless.

She wondered if York had succeeded in freeing Martin. If it weren't for Bea and the pups, she'd be home by now, perhaps in her own bed, but hardly sleeping.

She wondered what it would feel like returning home. She thought of Matty and Gerald greeting her, relieved, imagined her father coming out of his study expecting her to relate all that occurred, while he ranted about the horror of it all. She imagined that he would place guards around her day and night and she'd be forced to announce her every move.

As the night went on, her feelings hovered between the fear that York might not have succeeded, to fury that she was left to do nothing but mull over the entire calamity.

She was shaken from her wandering thoughts by the sound of horses. Bea's ears perked up, her senses fully alert, a low growl came from between her clenched teeth.

Could it be York? Her mind swarmed with anticipation, questions, relief. She stumbled forward, almost tripping over the huge gnarled roots of the old tree. Moving with abandon, thinking that York might be returning, she reached the path. Exhilaration consumed her as she stepped out onto the road. The light of the moon, no longer cloaked by the forest, gave her visibility just as two riders pulled up in front of her.

"Milady? Is it really you?" The man questioned, jumping from his horse for a closer look. "I can't believe it. It is you! Why are you here in the dead of night? We could have run you over."

"I...I was left here," Marielle answered faintly, recognizing one of her father's men. "I thought you were them. I..."

"Don't you worry milady. You're safe now. Your father's had us out combing the area, what with all the excitement today — one of the kidnappers being caught. We were hoping to find accomplices, never thought we'd bump into you. By God, it's almost what we did."

He dismounted, ready to offer assistance. "Come, we'll have you home in no time at all."

"No, I cannot leave Beatrice and her pups." As she spoke, she felt consumed with the haunting memory of saying those same words to a dark stranger. Everything began to lose its shape, her exhaustion finally taking hold. Her eyes glazed over, she felt as if she were staring down into murky water.

"Milady, are you all right?"

"Yes, I... Please collect my pets. I just want to go home."

As YORK RODE towards the spot where he had left Marielle, the land about him donned its morning robe, spilling dew like tiny crystals on shimmering leaves. The rising sun promised a clear day, but his mind ran behind and ahead of him. He'd just left his family estate, but as a trespasser, his path ahead uncertain, but his purpose resolute. He would use every opportunity possible to reclaim all that had been stolen from his father and Marielle must play a role. He hadn't wanted to leave her, but he'd had no choice and he didn't want to admit to himself that she'd made an uncomfortable imprint on his heart.

He rode cautiously, listening for search parties. The night had concealed him well and now as dawn's light melted the blackness, he was only a few minutes away. The closer he came, the more he realized how deeply she'd affected him. He wanted to see her there snuggled in with her pets, safe and hopefully relieved to see him.

When he reached the spot, he turned off the road and dismounted. It took only a few steps for him to realize that she was gone. He continued toward the ancient oak, looking about to be sure there was no sign of a struggle or footprints, or worse, animal prints.

But he knew she'd returned to her father where she belonged.

He stared for some time at the old oak, its giant limbs amassed with color as it stretched towards the sun. He envisioned Marielle as he'd last seen her standing there, watching him as he rode off. Turning his horse about, he led him out onto the path after scanning the countryside. Features hardened, lips clenched, he tugged hard on the reins, slapped the horse's flank and headed home.

IT WAS CLOSE to noon before Marielle awoke. She looked round her room, followed a slice of sunlight that slipped through a crack in the heavy tapestry curtains that graced the large window. She followed the bar of light that crossed the foot of her bed to her dressing table while collecting pieces of her past.

She forced herself to sit up, to think, to remember. As her mind gathered the scattered pieces, her new reality emerged with painful clarity. Her room looked exactly as she'd left it, but something was different, something inside of her. Slipping under the covers, she turned her face into the pillow. She no longer knew who she was or where she belonged, only that she was now truly a woman and one man, no longer a stranger, filled her mind and held her heart.

When she'd arrived home, all manner of excitement had filled the house. George and Matty were in tears, showering her with hugs. Her father, noticeably distraught, was overcome with relief. She feared he might have a heart attack. He wanted to know all but agreed to let her rest before questioning her.

A scratching at the door caught her attention, caused her to stop her rampant thoughts. Beatrice pushed open the door and trotted to her bedside, rubbing her cold nose against Marielle's outstretched hand.

LORD CRAYMORE MARCHED to the front of his house and waited restlessly for his carriage to be brought around and for his children to prepare themselves for a visit to the Henley estate. A messenger had arrived an hour earlier to inform them of Marielle's return, leaving him no time to deal with the men who'd allowed the prisoner to escape. Richard's efforts to follow the tyrants were futile. They seemed to have disappeared into thin air, but they would be found, he pledged and pay dearly. His mood was murderous, but he contained his rage.

The carriage appeared as Alaina emerged from the house with Richard following close behind.

"Father, I do not understand why you want me to come with you," Alaina complained, as she approached the steps. "I have not spoken to or seen Marielle in ages. Certainly, I cannot be of any help and mother needs me here."

"You will do as I say. I want to know as much about Marielle's capture as possible. She might open up to another woman, may have the need to confess any wrongdoings, any guilt."

"Father! What are you saying? She was taken by force. She's a victim!"

"If she allowed any one of them to take advantage, we must know."

"Allowed them?" Alaina glared at her father.

"A woman, particularly a fearful one, can be manipulated easily. Who knows how she may have reacted under pressure."

Alaina winced at his disparaging words.

"One of my men told me you became

inquisitive last night. Do you always sneak around in the darkness when we assume you've gone to bed? What have you done other nights when we have been asleep?"

As he questioned her, he lifted her chin roughly so that he could look directly into her eyes, his own filled with contempt. "I have no time right now to deal with your disreputable behavior, but I assure you, we'll discuss it later."

Alaina felt numbness rather than shock. She never knew what to expect. Since her mother became bedridden, he'd taken more notice of her. He'd begun to comment on her clothing or the way she wore her hair, not in a complimentary way, but with a leer that made her feel uncomfortable in his presence. She could only imagine what he thought of her, but she wouldn't allow fear to control her.

They rode in silence, each considering the best way to approach their particular mission. Lord Craymore, still outraged and humiliated at the loss of the prisoner, would be sure to let it be known that the imbeciles guarding him would be fired. Furthermore, he'd make certain that their names were spread throughout the *ton*. They would find it extremely difficult, if not impossible, to acquire decent employment in all of England. Richard sat tight lipped. The thought of his betrothed as a captive spending days with criminals, grated at his sensibilities, yet he must reassure her of his devotion and concern for her physical and emotional state. After all, they were to be wed, regardless of her condition and the sooner the better.

Alaina stared out the window wondering how she was to gain Marielle's trust when they'd spent so little time together. Nevertheless, she had no choice in the matter. Her rebellion would only enrage her father more and her mother would suffer the consequences of his foul mood.

The years had taken their toll on her mother. Bruises of the body and heart had weakened her, but it was the death of her spirit that was the most tragic. Her mother's once beautiful face never marred by her father's hand — he had his reputation to protect — was now thin and gaunt, her eyes lifeless. She seldom spoke and Alaina knew that she was waiting to die. She held on, though, in her weak state, eating little, her words barely audible.

Alaina wondered if she held onto threads of life for her daughter's sake, a frail attempt to protect her as she had in years past. She would stay with her mother until the end, even if it meant having to accept her father's cruelty in silence. She learned long ago how to escape in her mind. Her father's determination and cunning and her mother's courage were part of her too.

The day would come when she'd leave the estate and no longer be under her father's tyrannical hand. Her mother, through the years, hid whatever money she could. When she became bedridden, she told Alaina about her secret, made her promise that she would use it to run away before he destroyed her too. The knowledge that one day she might be free kept her strong and made life bearable.

Both stopped thinking as the carriage turned

into the long drive leading to the Henley estate and slowed to a stop in front of the elegant mansion. When the coachman opened the door Lord Craymore was the first to emerge. He gave his daughter his arm as she descended from the carriage and led her up the cobblestone path leading to the front portico.

Richard followed, after nodding to the coachman to wait.

Servants, expecting their arrival, greeted them while Gerald held the door for their entrance into the large foyer.

Lord Craymore continued to hold Alaina's arm firmly in his while he wore a facade of fatherly pride. He beseeched her, in a most concerned voice, to seek out Marielle, then ordered a housemaid to take his daughter to her.

Gerald wanted to protest, knew Marielle needed her rest, but remained silent and led the men to his lord's study.

Alaina followed her father's orders, at least until she entered Marielle's bedchamber. One glance at Marielle and she knew not to pry. She felt awkward at first, but to her relief, Marielle reached out to her.

They said little, but enough to seal a lost friendship, a friendship they both needed and before she left, pledged to protect.

Chapter Eight

MARIELLE LOOKED OUT at the lush gardens below her window while her mind replayed the events over the past few days. The sun, setting down for the night, cast a soft veil of translucent violet over the granite statues in the gardens and bathed distant hills in deep burgundy as the curtain of darkness descended.

Since her return, she felt as if she were watching the world she grew up in from the other side of a misted glass. Now her world would change again. She was leaving for London to begin preparation for her introduction into society, as a lady betrothed.

She'd thought that her father would want to spend more time with her. He'd repeatedly asked for her forgiveness for leaving her upbringing to Gerald and Matty and he seldom left her alone fearing that the kidnappers would return, yet, Lord Craymore's concerns seemed to take higher priority.

London was all abuzz over her kidnapping and the gossipmongers were creating scandalous stories about her days spent as a captive. Lord Craymore wanted his future daughter-in-law's reputation restored. Her father agreed.

With Aunt Cornelia as her chaperone, Richard

accompanying her to social gatherings and the announcement of their upcoming marriage, she'd be protected. Everything was taken into consideration, except for Marielle's desires, desires that she couldn't speak of to anyone.

Her visits with Richard were strained, but, thankfully, he didn't pressure her for information. She told them little, after all, she had no idea of the location of the cottage and her bland descriptions of her captives were of little help.

Her father remained frustrated at her vagueness, but Matty, bless her heart, continually reminded him of her "harrowing" experience and her need to heal.

Alaina Craymore's surprise visit on the day of her return puzzled her at first, but her warmth and sensitivity was heartfelt and it gave them the opportunity to rekindle their friendship. Fortunately, they'd been able to spend many afternoons together. Alaina never pressured her to talk about her captivity, instead, offered her friendship and companionship.

She smiled at the reality of finally having a friend, but grimaced at the thought of her exposure to the *ton*. Worse, she felt dishonest. She pleaded, even demanded that the marriage be delayed at least a year.

Her father was outraged. He reminded her that being alone with the kidnappers was already enough justification for many to accept that she was ruined. Her marriage would protect her from disgrace.

She knew it was a lost cause to argue and she

hoped that her visit with her aunt might help to unravel her confusion, find a course of action and, perhaps, give York more time... She held on to the hope that she would see him again.

Her aunt's letter, delivered a few hours earlier told about the news of the goings-on in London's elite circles. Wanting her to be prepared, she included some of the gossip about "that poor Henley girl's kidnapping". She looked forward to Marielle's visit to find out the truth and have the honor, she wrote, "of trimming off the peacock feathers that had grown on the old turkeys who crowed the loudest". Her aunt loved life in London, still making the round of parties and "old lady teas" as she called them. Cornelia enjoyed a bit of gossip. Her visits were always filled with stories of indiscreet affairs of the nobles or the escapades of foolish young debutantes.

Her aunt had favorites among members of the *ton* whose ongoing pursuits and scandals lit her up like a Christmas tree as she retold their antics, sounding at one moment like a soft spoken conspirator and the next like a babbling busybody. Marielle could well see why she refused to live a quieter life. She'd chosen not to marry and she despised being called an old maid, much preferring to be thought of as an eccentric who found men charming but childish. She enjoyed their company as a distraction. Only her real calling, she felt, was to be an historian.

Aunt Cornelia's letters defined her role exquisitely. "My dear, I am an avid collector of the myths of the moment, the relics of rogues and rapscallions and the tales of meek mice, married to old bores who give extravagant parties and scamper around at night in the guest rooms nipping on the tail of their newest catch."

She once told her niece that there was a special someone who was not meant to be hers. No other man could live up to him, so she preferred to "dabble in the art of the unexpected drama". Her meaning was never quite explained.

As a child, Marielle thought she meant the opera, or the theatre, perhaps, Shakespeare or Spenser. Much less naïve today, she looked forward to learning more about her aunt's pastimes.

EXPECTING HER CONSENT, Richard wanted their marriage date set at the close of the season. He agreed that a rush wedding would cause tongues to wag but waiting any longer, he insisted, was "unthinkable". Aunt Cornelia would make the necessary appointments to the dressmaker for her gowns and trousseau needs. Her mother's wedding gown had already been sent ahead to receive the needed alterations. It seemed everyone, except she, believed it was in her best interest to wed at the earliest socially acceptable date.

As darkness masked the landscape, York's dilemma invaded her thoughts. Her attempts to ask her father about the Blackstone legacy turned out to be impossible. If she did, she'd be divulging information that could lead to York's capture.

How was she to find out the truth? She believed York, didn't she? Hadn't George and the others confirmed the tragedy? No matter how many times she went over everything in her mind, she still could not make sense out of the entire ordeal. Perhaps Aunt Cornelia's knowledge of the past could unravel some of the mystery.

What stayed very real to her was the memory of York's touch and her own illicit behavior. Was she a wanton? Why couldn't she feel these same desires for Richard?

Despite York's obvious hatred for all Craymores, Richard treated her with courtesy and respect. He showed no sign of his father's vices.

She crawled into bed, wrapped the coverlet about her. The last image in her mind before her eyes closed in sleep was of York—his hair that curled at the nape of his neck, his deep blue eyes that sparkled in the sunlight when she sat with him and laughed at the water's edge, his strong chiseled chin, the brooding, dark looks when he told of his father's demise, the memory of their last kiss...before he rode out of her life.

HIDING IN A secluded area near the front entrance of the Henley estate, York watched as the footman lifted the boxes and chests onto the carriage. He'd already heard the footman discuss the trip to London, knew that Marielle was visiting an aunt there.

He'd come the morning of her return also, waited in the same spot, needed to see for himself that Marielle was safely home, not wanting to admit to himself that he hoped he'd get a glimpse of her. Instead, he watched Beatrice go for a run, smiled as he watched her fetch a stick thrown by one of the servants.

Satisfied that all was well, he turned to leave when he heard the sound of carriage wheels, saw the Craymore insignia as the carriage stopped at the front steps. He watched Craymore descend, noted the shock of white hair, the dark, aged complexion, recessed eyes under bushy brows, his stern expression as he held an arm out for his daughter, the one he'd seen conversing with Martin, as she descended the carriage. He watched as Richard joined them, stayed until they'd climbed the massive steps, were greeted by waiting servants and disappeared into the house.

Once back on the road, he urged his horse into a gallop, rode like the wind, needing to strip away the rage at seeing the man he wanted dead. He would have liked to have shot him, watched him as he groveled on the ground, but it would've been a waste. No, when the time came, Craymore would know why he was going to die. York would have the pleasure of watching him squirm, perhaps plead for his life.

His curiosity caused him to return a few more times, this time to find that Marielle was leaving for London. He'd already decided that he would find a way to see her after her arrival. He wondered about her feelings toward him, if they'd changed now that she was home. After all, he'd taken her virginity. She had every right to despise him, but he couldn't get her out of his head or his heart. She belonged to him. When matters were settled, he'd come for her, convince her to be his.

Meanwhile, he'd wait for the right time to strike, to bring Craymore to his knees, when he knew that nothing would stand in his way. He wouldn't endanger Marielle again, but he'd never forget her. He'd be back to claim her.

WHEN MARIELLE ARRIVED in London, the streets were bustling with activity. All manner of carriages were about the streets waiting for their parties or driving their passengers to and fro. The season was in full swing.

Aunt Cornelia had prepared for her visit by announcing her niece's imminent arrival to the more prominent members of the *ton* and many invitations were awaiting her. The first few days, she was given time to rest and chat with her aunt, but her life soon became consumed with activity.

Her aunt, wisely, didn't coerce her into talking about her kidnapping as she had feared. Marielle wanted to speak to her about the Blackstone family, knew that she must have some knowledge of the situation. Few events escaped Aunt Cornelia's notice or her involvement, but the time didn't seem right. Though she trusted her elderly aunt she feared she might repeat something without thinking. She couldn't take the chance.

Days passed in a blur of shopping and engagements. She was grateful for the busyness. For when she spent time alone, she thought only of York. When she was out and about the streets of London, she found herself glancing about hoping that she might see him, wishing that he, too, was thinking of her.

If he'd heard any of the news in London of Lord Craymore's relentless search, she suspected York would wait until things calmed down before making any moves. Richard told her that his father had made contacts throughout London — barkeepers, servants and even unsavory characters who might have some knowledge of the kidnappers. York was wise to stay hidden, but she knew he'd eventually carry out his mission. As time passed, doubts entered in. If only she could talk to him, clear the doubts.

Richard treated her with the highest regard and was a most gracious escort to the soirées of the season. He sent flowers, took her for drives in the park or simply walked with her in her aunt's garden. They spoke light pleasantries and he attempted many times to go beyond a kiss, but Marielle held him off, using the trauma of the kidnapping as an excuse.

She felt like a fraud, but she needed more time. His few awkward attempts to ask her subtle questions about the kidnappers' treatment of her received no reply. She'd express her need to put the experience behind her and though she sensed his frustration, he refrained from pressuring her further.

THE NEWS OF Lady Craymore's death came as no surprise. Since her initial visit, Alaina kept Marielle abreast of her mother's condition through her visits and an exchange of letters. Richard and his father returned to the estate to make arrangements, but were gone for only a few days.

The funeral was a quiet affair with only the immediate family present. Although Richard said little on his return to London, Alaina shared her deep sadness in her letters.

The good news was that Alaina was coming to London. With her mother deceased, her father felt it was time for her debut into society. At Marielle's request, Aunt Cornelia graciously agreed to have her stay with them and happily offered to be her chaperone. Marielle looked forward to their time together and secretly hoped that she might be able to gain more insight into the Craymore family's background.

As the servants prepared her luggage, Alaina Craymore carefully packed those of her mother's jewels she had been allowed to keep and her mother's secret savings. She hoped never to return to this dismal home. A new world was opening up to her and she was ready to make it her own.

She mourned the loss of her mother, but knew it was for the best. In the end, Alaina was the only one by her bedside. Her father had no desire to see his wife waste away and Richard was unable to stay for more than a few minutes.

Although her brother seldom revealed his emotions, she saw his eyes fill with tears on his last visit before he turned quickly and left. He was his father's son and whether through admiration or fear, he refused to show weakness and would continue to follow his dictates.

Alaina wondered if Richard's avoidance of his mother and sister grew more from guilt than disregard. After all, he received their mother's loving care and knew all too well of his father's abuse. She remembered the time years before when he attempted to stand in front of his mother to protect her from their father's brutality. He was no more than ten. Their father had lifted him in the air and thrown him to the floor, then gave him a strapping that left him bleeding.

Her mother pleaded with him to stop, but she was thrust aside. Later, when her father stormed out, her mother ran to comfort her son. Richard refused to cry or allow her to comfort him. Instead, he turned away. From that day on, he was no longer the brother she knew. He obeyed his father's every command and disappeared the moment any controversy between his parents became evident. He remained uncommunicative to his mother and sister, choosing instead to seek his father's respect and avoid his wrath.

Her mother seemed to understand her son's need to keep his father's love and distance himself from his emotions and from her, but Alaina felt disgust at her brother's cruel behavior. The distance grew between them until they barely spoke a civil word to one another.

She would see more of him now that she'd be joining Marielle in London. Both her father and brother hoped that Marielle would confide in her about the men who'd kidnapped her. Alaina had succeeded in convincing them that it would take time for her to gain Marielle's confidence and that Marielle appeared to be in shock about the whole incident during her visits with her at the Henley estate. Only compassion and patience would cause her to open up.

They reluctantly accepted her reasoning and other concerns kept both of them occupied. Ironically, their ploy to use Alaina as bait had turned into a blessing. She now had a friend.

"YORK, YOUR SILENCE is deafening. What is going on in that head of yours?" Martin asked, as he walked onto the porch and saw his brother staring out into the distance. His face, set like chiseled stone, was grim, unreadable.

"I'm thinking that you need to find more things to occupy yourself with instead of my thoughts."

"Your thoughts are no doubt murderous if your moods are any indication. Let's have it." He knew York would not rest now that Craymore was no longer a ghost from the past, but alive and well and now there was an added complication, Marielle. "So what is our next move?"

"Our next move?" York arched his brow.

"Whether I like it or not, I'm very much involved. After my extremely unpleasant visit with the man, I have my own matters to settle."

York nodded, understood. Martin's bruises were healing, but still visible. "Though I despise the waiting, we must. I'll find out what I can from Jeremy tonight."

"I fear this London trip is a mistake. Craymore most likely has our names now since he has all of London looking for us. You're taking too big of a chance."

"We need supplies and I want to find out as

much as I can about his whereabouts. He's not at the estate and I want him there when the times is right."

"So you've checked out the estate as well?"

"Certainly. Craymore will let down his guard sooner or later and I'll know when and where."

"Have you also checked on Marielle?"

"That, brother, is my personal business."

MARIELLE HAD TO admit Aunt Cornelia was right. Her attendance at the plethora of gatherings of the *haute ton* did manage to assuage a good deal of the gossip. On Richard's arm and with his devoted attentiveness and her father's attendance at a couple of the affairs, the talk lessened, just as they had hoped. Other scandalous stories erupted concerning one of the season's newest debutantes and it seemed that Marielle's kidnapping was slowly becoming old news.

Tonight's ball would be one of the biggest of the season. Marielle's attempt to feign a headache failed. Her aunt saw through her easily and urged her to attend not only to quiet any residue of gossip, but, she reminded Marielle, Alaina needed her support.

Aunt Cornelia was well aware that she, like Marielle, preferred to stay home but her father had sent strict orders, even insisted that she forego the darkest colors of mourning, suggesting lilac or grey. The exposure to the *ton* meant being introduced to the most prominent eligible bachelors and he didn't want her to miss the opportunity. Some members of the *ton* would find her presence a sign of disrespect, but Cornelia was quite adept at handling the most straight-laced of them. She knew Alaina would continue to grieve the loss of her mother. However, going against her father's wishes would mean sending her back to him and that would be worse.

Alaina accepted Aunt Cornelia's wisdom. She feared being under her father's control again and needed time to create a plan for her life. She loved being with Marielle and her delightful aunt and wanted nothing to cause him to change the arrangement.

It was close to midnight and people were still arriving. Marielle and Richard shared many dances and she'd dutifully spent time chatting with two of the more elderly dowager viscountesses.

Leaving Marielle to rest, Richard left to speak with his father. Since Alaina was on the dance floor with a very eligible bachelor and Aunt Cornelia sat watching her with other chaperones, Marielle found an opportunity to walk out on the patio. The blackness of the night made it impossible for her to see much beyond the balcony steps. She could hear the music and the laughter and wanted no part of it.

"Not enjoying the party, milady?" A voice from the shadows shocked her into attention.

"*York?*" Her voice a shaky whisper.

"Come here, away from the light."

Marielle followed the voice, moved blindly toward the darkest corner of the terrace, her heart pounding. A hand reached for her, she allowed him to draw her close. "York, it is truly you. How did you know I was here? And *why* are you here? It's much too dangerous."

York raised his finger to her lips to calm and quiet her. "I *do* read an occasional paper. Your escapades with your betrothed have been well publicized, even the expectation that you would be attending this monstrous affair. I thought I'd see only a glimpse of you, but fortune was with me." With that, he pulled her into his arms, crushed her to him, before she could utter a sound.

Marielle melted into his arms. His kiss was just as she remembered. Time and place disappeared, only his embrace and the feel of his lips on hers mattered.

York finally, regretfully, broke the kiss, knew if he didn't he'd be tempted to take her with him, find a hidden place to ravish her. "My midnight miss, you look ravishingly beautiful."

Her silver gown enhanced her shapely figure and, in York's opinion, revealed much too much cleavage. "The thought of kidnapping you once again is very tempting." York restrained himself from pulling at her gown to reveal her hidden treasures. He focused his eyes on hers, forced his mind to remain clear, but he saw even in the dim light that her desire was as deep as his own.

The sound of footsteps broke the spell. York turned to see a figure standing just outside the doors. "Pity, my sweet Marielle, but I must leave."

"But *where* are you going? What do you plan to do?"

"As usual, you ask too many questions," York whispered. "I look forward to seeing you again…one day soon, *if* you're not married off."

"York, I must tell you…"

"Good night, Marielle."

Before she could utter another word, he brushed her lips with one last kiss and he was gone, once again, out of her life.

She stood in the darkness, saw Richard at the balcony doors looking about. If only she could have told York what she felt, that she didn't know how to proceed without affecting the lives of everyone about her, or worse, revealing too much, endangering his life. If only she could have warned him of Lord Craymore's aggressive search. The moment with him was gone and she knew nothing more than before, only his touch, once again, that lingered. She wrapped her arms about her, forced herself to step back into the light, back to her life with Richard, to live the lie, until she knew what to do.

CORNELIA SAT IN her private drawing room shuffling through the many invitations that had arrived that morning. Tonight they would be at Almack's and, no doubt, the eligible bachelors would be filling Alaina's dance card. She was a beautiful girl and much sought after, yet, she seemed to be completely uninterested in any of the young men seeking her attention. Richard, as expected, would accompany Marielle.

Young Craymore, she mused, did his best to silence any sordid rumors. His father, too, made it his business to assure others that his future daughter-in-law had escaped unharmed from her captors, her virginity intact.

Cornelia, personally, had no use for Lord Craymore. His background was far from being free of scandal, but he always managed to find his way into the most elite circles. His humorless and often condescending comments made him an unpopular guest, but he did know how to flatter the married ladies bored with their husbands. His name was too often attached to gossip concerning clandestine visits to the bedrooms of "proper" wives who enjoyed illicit sexual encounters, though she guessed he was getting a bit old to satisfy them.

His own marriage had never gotten in the way of his sexual exploits. Now with his wife deceased, she expected that he'd be even more visible and irritating to the extreme. Something about his demeanor sent chills up her spine, even since the day she'd first met him decades earlier. He was gracious enough, but her sensitivities led her to be wary of him.

Her present concerns were the two lovely young ladies in her charge. She was determined to bring Marielle out of her doldrums. Richard had been unable to lift her spirits. On previous visits to the country estate, she found her niece to be a fiery young thing, but the fire was gone and Cornelia didn't like it one bit. Alaina was as much in need of her expertise. With a father like Ward Craymore, she suspected she had a great deal of work to do.

Cornelia was interrupted in her thoughts by her servant tapping on the door.

"Milady, Master Craymore has arrived and is now speaking to Alaina. They have called Marielle from her room and would like you to be present."

"Send the three of them in to see me as soon as my niece appears."

"Yes milady. I..." Before the servant could finish, Marielle walked through the door looking visibly upset. Alaina followed, with Richard close behind.

"Forgive our intrusion, Aunt Cornelia." Richard has something to tell me, but refuses to say a word without your presence."

"Well, here I am, so get on with it young man. Don't leave us in suspense."

Richard bowed before speaking. "I thought you might want to be part of the celebration."

"Celebration? What news do you have for me?" Marielle asked, uncomfortable with Richard's abrupt visit and unusual behavior.

"Please, Marielle, won't you have a seat?"

"I'd prefer it if you would just tell me what this is all about." Marielle said exasperated, but allowed him to lead her to the nearest settee.

"My father, as you know, has actively sought the whereabouts of your kidnappers and..." He paused, an obvious gloat settling on his face. "I'm pleased to announce, he has succeeded! Two are now under arrest, the older brother, I believe and one of his partners in crime."

York captured? Marielle stared at Richard in shock. Her mind reeled with the implications. My God, what will happen to him? Had he been captured after the ball last night, after he'd left her?

Richard bent down beside her. "Marielle, are you all right? You seemed dazed by the news."

Marielle covered her face with her hands, unable to respond to his question.

He hadn't realized she still held so much emotion over the entire affair. He wanted to forget it, hoped their time in London together had helped to erase the memories. He thought this with irritation since they'd spent very little time alone over the past two months. He was either presenting her at a ball, or she was off to the dressmakers or having tea with the ladies of the *ton*. Her overprotective aunt was like a mother hen. He found it a relief to go off to the clubs or visit Jeanette after their social obligations were over and Marielle was safely home. His new mistress was quite satisfying, to say the least.

Capturing the two men turned out to be a delightful achievement, considering it came through Jeanette, a delectable companion he found at Sherry's brothel. He'd reward her well for her keen observances.

His father's reaction was even more surprising after he'd told him the name of the captured brother was Blackstone, an infamous name he'd remembered from childhood. Richard knew the name was that of a traitor, one who his father helped to put in prison and who had once been the master of the estate they now enjoyed. Richard found it mind-boggling. He couldn't tell if his father was relieved over the capture or ready to have a seizure. Now Marielle, too, reacted strangely.

He pushed away his feelings of uneasiness. Now that at least two of the tyrants were behind bars, their marriage plans could go forward without ghosts. The kidnapping actually worked to his benefit. Desiring to keep his daughter near him, Lord Henley had no problem agreeing to have Richard move onto the estate rather than to have Marielle live at Craymore. In no time at all, he would be running the Henley estate, be out from under his father's thumb.

Breaking the uncomfortable silence, Aunt Cornelia called for a maid to bring refreshment.

Meanwhile, Marielle struggled to reestablish her self-control and respond to the news. "Thank you, Richard," she paused to gather her nerves, "for informing me, but how can you be certain that these are the kidnappers?"

"My dear, my father paid handsomely for any information to identify the kidnappers. Blackstone was clearly identified by the man used by the kidnappers to bring the ransom note. His partner, captured with him, is well known in London as a street thief."

"Braum," Marielle whispered, looking away.

"Why, yes," Richard said stiffly, disgusted by his fiancée's mention of the name. "Might you tell me something about them now that they are captured, darling? It might help us find the brother who is still on the loose."

"Martin has not been found?"

"No," Richard said curtly clenching his teeth, "but we'll not rest until he too is imprisoned."

Marielle realized her vulnerability, feared he might read too much into her reactions. Her heart felt caught in a web of deceit. She couldn't deny what she felt for York, or their intimacy, but Richard must not know of her conflicting emotions.

"I'm greatly relieved, Richard. I must know, however, that you have truly captured the right men. Otherwise, I should still be afraid."

"I understand, darling," he said, relieved at her words, "but you say their names as if you've known them, well, more intimately," Richard responded, a forced smile frozen on his face.

"Richard!" Alaina scolded. "How dare you speak so accusingly? Marielle is obviously relieved, but no doubt upset that this horrid time in her life must be relived."

"Please, Alaina, I can speak for myself. They saw me as a lucrative venture, Richard. They took care not to harm me. I've realized since my return that it could have been much worse. I expect that you are also relieved that they were not bloodthirsty animals."

"Of course," Richard said cloaking his anger. "They were wise not to harm you. Regardless, they deserve to be punished with the greatest severity for their crime. My father and I will see to it that they are."

"And how were they captured? Did they attempt another kidnapping?" Marielle asked innocently. She needed to know if York was physically harmed.

Richard laughed, surprising both Marielle and Alaina. "Actually, it was my father's ingenious idea to spread the word through London's houses of ill repute. Money, I dare say, is more alluring to the ladies of the house than their clientele. It seems this

Blackstone and his fellow scoundrel couldn't stay away. Fortunately, my...ah...father found the right contacts. While the two culprits thought they were safe in the arms of their whores, they were seized." Richard grinned. "I wished I could have been there to see their humiliation.

Richard seemed completely unaware of how inappropriate it was to tell such a story to single young ladies.

"Now, my dear, I suggest that you take some needed rest, for it may be necessary for you to identify them." Richard didn't notice Marielle's stunned expression. His obvious delight that the kidnappers were found in such compromising positions in a brothel caused him to forget his audience.

"Thank you, Richard, for your consideration. The news, I must admit, has upset me more than I thought." Marielle held her hand to her forehead and gave Richard a weak smile. "You've been kind and understanding throughout this entire ordeal. Why, I believed for a short time with you by my side here in London, the frightening experience had begun to fade away. This news has brought it all back and I am afraid that it will now overshadow our plans," Marielle said with a feigned sigh. "Perhaps it would be best to hold off the wedding plans until the criminals have been dealt with, so I may feel free to go on without fear. I'm afraid that you've become embroiled in a situation a man to be wed should not have to deal with."

Richard's face softened a bit at Marielle's tender words, but her suggestion was unthinkable.

"My dear," he spoke softly reaching for Marielle's hand and bringing it to his lips. "Their arrest should bring some closure to the pain you've been subjected to through this entire ordeal. Postponing our wedding serves no purpose and may only cause added rumors to those already circulating. And darling," Richard pressed his lips to her palm and kissed it lightly, "I look forward to the day when I can make you as happy as you have made me. The wedding date will not be changed."

Marielle noted the determination in his voice and had no strength to argue. "Forgive me, Richard, but I suddenly feel quite unwell. Please excuse me. I need to retire to my room."

"I agree with my niece." Lady Cornelia, who'd been standing aside watching in silence as the episode unfolded before her, noted specifically Marielle's changing demeanor. *The girl is more upset than she is letting on. I must find out what she is hiding.* "The news has obviously brought back fearful memories." Lady Cornelia continued as she moved to the door, opened it, waited.

Richard, realizing he was being dismissed, reached out once again to Marielle only to have her gather her skirts, stand and turn to join her aunt.

"Forgive my lack of courtesy, but I really need time alone. Please keep me informed of any new developments." She walked quickly through the door and ascended the staircase without a backward glance.

Richard turned to Alaina. "Tell Marielle that I will find Father and see to it that the arraignment is speedy and their punishment deserving of the crime."

Alaina, stunned at the interchange and at Marielle's reaction, nodded and watched as her brother bowed to Aunt Cornelia and turned to leave, slamming the door behind him.

Aunt Cornelia watched Richard through the glass as he rode off, her mind filled with every detail of the encounter. Richard's obvious pleasure in the capture, Marielle's unusual behavior and Alaina's facial expressions as she watched the interaction, gave her much to mull over. She needed time to consider her response to the new and interesting developments.

An unsettling feeling washed over her as memories of the past and the Blackstone name rose in her mind like whitecaps on a stormy sea. Lord Blackstone, his wife and family, were devoted to one another, that she remembered well. How shocking it was when she found out that Blackstone had been accused of treason and Craymore granted his estate.

King George, having lost his reason, made Blackstone's loyalty to him of no account. The Prince Regent held little interest in the affair. How strange that Marielle's reaction to the imprisonment of the young Blackstone was very like her own when she heard of the elder Blackstone's arrest. How strange indeed.

SETTLING IN FOR the ride to Sherry's Place that evening, Richard mulled over the events of the day. The news of the capture would be made public in no time and fuel the gossip mill. It made little difference whether the facts were accurate or the informant trustworthy, only that afternoon teas became tastier and evening performances more palatable.

The irritation he felt when Marielle had shown such scant relief hearing the news of her assailants' capture, still rankled. He'd hoped the news would have made him more of a hero in her eyes. Her reaction only fueled his uncertainty of her devotion and injured his pride.

A visit to Jeanette would lift his spirits. His discomfort needed some respite and quite possibly, with a little coaxing, his French doxy might remember more about this Braum fellow. A man who indulges in too much whiskey and then pays for sexual favors might talk more than he can perform, Richard mused.

Through Braum, she knew of the brothers. The tyrant may have mentioned where they lived. *How ironic that she should be acquainted with one of the scoundrels*, he thought. Obviously this Braum did not please her, or she found Father's grand idea of a reward much more enticing. Regardless, she might remember something that would lead him to the brother who'd escaped. He knew he would recognize him on the spot.

If only he'd known then that he was a Blackstone. Richard remembered finding toys, books and other signs that children had lived in the house before his family moved onto the estate. He was too young to understand the circumstances only that the Blackstone name was never to be mentioned. As he gained more of his father's trust, he learned vague details of his father's part in bringing a traitor to justice. The elder Craymore wanted him to know the truth, he told his son, to protect him from false rumors.

The security of England was at stake, Richard could hear his father words reverberate in his brain and Blackstone's popularity made him more dangerous. Who could be a better spy than a trusted advisor? Knowing of too many of his father's questionable actions, he had to admit that his father's strong allegiance to fight for justice and the security of the country was out of character.

His father's pride, however, at becoming the lord of Blackstone's most magnificent estate was obvious. He thought, now as he sat in his carriage that rumbled over the cobble stoned streets, of conflicting details of his father's role that he'd earlier ignored.

Lord Blackstone most likely died in prison. Why is it that his sons have come back into their lives in such a strange way? His father had turned pale at the news of the identity of Marielle's captors. Did he fear revenge? Might Marielle's kidnapping have other ramifications? There were too many questions. Finding the younger brother might be more important than he'd originally thought.

The carriage pulled up at Sherry's Place, but he changed his mind. He directed his coachman to his father's London address. The chain of events carried missing links and scandal weaved through it with more than a single thread. He was his father's son, not out of admiration, but from fear —

fear that turned to acceptance of his father's ways and even pride at his father's ruthlessness. He still carried the guilt of turning his back on his mother's needs. He remembered, with disgust, how he fled the house, rather than stay at his dying mother's bedside. He'd mounted his horse and rode for hours, tears of regret stinging his face while the wind turned his skin raw. The faster he rode, the more his emotions surfaced until he stopped and collapsed on the ground groveling in the dirt like a worm.

He felt like one.

At times he felt hatred for his mother, even more than for his father. Her gentleness gave him weakness rather than strength, confusion rather than peace. He came to believe that the path of self-preservation was power and wielding it brought him satisfaction for a time.

He could pretend indifference toward his mother and his sister and took pride in ordering his father's men to do his bidding, but he could never stand up to his father. The pain of this truth was too unbearable to think about. When his will lost the battle and his thoughts strayed in that direction, he'd take off, find pleasure in women or drink himself into a state of oblivion. The next morning he'd resolve to be more like his father so he could escape the hell of his emotions. *Leave them to the women who could carry them like babies in their bellies*, he'd thought.

Although he felt incapable of love, Richard hoped that after the wedding, he and Marielle might learn to live together in a way that would bring satisfaction to both of them and free him from his father's control. Once he married, his sister could live with them. Too often he'd been forced to turn his father's attention to business affairs in order to protect Alaina from his father's rages. As she grew older and their mother's health weakened, Alaina took on the role of her mother's protector and even found the courage to stand against their father if her mother's welfare or safety was endangered.

As the carriage rolled on through the cobblestoned streets, he thought of his sister and the family role she chose, so different from his own. She'd figured out ways to keep their father away from their mother, remembering once how she rang a bell, deliberately, to call a servant when her father was close to striking their mother. In another instance, she caused a vase to crash to the floor to draw her father's attention when he was beginning to turn violent. Father would rage at Alaina, but with the broken glass in her hand or the bell cord pulled to call a servant, he would storm out swearing to take care of both of them later.

His mother's illness kept both of them safe, for his father despised sickness and Alaina was most often found near her mother's bedside. He feared that after his marriage to Marielle and with his mother gone, that Alaina might be in danger if she returned to the estate.

Since his sister had come to London, Richard noticed the admiring glances of the young men standing in line to be introduced or grateful for a dance with this new beauty who had been hidden away. He felt a newfound pride when he walked into a room with Marielle on one arm and Alaina on the other. She would smile gracefully at him before the eyes of the *ton* and before being whisked off by Marielle's old maid aunt for introductions or for a dance with one of the hopeful young men. But he knew Alaina held little respect for him.

His sister could not possibly understand what it was like to be the only begotten son who was to carry on the family name, he reasoned, or the pressure he felt to bend to his father's wishes. He'd learned to rationalize every illegal maneuver his father made. He chose to believe that all men in power must play a game in order to wield that power. Hadn't his father voiced just that to him since he was old enough to recognize that power brought obedience?

Knowing his father's methods of operation, it was difficult not to question his father's patriotic role in the treason trial of Lord Blackstone. His father always had an ulterior motive that fit his own best interests. Although he was quite young when his family moved into the former Blackstone estate, he was old enough to recognize his mother's unhappiness. He clearly remembered his father's demand for her to keep silent when she attempted to discuss the fate of the Lady Blackstone and the children.

Why were all these memories invading his mind now? He wanted no part of his father's past deeds, or his father's demons. He carried enough of his own.

As much as his father sought to mold him into

his own image, his mother's influence followed him like a dark shadow. He'd learned to stifle contradictory emotions, mask his feelings. Even the passionate fury he should have felt over Marielle's kidnapping or tears of relief when she'd been found, escaped him. His laughter or congeniality at the events of the *ton* was that of a good actor.

He felt nothing.

Something changed in him when his mother died, guilt, anger, his father's caustic reaction. He still played the role of dutiful son, but it no longer brought satisfaction. His father disgusted him, therefore, his own self loathing became a daily demon to fight off.

Lately, he was losing the battle.

As the carriage turned into his father's drive, Richard stared blankly at the red velvet curtain that blocked his view of the coachman. He wondered where his thoughts were taking him. An emotion he couldn't name coursed through his body, surprised him, caused his body to shudder.

ALONE IN HER bedchamber, Marielle replayed Richard's words in her mind. York captured while in the arms of a harlot... *Why he'd just left me, waited for me. I thought he'd chanced capture by returning to London to see me. It seems his weakness for women created his downfall, Marielle thought indignantly.*

If he loved me... She realized where her thoughts were leading. *How foolish of me. He'd never used those words. He wanted me only to satisfy his lust and now his lust has led to his capture.* She pounded the bedding with a fist silently cursing his name. *Even*

Richard, she thought, had never professed love, only admiration and gentlemanly courtesy. She realized the men in her life controlled her and her own desire for love blinded her, allowed her to be used. Her anger magnified at the thought. He deserved to be caught, he's a disreputable tyrant. She forced herself to push away any thoughts of concern for him, especially the feeling she refused to identify, that she'd fallen in love with her kidnapper.

ALAINA CRAYMORE CHOSE to spend the remainder of the afternoon in her room. She couldn't shake off a strange feeling that bordered on fear. It had something to do with the name Blackstone. She lay in bed for a long time, refusing dinner. When darkness fell, she tossed and turned, finally falling to sleep.

In her dream, she was just a child, no more than seven. She crouched in a corner, her small hands covering her ears. The floor rumbled and the chandelier swayed above her. At the moment of her deepest fright, her mother appeared. She came towards her with her arms extended, bloody arms. Alaina tried to reach out, but a large shadow appeared. Her mother stared down at her with fearful eyes, then turned away to face the shadow. She watched as her mother picked up a candle stick which had fallen from a mantle and placed it back in its original spot. As she did so, the shadow disappeared.

Alaina awoke, her body drenched in sweat. She rose quickly from the bed and went to the water basin and splashed her face repeatedly. What did the dream mean?

The shadow had to be her father, for he overpowered her mother and controlled her actions. She recognized her home, the Craymore estate, though everything around her appeared changed. She remembered her mother's pleading and felt the power of her father's wrath. She sat on the edge of the bed and held her head in her hands.

There was something else, something more. She felt her mother wanted to tell her something, but what?

Chapter Nine

IT WAS NOON of the third day of his imprisonment, though the darkness in the cell gave the appearance of night. Time held no significance for York. He could barely move in the small damp space where he'd spent the last few days. Braum was in a nearby cell, out of sight. They spoke only an occasional word to see how each was faring. Little else needed to be said.

Except for stale bread and water, the food given them was rancid. The odor of feces and urine caused him to vomit the little that was in his stomach. He forced himself to eat the stale bread and drink the dank water while he prayed that Martin would stay away.

They'd come into town for much needed supplies. They were taking a chance being seen, but they'd eluded the law more times than he could remember. He also couldn't deny that he wanted to see Marielle, even if it was only a glimpse.

It was late evening when they met their trusted ally, Jeremy Duggins and made arrangements for supplies. They had a few hours to wait and Braum became unbearable knowing they were only a short distance from his favorite doxy, the French import, Jeanette.

York couldn't stop him and knowing where

Marielle might be, York gave in to his own need to see her. The darkness and the heavy fog would conceal them well enough.

After his brief visit with Marielle, York returned to the docks only to find that Braum was still at the brothel and Jeremy hadn't returned. He became restless. He decided it was time to coax Braum away, hoping by the time he returned, Jeremy would be back. The streets were empty and it took only a few minutes to reach the brothel's discreet entrance.

Clarisse, York's usual companion when he visited, appeared as York entered the parlor. She rushed to him, clenched his coat sleeves. York pulled her away, but before he could tell her he wasn't interested, she whispered, pleaded with him to follow her into one of the rooms. Something was wrong. With the door closed, she quickly told him the dreaded news.

Jeanette had been available when Braum arrived earlier. She'd asked for a few minutes to freshen up. That must have been when she sent a runner to bring the authorities, Clarisse explained. They arrived shortly after she joined Braum and he was taken into custody.

Before she could go on, a commotion in the hall drew their attention. York had no time to react. The authorities stormed through the door. Clarisse threw herself at York wrapping her arms around him, kissing him, hoping to protect him. York appreciated her ploy, but it was too late. Two men grabbed him, pushing Clarisse to the floor.

York knew that Clarisse wanted to help, but

Jeanette thought only of the reward. It did no good now to think about what should have been done.

His thoughts turned to Marielle and the words of the men who had brought him to the jail cell. "So you thought you'd get away with capturing an heiress. Figured you'd be enjoying the fruits of your crime. But she got the better of you, she did. Her description must o' did you in. She'll enjoy seeing you hanged from the gallows." They'd pushed him into the cell, locked it and left, still mocking him.

Marielle. York pictured her, as he had seen her tonight in her silver, jeweled gown. *Why wouldn't she tell what she knows? I took advantage of her innocence, ruined her. Her marriage plans were publicized enough. She'd want to get on with her life, forget... She'd wanted to tell him something before he'd left her on the balcony, or did she want to entice him to stay long enough to be caught?*

He turned his thoughts from her, to his brother. York left Jeremy with instructions in case of trouble. He knew his friend would follow his directives and, hopefully, before Martin took it upon himself to come to London and search for him. York's fears of what he would do made his captivity all the worse.

JEREMY HAD PACKED the wagon with the supplies York requested and arrived at the docks shortly after York left to find Braum. He dozed for a time, but when he woke to the damp chill of daybreak, he knew something was wrong.

Leaving the supplies behind, he trudged off to

Shipley's Tavern, a short distance from Sherry's Place. He figured if anything bad had happened, someone there was sure to know. It didn't take him long to find out.

He knew what he needed to do as he muttered to himself. *I'll see who I can dig up. A meetin' at Devil's Dam... It's been awhile since we been there, but it's needed fer sure.*

Jeremy went off to gather what was left of the men who'd lived off the streets together, the men selected by York to be part of the pact made in blood years before, the ones who knew of Devil's Dam.

Some of the old crowd wouldn't be available, Jeremy grimaced. Lester had been shot. Jake was locked up again for getting drunk and brawling and Arthur got himself married to a shopkeeper's daughter. Jeremy laughed thinking about Arthur, since they had done their share of robbing his new father-in-law more times than he could count. The old gang had their share of wild adventures together and misery as well.

He found only two men available in such short notice, Bates and Willie. Others would be rounded up soon enough. Jeremy filled both men in and with few words spoken, they readily agreed to help. The men came to accept each other's rough edges over the years and looked out for one another. If any one of them was captured, if a cooling-off period was needed, or if a plan had to be made, news would travel swiftly through the streets and those who were available would meet on the nearest Saturday at midnight, unless news spread for a more urgent meeting. It turned out to be an ingenious setup that had been used many times over the years.

Since there was no other way to contact Martin—York kept their living quarters sacred wanting no one to intrude—Jeremy could only hope that he'd question York's absence, suspect trouble and show at their historic meeting place. He had bad news for Martin and little to offer for help.

SOMETHING WAS VERY wrong. Martin's emotions warred with his common sense. He was ready to ride to London at lightning speed. George used what persuasion he could muster to beg him to heed his brother's advice. As difficult as it was, Martin knew he was right. He knew York's plan was to meet Jeremy for supplies. Whatever happened, Jeremy would know and he'd show up at the meeting place tonight.

By late afternoon, Martin was on his way. As he rode on, he feared what he would find. If no one showed up at Devil's Dam, he'd ride into London. Contacts in Bethnal Green or Whitechapel might know something.

It was close to midnight when Martin reached his destination. The moon lit his path until he reached a fork in the road. He brought his horse to a halt, looked around and listened for any uncommon sounds. Hearing nothing unusual, he nudged his horse, leading him off the main path into the woods. He followed a narrow path that led up through rough terrain until he could hear the sound of water trickling through rocks. Moving slowly in the darkness, he reached the great wall of rugged rock. He dismounted and walked the horse around the wall to a clearing where a small spring lapped at nearby rocks, barely visible in the darkness.

York discovered the place years before and brought Martin and trusted others back to it to share his find. The rock wall was obviously an old ruin, probably built by the Romans when they inhabited the land over a thousand years earlier. They were master builders who cut through forests to build roads as well as fortresses. They probably chose this spot because of the availability of water and the incline which would allow them to see invaders. York had studied Latin and the history of the Roman conquests before his family was turned out of their estate. He shared what he could with Martin who'd been denied higher learning when they'd been removed from their home. When he found this spot, he couldn't wait to bring Martin to see it.

It was Martin who dubbed it Devil's Dam.

York considered it a marvel. Their friends showed little interest in the decrepit crumbling wall, but all agreed that it was a fine hideout. A fire could be blazing and remain unseen from the road and the wall gave protection from wind or the night's chill. In time it became a sacred meeting place—tonight Martin hoped that time had not weakened their pact.

Those who remained in London would most likely know if York and Braum were in danger. News sails through London like a handkerchief caught in a breeze and information can be easily purchased for a few pounds, Martin thought, as he collected wood to build a fire.

Before long, he heard the sounds of horses coming from behind the wall. He moved to the opposite edge where a chink in the wall allowed him to see, while remaining hidden from view. Once the riders became visible, he sighed with relief.

The men, as they approached the wall and could see Martin's face in the light of the fire, grinned with satisfaction.

Jeremy broke the news immediately of York and Braum's capture. They were being kept at Kingston Prison for the time being. He suspected that they'd be moved to a higher security prison, probably Newgate, after the trial. Jeremy knew a jailer at Kingston who owed him a favor, but the men had little else to offer.

Seeing that Martin had already started to build a fire, Bates and Willie searched around for more wood to keep it going. Jeremy added a couple more pieces and stoked it until the flames began to take on a life of their own.

Soon the men were settled around the fire watching the flames dance in the brisk night air. Martin took little notice. He was anxious to get on with a plan. Bates pulled out two bottles of whiskey, one from each pocket and passed one around while he opened the second and took two long gulps. Jeremy opened a sack of dried beef and mutton and passed it around. Warmed by the fire and the whisky, they were ready to answer Martin's questions and help in whatever way they could.

Jeremy began with the events on the night he met York and Braum and added the information he collected. Willie and Bates nodded their heads grimly in agreement, adding other bits of news, none of them hopeful.

Martin listened without interruption, his mind absorbing each detail. The thought of York being in a prison cell appalled him. Much of the time his father was imprisoned was a blur, but not the sight of his father when he was finally released.

He remembered being led over to his father's bedside by his mother's coaxing hand and the cold, thin feel of his father's skin. He wanted to pull away, but his mother held his shoulders securely, urging him to stay. He remembered tears filling his father's tired, weary eyes and how his father's body appeared shriveled beneath worn, oversized clothing, his large bootless feet hanging over his mother's small cot.

In Martin's mind the memory of that one moment stretched on through the years, mixed with earlier, more pleasant memories. He remembered his father's deep laughter as he lifted his younger son on a horse for his first ride and wrapped the leather reins about his fingers as he slid sideways, his father large hands securing him in the center. He'd been sickly and scrawny. Flesh, his mother would say just wouldn't stick to his bones. His mother feared he would fall, but his father won out and for weeks his father patiently walked beside him until he could ride the horse around the stable yard with confidence. The memories swept through him as swiftly as the fire raced over the dry brush before him. How strange these memories, which had been like fog in his mind over the years should now be as vivid and poignant as if they happened yesterday.

His thoughts returned to the last night he saw his father alive. He remembered York standing by their father's bedside. With great effort, his father turned toward York and Martin swore he saw a grin form on his dry crusted lips. His brother, unafraid of the sight before him and with tear-filled eyes, wrapped his arms around his dying father's body. Martin would never forget the anguished sound of his brother's cries, nor his mother's weeping, or the hours they hovered by the body of his father until he took his last breath.

The courts, Martin heard later, were considered by some to be most merciful. They released the traitor, not because of his mother's constant letters professing her husband's innocence and pleading for his release, but because his sentence had not been death.

With his health deteriorating, some older members of Parliament who doubted his alliance with the French, called for a vote in Parliament for his release. Perhaps one of his mother's letters may have reached them. Regardless of their sympathies, only one argument won support. Sending him back to his family meant they didn't have to concern themselves with burial costs. The vote to release him passed and he was sent home to die.

Martin shivered at the memories and the thought of his own brother now behind prison walls. He'd do whatever possible so York wouldn't suffer the same fate.

THE MEN WATCHED Martin's face as he stared into the fire. His blank stare gave no clue to his thoughts. Jeremy finally broke the silence.

"Martin, we ain't been defeated before by the authorities or prison walls. As it is, the foot patrol has dwindled in the boroughs, money being tight and I'm well acquainted with the jailer who owes me a big favor. It was him I came upon being beaten up in an alley for not paying his gambling debts. Why we chased those bullies out of there and this chump was practically crying in my arms, thanking me for saving him.

"Can't say what I can get him to do, but I'm sure to get some news. There have been a few riots lately with all the cut down in patrols and such. You know, jailers complaining they can't keep up with the numbers of prisoners and all. We have opportunities here if we can get them at Kingston before they lock them up at Newgate or the Tower.

Martin cringed at the mention of Newgate, breaking him free from his thoughts that did nothing to help the present situation. Jeremy was right—they'd accomplished what seemed impossible more than once.

"Jeremy, find out what you can from this jailer and anyone else that might know about the prison conditions and layout and find out if York or Braum were injured.

"Bates, you say you've been keeping an eye on the Henley townhouse and you've seen Henley's daughter? Tell me every detail."

"Well, Marty," Bates spoke up. "Jeremy told me to keep an eye on the lady's place after he heard about York and Braum. We knew enough from the papers that the younger Craymore and the kidnapped girl were planning a wedding. We thought that since we couldn't help York, we might be able to hear some news through the girl. I can tell ya' what I've seen first and what's been rumored around."

Bates' voice was slurring a bit from the whisky and before he could take another gulp, Jeremy grabbed the near empty bottle.

"Oh, don't ya' worry there, Jeremy, I can hold a lot more than that before I lose my head. Anyways, I watched the Henley house for the past couple of days. I talked to one of the maids that came to and fro from the nearby pub. It seems she has a taste for ale and a goodly jiggle in her behind when she sneaks out the back door. I bought her a couple of rounds and she was as chatty as an old hen being rousted by a rooster. I hope to spend a little more time with her when this is over. Why, when she gets going her bosoms just rise and fall like waves on a windy day. It was all I could do to keep my hands to m'self."

"Get on with it," Jeremy interrupted. We need to keep our heads on the problem at hand as York always reminded us when we'd go off. I'd like to find out who was the snitch that identified York."

"It could have been Marielle, I suppose, or

Griggs," Martin interrupted. "You were wise to watch the house. Her connection to Craymore was a surprise to us and it's led to this catastrophe.

He turned to Bates. "Tell me what you found out."

"I stayed out and around the place until I knew we were meeting tonight. I seen the two young ladies. One's that Miss Henley, York and Braum took off with and Craymore's daughter's the other one, according to the well bosomed Bess, Lady Henley's kitchen helper." Bates stopped to emphasize, with his hands, her endowments. "The ladies are staying with Miss Henley's aunt who's helpin' the young miss, Marielle's her name, prepare for the wedding with Craymore's whelp. Richard's his name. Bess don't seem to like him much or his sire for that matter. Anyhow, it seems the news of the capture was given to the ladies this morning by the younger Craymore.

"Bessie said she didn't hear much, but after a couple of ales, her details improved. It seems Richard was quite pleased that the capture had taken place and he figured Marielle could have some measure of peace and focus on the upcoming wedding. I got more to tell, but I'm getting a bit thirsty."

"Keep your mind off the bottle, Bates. Don't forget what you're here for. See what else this Bess can find out and try to keep your pants on," Willie said.

"I hear ya, Willie. I won't let York or Martin down. Not Bates. As I was saying, Bess could tell Craymore was anxious to wed this Marielle. She figured he was getting hot under the collar and tired o' waiting for the wedding night. I must admit there were a few moments there when I could see Bess had her mind right where I'd like it to be. Anyways, the young lady, according to Bess, got upset. The house was pretty quiet after that.

"Didn't see Bess around today, or the ladies, but I did notice that Lady Henley was out bright and early. Her carriage was waiting out in front before nine and she didn't return until noon. Seeing I was on foot at the time, I couldn't follow her, but I'll see if I can buy Bess a few ales tomorrow and find out more."

"I'm not waiting," Martin said, angrily. "I'm paying Marielle a visit. I can still make it there before dawn. I want to know what part she played and how much influence she has with Richard."

"You're courting danger, but I'll bring you there, Marty," Jeremy replied, "but what plan have you got in your head?"

"I don't know yet, but I must talk to Marielle."

"And may I ask how you think she'll greet you?" Jeremy asked.

"I won't know until I face her, but I do know that she and my brother took a liking to one another."

The men gave each other knowing glances. "Leave it to York to turn a kidnapping into an entertaining experience for the wench," Bates laughed, coughed and then spit into the fire.

"I didn't mean to infer that it was more than an attraction. Our time with Miss Henley was well spent. Information that concerned my father's demise and Craymore's connection gave rise to much thought and anticipation on York's part concerning our father."

"I'll bet it gave rise to something else as well," Bates snorted.

Jeremy stifled a laugh, smacking Bates in the arm, as he considered Martin's words. "I'm beginning to understand."

Years earlier, as the men drank together York had entered one of his dark moods. Jeremy had asked York the same question he'd asked him many times before. "Where did they come from?" Certainly they were not born to poverty. Though the streets toughened York's and Martin's speech and actions, their manners and intellect were often beyond what the rest could even fathom.

That was the night York told them his name and his birthright. After uttering the name Craymore, York took the bottle he held in his hand and smashed it against the brick wall of the alley. York never opened up again, but he'd said enough. Yes, Jeremy thought, it was a strange situation to be sure.

Jeremy's contemplation was interrupted by Martin's decisive words as he rose and began kicking dirt into the fire. "I will find out what Marielle has told them. If she can help in any way, I need to know."

"She ain't going to be on our side, Martin. She's been seen gadding about with a Craymore and she's marrying him. I'd not be trusting her words."

"I don't know what to expect from her. She may have helped to incarcerate my brother.

Cooperative or not, I want to hear what she has to say. I want Bates to come with me.

"Jeremy, find out what you can about this jailer and his activities. How close can this man get to York and Braum? See if he's heard of any plans for their disposition with the courts. Can you dig up more men to keep a watch on the prison?"

"Sure can. Just need a little more time."

"Find out the setup, the guards' duties and rounds and if an escape is possible. If this jailer owes you his life, it's time he repaid his debt." Martin said decisively then turned to Bates.

"Bates, on the way to the aunt's, tell me what you know of the entrances and the setup of her house. Willie, I want you to find and follow the elder Craymore."

"Not a problem, Martin. I'd be happy to take care of him for you in any way you'd like."

"Just follow him for the time being. Don't let him out of your sight. Send out some feelers about Richard Craymore's activities. Whatever information you can pick up at the taverns or through some of the local gossip, collect it. Jeremy, we'll get a message to you for another meeting. No doubt Bates knows where to find you. Let's hope by then we have more to go on. I'll see Craymore dead before I see my brother sentenced."

The men said little after their instructions. They doused the fire, slapped each other on the back and rode off.

Bates rode alongside Martin when the path made it possible. When they reached London, they left the horses secured in a stable near a tavern they knew well and traveled by foot. The lamplights in the drear sections of the city had already been doused. Each picked up an empty bottle they found dropped by the side of the road which gave them an appearance of two rummies wandering about with no place to go. Jeremy was right about the lack of night watchmen. None were about.

When they reached Piccadilly and drew closer to Lady Henley's townhouse, the new gaslights caused them some difficulty in remaining unseen. An occasional carriage rolled by, most likely bringing party revelers home for the night. They turned off the main thoroughfare, instead making their way behind stables and churchyards until they reached their destination. Crouched behind nearby shrubbery, they watched for movement in the dimly lit windows of Lady Cornelia's townhouse.

Martin assumed everyone was asleep. Bates pointed out a bedroom of one of the ladies. He'd seen her looking out the window the previous night. She was brushing her long hair and it was obvious she was in her dressing gown, probably preparing for bed. He couldn't tell Martin who it was, but only that she was young and created quite an attractive image in the dim light.

Martin recollected his meeting with the young Miss Craymore during his brief imprisonment in her father's stable and wondered if it might have been her. He remembered her dark, lustrous hair and the long tendrils curling and resting on the bodice of her gown. She'd left an unforgettable impression.

His thoughts returned to the moment at hand. Passing the clock tower about a half hour earlier, Martin knew it to be about three o'clock. Fortunately, the fog was thickening and though the blackness of night had begun to gray, the fog made it possible to move easily about unseen. No Charleys with their staves and lanterns could be seen patrolling the streets. After raising their age-old chant, "Twelve o' clock and all's well" they too had probably turned in for the night.

Martin thought about how he would approach Marielle and how she might respond to him. *She's been in London for some time, he thought, preparing for her upcoming marriage. Her time with York may now be a painful memory she'd like to forget.* Marielle's station in life and her betrothal created a wall between them that would be difficult to surmount even in normal circumstances.

Despite York's sullenness, women found him appealing, Martin acknowledged. Marielle's attraction to his brother may have been temporary madness. In fact, he feared his brother, usually so in control of his emotions, had lost his senses over the girl.

If it weren't for his determination to avenge our father's disgrace, he might have been tempted to take advantage of her innocence. Thank heavens he hadn't been that foolish, Martin thought. *At least I don't think... The marriage is still going forward.* Martin turned from his thoughts and sharpened his focus, preparing for his next move.

HE WOULD HAVE been surprised to know what had been transpiring inside Aunt Cornelia's residence throughout the day. Late in the afternoon, Cornelia had encouraged both girls to take a carriage ride with her through the park. They needed some respite from the harrowing day and a ride in the park, she thought, would refresh them. They would return to dine at home rather than participate in evening's festivities.

The ladies reluctantly agreed to Aunt Cornelia's suggestion. They gave the necessary nods to familiar faces in the park and except for one aggressive bachelor on horseback who insisted on stopping the carriage to greet the young ladies, particularly Alaina, they were undisturbed.

Cornelia had requested that dinner be served immediately on their return, for she had her own plan in mind for the evening. Too many situations were sprouting up around her leading her to some uncomfortable conclusion and opening her mind to some puzzling questions.

Marielle's reaction to the news of the capture of York Blackstone and his partner in crime puzzled Cornelia and she hoped that with tact she might encourage Marielle to open up to her. Other thoughts that she had reluctantly put aside years before were now squirreling around in her own mind, thoughts specifically concerning Lord Craymore and his involvement in the famous Blackstone affair.

She hoped for an opportunity to talk with Alaina. She knew this would take even more tact and diplomacy, for Alaina had been a small child when her family took possession of the Blackstone estate. Alaina, however, was an extremely intelligent and intuitive young woman, who no doubt had borne much of the family's burdens. Cornelia knew of her great devotion towards her mother as well as her father's influence on her brother. She wondered if Alaina might be able to add pieces to the puzzle that now lay quite scrambled in her mind.

But, oh, how she loved puzzles and the intrigue of solving them.

Her own memories, the gossip of the *ton* that had run rampant through the years and now these latest developments were too much for her to ignore. She must find answers to the questions plaguing her.

Even in the midst of the turmoil, Cornelia found herself shamelessly smiling in delight. This was just up her alley. Gossip she enjoyed, mysteries were marvelous, but combined with situations that involved love, scandal and criminal activities, why she was in her element. She was anxious to see how the night would progress. The girls were simply carrying too many secrets and it was her duty to uncover them. For their own good, of course.

Chapter Ten

DINNER WAS A quiet affair. Marielle barely touched her meal before pleading exhaustion and asking to be excused. When she left the dining room, Aunt Cornelia found her opportunity to talk to Alaina. First, she rang for the kitchen maid to bring her accustomed brandy.

Alaina smiled as her newfound "aunt" sipped her brandy, daintily, but with slow deliberation, obviously savoring its taste. Aunt Cornelia's acceptance of her brought her not only delight but a warm feeling within her, perhaps not unlike the warmth of the golden brandy Cornelia now swirled delicately in its crystal goblet.

She couldn't remember when she'd laughed so much, especially at some of Aunt Cornelia's bawdy tales, some borrowed from Chaucer or paraphrased from Shakespeare, not to mention the gossip she relayed with relish concerning "virtuous" members of the ton.

Tonight, however, both sat quietly wrapped in their thoughts, the day and Marielle's strange behavior. Alaina felt especially close to Marielle, but today a wall of silence had grown between them. Marielle's reaction to her kidnappers' arrest was strange. She seemed visibly upset, not relieved. She wondered what Aunt Cornelia's thoughts were about the day's events and wanted desperately to share her own misgivings.

"Aunt Cornelia, you seem quite deep in thought this evening."

"Why, I was just thinking the same of you, my dear. Your facial expressions tell me that you may be having some inner struggles going on. I must admit I do as well now that the events of the day have ceased and I have some space to ruminate about their significance."

"To be honest, I find myself quite puzzled by Marielle's response to Richard's news concerning the arrest."

It was just what the old aunt needed to begin her quest.

"I agree, my dear. I do have questions about Marielle's behavior, but the news also brought up some "attic" memories. Tonight, I find myself caught in cobwebs, like a tiny fly caught within the spider's grasp, attempting to reach the next thread that might lead me out."

Alaina smiled at the visual description of Aunt Cornelia's thoughts and waited to hear more.

"You know, Alaina, it seems just yesterday when your father and your dear mother... Oh, she was such a darling. I do remember her beauty and her compassion and how she loved her children. How her eyes would light up when she was allowed to join the festivities. Oh, forgive me. Perhaps, *allowed* is too strong a word."

"No, Aunt Cornelia, it is quite correct."

Cornelia continued as if there'd been no interruption. "Your mother thought nothing of getting right into the midst of play between the children when we gathered with neighboring families during holidays or an occasional summer outing. It was a time before Lord Blackstone's disgrace, before his family became outcasts, before Lady Blackstone and her children disappeared into the London streets." Cornelia paused for a moment to observe Alaina's reaction.

Alaina remained silent, surprised at the turn in the conversation.

"How tragic a time it was. You were such a little thing," Cornelia continued, patting Alaina's hand. "Your mother dressed you up with ribbons and lace, yet she still allowed you to tumble around with the other rambunctious children. I'd watch her try to disentangle your disheveled hair after you played a round of games.

"We chatted often, your mother and I, of mundane things, but I could not help but observe her sad countenance. She could not mask it, except when her face brightened at the antics of the children. Your father was usually off with the men, so I remember little of his involvement with you. He did seem to enjoy being included in the events, for at the time his own title was questionable. "Oh dear, I am so sorry, I am being insensitive."

"No, please go on," Alaina said softly. "I'm aware that my father's rise in title and lands and his acceptance in the upper echelons of society were in some way associated with Lord Blackstone's covert activities."

"If you insist, my dear, I do not want to upset you or cause you undue anguish."

"I have not been blinded to my father's ways.

Please…"

"I fear I'm rambling too much," Cornelia said feigning dismay, "but I do find pleasure remembering the visits to the seaside where we picnicked, the children playing games or being "dipped" in the waves. Such a lovely time it was and the Blackstone boys, such little gentlemen. The little one always tugged at his big brother's sleeve. After the scandal and the disappearance of the Blackstone family, we, of course, continued the traditions of the past. For life must go on. Scandal is given its glory and the gossip its audience. But their presence was sorely missed and grieved by those who knew them well. When your father was given the Blackstone estate and lands as a reward for his information, he isolated himself from the *ton* for a time, probably to allow others to adjust to his new position. He was well aware that Lord Blackstone and his family were highly respected.

"In time, he attended events, bringing his family along. I must confess he was still ignored by a few, but your mother and, of course, you and Richard were accepted easily enough." Aunt Cornelia stopped, took a sip of her brandy and gauged Alaina's reaction.

"As the seasons went by, we saw less and less of your family. Your father came alone to most events and sent your mother's regrets. If we offered to visit her, he discouraged our offers, saying only that he would pass on our kindly thoughts. He insisted that your mother needed rest. After a time, it was accepted as all things are in the ton, when everyone focuses in on their own desires. If only she had been able to join us. Why, I would have come to know you so much sooner," Aunt Cornelia squeezed Alaina's hand and smiled affectionately. Alaina encouraged her to go on, needing to hear more.

When Cornelia turned her musings to the arrest and imprisonment of Lord Blackstone and the disappearance of the family, Alaina's face turned grave and her eyes moist. Aunt Cornelia, aware of the emotions rising in Alaina chose to continue on, knowing she was causing the girl discomfort, but feeling the necessity to bring her to a point where she might reveal her thoughts. Hurtful as it might be, Aunt Cornelia sensed the girl had years of stifled emotion that needed airing for her own sake and might lead to a joining of some of the scattered puzzle pieces.

Leaving only a few moments of silence, Aunt Cornelia continued. "*The Blackstone Scandal* it was called and what a scandal it was. During King George's illness—he was a bit funny in the head you know—he went in and out of sanity. The country never knew what to expect from him. Sadly, he was a most intelligent king when he had his senses. Lord Blackstone, before the king's more recurring lapses of insanity, was one of his trusted advisors and admired for his keen intellect and wisdom in affairs.

"I do remember my own father, bless his soul, lauding Blackstone for his intervention during heated arguments on the floor of the House of Commons, particularly when France threatened an invasion of England. Blackstone, as my father would say, *'Knew how to maintain calm when others would be hopping out of their seats and flurrying around like hens being chased by a rooster'*. Aunt Cornelia fell into a bout of laughter as she recalled her father's words. Alaina laughed with her, but more at Cornelia's high pitched moment of jollity. It didn't take long before the elderly, but childlike little woman sitting in the massive chair continued.

"He was quite brilliant you know—Lord Blackstone, I mean. He loved to delve into antiquities, particularly ancient manuscripts. I remember his excitement at obtaining a prized classic while on an errand for his wife. Lady Blackstone had sent him off to *'Get him out of her bonnet'*, I remember her saying and to pick up a set of *Minerva* novels at the circulating library. As we were having tea, he rushed into the sitting room overjoyed that he'd purchased a magnificent classic at some ridiculous price and amazed that the book had found its way into London when it was purported to be part of the Pope's collection.

"He picked up his wife and twirled her around thanking her for sending him on such a ridiculous errand." Aunt Cornelia hesitated, looking off toward the drawn velvet curtains. "I still find it unimaginable that this jovial and warm-hearted gentleman could have been a traitor to the crown and now, his young sons are all grown up and found to be kidnappers! Why, the absurdity of it all. I have always thought of myself as a good judge of character. Mayhap my ruminations of the past have taken on a soft patina in my golden years, but Lord Blackstone seemed so gallant at the time and his children so well behaved. I must admit..." Cornelia giggled into her lace handkerchief, "I found him most attractive. I even attempted a shameful flirtation, hoping to catch his eye. I was young, foolish and infatuated, but his eyes were only for his wife."

Cornelia peeked up from her hankie to see Alaina's reaction. She only smiled, but her eyes spoke volumes. "When the accusations of treason arose after King George had gone off to his retreat, we were certain it was most likely one of the king's hallucinations, but your father presented convincing evidence. With the king taken off to Weymouth to convalesce, the Regent took control. His fancies were to decorate England. While he and his devoted architect, John Nash, cleaned the coffers to build grandiose facades and oriental gardens, the trial came and went. The Blackstone's were gone and King George never regained his sanity."

Aunt Cornelia could see that her last reminiscences caused Alaina great agitation.

"Alaina, I am sure your father did what he felt had to be done. Please forgive this old woman for delving too far into the past and rambling on. I'm being insensitive to your connection to all this. Why, you were just a child at the time. I'm sure you have no recollection of the affair." She was pushing and Alaina was strong, but was she being too cruel in her desire to discover the truth?

Alaina remained silent, wrapped in her own thoughts.

Cornelia knew she'd said enough for tonight,

despite her desire to probe further. "My dear, I've tired myself out. Please help me to my room. I think it's time we both rested." Without another word said, both ladies stood. Alaina took the elderly aunt's arm and led her upstairs to her bedchamber.

When they reached the door leading into Aunt Cornelia's bedchamber, Alaina paused. She leaned against the wall to support her body as well as her emotions." I do remember some things that have puzzled me through the years. I remember Father and Mother arguing. My mother spoke the name *Blackstone* aloud in the presence of my father and it was if she'd cursed. My father became furious and forbade the mention of the name. As a child I did not connect it to a person, but to some mysterious, dreaded object."

Aunt Cornelia could see that the girl was upset and searching her mind for more. Though she wanted to press her, hoped she'd remember other situations, she could see it wasn't wise, tonight.

"My dear, let us rest for tonight. Perhaps in the morning you might remember other things that may be helpful. Finding the truth remains the important issue. Two men may be hanged if Marielle identifies them as her kidnappers. But you, Alaina, mustn't upset yourself. Lord Blackstone may very well have been a traitor and your father the one who brought him to justice, nothing more. The mind of an old woman easily slips into the past where the color of things may take on strange hues. I'm sure the morning will help all of us to see more clearly. Goodnight

Alaina."

Before Alaina could respond, Aunt Cornelia disappeared behind her door.

Alaina walked slowly to her room, shut the bedroom door behind her and leaned against it. She found herself almost laughing, even with tears forming, to think of her father as a humble, patriotic servant looking to the best interest of the kingdom. She knew her father thought only of his own selfish interests. The kidnapping may or may not have been a coincidence, but she could not rid herself of the disturbing sense that the estate she grew up in may have been acquired by devious means. The thought brought shivers up her spine.

She too, wanted to know the truth.

Another memory surfaced as she sat at her dresser combing her hair. She was quite young, standing outside the door of the library and listening to her parents arguing. She heard her mother ask what had become of the Blackstones, then the sound of a slap and her mother's sobs. She remembered running away from the door and up the large winding staircase. The incident left her believing that the *blackstones*, whatever they were, were to be feared.

She prepared for bed, her mind in turmoil. She wanted to begin a new life in London and not allow her father to wield any more power over her. She now faced the realization that like a ghost that haunts its former abode, there was no escape from her father's deeds. Freedom now seemed a fleeting fantasy.

The Blackstone brothers chose the wrong

captive. She knew her father would not rest until they were punished to his satisfaction. Most probably not because of Marielle, for she doubted her father could have any feelings for his future daughter-in-law, or any woman for that matter, but because of their name.

What was the truth behind the Lord Blackstone's demise? Could her father have manufactured evidence? Could he be that ruthless? Nothing, she had to admit, would surprise her.

As Alaina crawled under the bedcovers, her mother's face appeared in her mind's eye, one moment kneeling in the garden surrounded by her roses, the sun spilling its gold on her silky hair as she smiled up at her daughter, the next moment she saw only her tired, gaunt face and blank, lifeless eyes and she knew the answer.

Dear God, she murmured as she clenched her knees tightly to her chest, tears spilling down her cheeks.

MARTIN AND BATES slipped easily into the courtyard, climbed over the ivy-covered wall and into the small garden that led to the side entrance of the Georgian style townhouse. With little trouble, they unlatched the door and entered silently into a dark corridor. The servants' quarters at the rear of the house were far enough away from the upper bedrooms to create little concern. Groping their way in the darkness, they reached the staircase and climbed to the upper level with the deft expertise of experienced criminals and moved cautiously towards one of the front bedrooms.

Neither of the men knew if they would find Marielle or Alaina, only that it belonged to one of the young ladies.

Martin signaled to Bates to stay outside the door and keep watch. He turned the handle, slowly opening the door that led into Alaina's bedroom. Just enough moonlight streamed through the window for him to see the shape of a woman asleep beneath the coverlet.

Seeing the soft, dark curls spread on the pillow, he knew immediately that it was Alaina, not Marielle and he found himself close enough for the scent of lavender to fill his nostrils.

It reminded him of their last meeting.

Watching her sleep, he could see her tear-stained face and wondered what had caused her such sadness. Even with her face reflecting anguish as she slept, his body naturally responded to her beauty and the curves of her figure molded beneath the covers.

The thought of leaning down and kissing her full lips, still swollen from crying, flitted through his mind only to be immediately snuffed out by the larger purpose of his mission. There was no time to search other bedrooms to find Marielle. York was his concern and Alaina would have to lead him to her.

Bates waited restlessly outside the door, his thoughts roaming to the servants' quarters. He'd have to save the wench for another day, but his thoughts remained on Bess' rounded backside and her bountiful bosom, creating much imaginative meandering in his mind and much frustration in his loins.

A light sleeper, Aunt Cornelia knew the sounds of her house as well as her own breathing. Something was amiss and she knew exactly what to do, for she often mused about how she might confront a burglar if the need arose. The excitement of it seemed more invigorating, than the danger. If she rang for a servant, it would certainly cause a calamity and it might only be one of the girls roaming about.

There was a distinct change in the air and she wasn't going to wait to find out what caused the change. Finding the set of dueling pistols inherited from her father, she set them on the bed while she retrieved her robe and slippers.

Meanwhile, Martin kneeled over Alaina and gently but firmly covered her mouth with his hand. Her eyes flew open.

He brought his mouth close to her face and whispered as he stared into her fearful eyes. "Shh, do not be afraid, Alaina. I promise I am not here to hurt you. Do you remember me, sweet lavender lady?"

Unresponsive at first, her body frozen in place, she eventually moved her head up and down, answering his question.

"I remember our pleasurable meeting in the horse stall," Martin said softly, a slight smile playing on his lips. I've thought of you often, for you brought me a measure of comfort, until you ran off, that is. I would enjoy continuing our conversation, but my purpose here cannot be diverted. Now, unless I am mistaken, your fear is turning into anger if your gritted teeth are any indication. I much prefer anger, fear immobilizes while anger brings passion."

Wide awake, Alaina had no absence of fear, but his words *were* arousing anger, causing at least some of her fear to subside.

"Alaina, I must see Marielle. As you're probably aware, my brother is imprisoned thanks to your father's conspiring cohorts. I'll let nothing stand in my way to free him. Do you understand?"

Alaina, still wide-eyed, nodded.

"Marielle may be able to help. I'll not leave until I speak with her. If I lift my hand and you choose to scream, you'll wake her and everyone else causing danger not only to yourself and Marielle, but also to her aunt. I have a bodyguard standing right outside your door."

Alaina's eyes darted towards the door, but it was closed. She knew she had no choice but to obey.

"I want you to lead me to her bedchamber. No harm will come to her. That would be of no use to me or to my brother. I only want to talk to her."

Alaina nodded and Martin lifted his hand slowly from her mouth.

MEANWHILE, AUNT CORNELIA slipped out of her bedchamber carrying the two heavy pistols. Their weight created discomfort for her tiny frame, but her determination gave her strength. She passed Marielle's bedroom, which was the closest to her own and found nothing amiss, but as she silently turned the corner to face Alaina's room, she spotted Bates leaning against the door.

The darkness covered her, but the soft glow coming from an overhead window, made his outline clear. She took feathery soft steps towards the intruder, the pistols aimed directly at him.

Bates, suddenly aware of movement, lifted his head, which had been resting against the door frame. His first sight was a shadow moving forward and then, to his amazement, he spotted the mere slip of a woman holding two large pistols in clenched hands, one aimed directly at his groin. He instinctively clasped his crotch, which only a short time before was quite aroused at the thought of Cornelia's servant, Bess. He regained his senses and reached clumsily for his own revolver, but stopped short when Aunt Cornelia spoke.

Her whisper carried no fear, only a demand to know what he was doing in her home.

Eyeing the pistols as they came closer, he began to stutter a response and, instead, fell backwards into Alaina's bedchamber.

Landing, with a loud thud on the floor, he startled Martin and gave freedom to Alaina to let out the scream she'd been holding in.

As Bates groveled around the floor to gain his footing, Martin grabbed Alaina to squelch her cries.

Aunt Cornelia stood in the open doorway with the pistols leaning against her side, the moon creating a larger shadow around her and demanded he let her go.

Alaina, now sitting up, her coverlet lifted up around her neck, stared with shock at her aunt's boldness and the two large pistols in her hands.

Aunt Cornelia directed Martin and Bates to move towards the window as she moved closer to Alaina and handed her one of the pistols. Before Martin could attempt an explanation, Aunt Cornelia looked at the stranger, then into his eyes and immediately knew his identity.

She almost cackled with delight at the recognition.

"I'd remember those eyes anywhere," she said, smiling and promptly settled herself on the edge of Alaina's bed.

She looked towards Bates and back at Martin. "Why don't you send this big buffoon out of here so that we can converse? He seems to be in shock."

Martin, overcoming his surprise, instructed Bates to wait at the foot of the staircase until he called for him.

Bates, without hesitation, his hands still covering his groin, stumbled out of the room and hurried down the staircase.

Aunt Cornelia barely hesitated before sharing her thoughts. "Why, I would swoon when your father would gaze at me with those eyes and those lashes. Of course, he only had eyes for your mother, but as a young girl I couldn't help but dream. I would guess that you are Martin Blackstone, unless your brother has already escaped, though I doubt he would have the opportunity for another few hours.

Martin stared at her in total confusion.

Alaina, too, sat up straighter, forgetful of the thin nightgown that she wore and stared at her aunt.

The noise created by Bates' clumsy entrance into Alaina's bedroom woke Marielle with a start. She grabbed her robe, wrapped it around her and rushed from her room. Entering the hallway, she heard the voices and saw the top of Bates' head as he scrambled down the stairs. Her fears mounted as she rushed first to her aunt's bedroom to find it empty and then to Alaina's. When she reached the open door, she froze at the sight before her.

Alaina sat on the bed holding a large pistol. Her aunt rested on the corner of the bed, an identical pistol on her lap. In the soft light that now filled the room, she saw Martin.

"Martin!" She rushed over to him, reached out to grab his arms, blurting out her questions. "How did you find me? York, he's been captured. What are we to do?"

Martin wrapped one arm about her as he kept his eyes on the other two women. He felt great relief that she seemed genuinely concerned. At the same time, he knew he couldn't answer her questions adequately and only wanted to ask his own.

Marielle, suddenly aware of her reactive behavior in the presence of her aunt and Alaina, turned to them, embarrassed.

"Do you think you could put down those pistols before somebody gets hurt?" Martin asked, with a hint of a grin.

Cornelia, now recovered from the shock of her niece's impulsive behavior, answered. "Needn't worry. They're not loaded, too old and in need of repair.

At that, everyone else glared at her and laughed, releasing much of the tension in the room.

Bates, who'd been creeping up the stairs to aid Martin, heard the laughter and sat on the steps mystified. Realizing all was well for the moment, even if a bit strange, turned his mind to Bess. Without a second thought, he set out to find the servants' quarters, assuring himself that he would be back before Martin finished his business.

The seriousness of the situation returned as Martin led Marielle to a nearby chair. He turned to Lady Henley, questions in his eyes. "What did you mean by your comment concerning my brother?"

The aunt, presenting an innocent façade, responded. "Whatever do you mean, young man?"

"You said that York couldn't possibly have escaped, *yet*? Do you know something that I don't?"

"Well," Aunt Cornelia began, "I knew full well that Marielle was overly upset over your brother's imprisonment. I've also heard of the slack conditions at Kingston, what with all the construction going on. Three men have already escaped, you know, it's a mass of confusion. I'm surprised they didn't choose a more secure prison, but with the overcrowded conditions everywhere, it was probably the first choice.

"I took it upon myself, this morning, to find out who was responsible for the prisoners' lodgings. My trusted servant convinced him, with some gold coins, to move your brother and his associate to an area with better accommodations. Gold does carry much weight, you know. It is a privilege of the rich to be granted better quarters, even in prison. I felt impelled to offer Lord Blackstone's son some assistance, though I must say I do not yet know if he deserves such a courtesy.

"He's to be moved in the next few hours. How this will help him I do not know, but I'd hoped it might be of some benefit. Money has the might to move the earth being imbued with muscle that men bend for," Cornelia added. "Now that I see you are well and that Marielle demonstrates goodwill towards you, I suspect your brother may not be the tyrant he's been purported to be. Perhaps, if we put our heads together we might come up with a plan which might be of help to your brother and end this calamity."

The small group stared, unbelieving, at the wee woman propped up on the large bed until Alaina broke the silence.

"Aunt Cornelia, you are incorrigible!"

"Why thank you, dear, I take that as a compliment. I am truly sorry for upsetting you earlier. It's unfortunate that your father and brother are so deeply involved in the entire situation, but it's the truth of the matter and we do need to get at the roots of the truth. From what I see before me, Marielle did not suffer any ruthlessness during her captivity. My guess is Marielle would agree."

Marielle nodded her head and give her aunt a reassuring smile.

"I also do not believe," Aunt Cornelia continued, staring directly at Martin, "that your sire, Lord Blackstone, ever committed treason. I do not know where we go from here," she continued, "for many ill-fitting puzzle pieces must be studied before we can figure out how your father was framed, but I feel confident we will figure it out."

Martin responded, mystified, "We?"

"Why yes," Aunt Cornelia said, her eyes sparkling. "This may be a dreadful business, but it does lend some excitement to an old woman's days. I will not be left out for a minute."

Martin walked over to Cornelia and wrapped her in a big hug.

When he released her, a crimson blush covered her face.

"Young man, I think I will melt into this bed right now from the heat." The room exploded in laughter at her words. "Now let us come up with a plan."

"I need to find Bates," Martin interrupted. "Our friends are waiting for news and are prepared to do whatever needs to be done to help York. There is a jailer, who owes a favor. He might just be the key needed to gain their freedom and your action may have set the perfect stage."

"*I'll* find Bates." Aunt Cornelia offered as she stood and walked to the door. "Why don't you and Marielle take a few minutes to catch up?"

"No, I must go with him. I may be able to help."

"Nonsense, young man, it's nearly dawn. Do you trust this Bates?"

Martin nodded.

"If you're caught, what good will it do your brother? Now is the time that you need to trust your friends. You did say that they are awaiting news. Can you not trust that they will act as needed, at least until we have time to create a plan of action?"

"Yes, they're wise to the ways of the prisons and they'll do whatever they can to help York." Martin couldn't help but imagine that York would be impressed at this elegant little lady's shrewdness.

"Fine, then let's take some time before morning comes to sort things out. I shall return with your friend Bates." Without waiting for a reply, Aunt Cornelia walked out and shut the door firmly behind her.

Alaina, now searching for her robe, felt the discomfort of the situation and prepared to leave the room.

Martin reached over to her and laid his hand on her shoulder. "Alaina, do you understand what we must do and why?"

"I know my father and I know what he is capable of. I fear for all involved. If my father is to blame for the tragedy laid upon your family..." Alaina turned away feeling shame and revulsion at the thought of her father's involvement.

Martin turned her face towards his own and stared into her eyes. "You were just a child—we both were. But, now I must do whatever I can to find out the truth and to free my brother, not only from prison, but from the prison that he has lived in since our father was accused."

Marielle could see the anguish in Martin's face and Alaina's silent understanding. She quietly touched Martin's hand before reaching out to her friend. They hugged each other as Martin looked on.

Aunt Cornelia's search for Bates meant following soiled footprints that led to the servants' quarters and finally to Bess' bedroom. Cornelia chose to knock once before entering.

The knock was enough to alarm both Bess and Bates but gave them no time to avoid Cornelia's perusal of their awkward positions.

Seeming nonplussed, Cornelia instructed Bates to put his pants on and go to Martin. To Bess, she only shook her head and told her to get herself up, since she demonstrated so much excess energy and make coffee for the guests. Cornelia waited until Bates found his pants before returning to the upper floors.

Why this night is just full of surprises, she thought, as she giggled at the sight she'd just observed.

BATES STUMBLED INTO Alaina's bedroom looking confused and avoiding Cornelia's eyes.

Martin gave him a quizzical stare and wondered what he'd gotten himself into, but he knew that now was not the time for questions. He filled Bates in on the new development and sent him off to find the other men and to seek the jailer who owed Jeremy a favor. Martin prayed his old friends would come through and wondered what else he might be able to do in the meantime.

Cornelia, noting Martin's pained silence after Bates' exit, walked over to him and placed her arm in his.

"Please escort me to the dining room. My maid, Bess, is making some coffee. The girls, I'm sure, will join us when they make themselves presentable."

Marielle and Alaina, suddenly aware of their flimsy attire, self-consciously reached for the coverlet.

Martin walked out with Cornelia after bowing slightly to the young ladies. Even through the turmoil, he hadn't missed the lovely visions propped on the bed. Marielle wore a delicate robe, but Alaina's nightdress did little to hide her firm, uplifted breasts and the dark shadow of her nipples.

He would relish the memory.

Chapter Eleven

IT WAS CLOSE to midnight when Richard reached his father's townhouse. Carver, his father's butler, ushered him in and informed him that Lord Craymore's behavior for most of the day was uncharacteristic. In fact, he was most likely inebriated and asleep in his study. Richard refused the butler's suggestion to return in the morning. Instead, encouraged Carver to retire. The butler gratefully obliged.

As Richard entered the room, the glow from dying embers and dimly lit candles sent shadows shivering about the walls of books. The large leather chair pulled close to the fireplace hid his father's figure, but created a larger shadow that stretched across the room. When Richard's eyes adjusted to the distortions of light and shadow, he could see his father's grim profile and a glass resting in his hands. He seemed barely awake, but Richard was determined to gain his full attention.

"Father, forgive the lateness of the hour, but I must speak with you."

Craymore lifted his head and through glazed eyes acknowledged his son's presence. "Ah, Richard, you've come at last. I've been waiting for you. I have everything worked out," he said in a slurred voice, before taking a sip from his glass.

Finding it empty, he reached for the bottle of scotch propped snugly between his arm and the soft leather cushions of the armchair. With shaking hands, he filled it half full then stared ahead at the dying flames, a strange look on his face as if were searching his mind for a message he wanted to relay, but couldn't find.

Silence ensued while Richard watched his father's machinations. Though his father always enjoyed his scotch, he'd never seen him quite so inebriated. *In fact*, Richard thought, *he seems to have aged ten years.*

With a fresh sip from his glass, his father's voice became more audible, though he barely looked at his son. "You must go and speak to the magistrate in the morning. Blackstone must not go to trial. Do you understand? He must not go to trial."

Richard absorbed his father's words and chose his own carefully. "Yes, I hear what you're saying but in a case such as this, the high court decides the punishment. Men have been hanged for lesser crimes. I doubt he'll see the light of day until he walks to the gallows."

"Blackstone's crime deserves immediate execution," his father spit out bitterly. "He's insulted us and most likely ruined Marielle. You do realize that, don't you, son?" He glared at Richard.

"Yes, Father, even if they haven't touched her, her reputation... Regardless, she's alive."

"True. She could have been killed, all our plans destroyed. It's your duty to demand immediate reprisal. Richard, do you understand what needs to be done?"

Richard could tell his father had been mulling over these thoughts for some time, for even in his drunken stupor, they came through well rehearsed. He needed to play along if he was to find out what he wanted to know.

"Yes, Father, I understand your reasoning, but you should be relieved and pleased at your accomplishment. At least two of the men who kidnapped Marielle are imprisoned. Marielle need only identify them and the courts will certainly act swiftly to mete out punishment."

"Don't tell me what I should be feeling, Richard!" his father growled. "We must get rid of Blackstone immediately. There must not be a trial. We cannot take the chance!"

"Chance? What chance? We've nothing to fear from the scoundrels. The criminals are behind bars and Marielle and I can proceed with our plans."

"You foolish boy. The Blackstones could ruin us, just as their father tried to do."

"What are you saying? His father was a traitor. You did your duty to have him arrested and thrown in prison. It seems his sons are just as ruthless. Soon we'll find the younger one and this mess will be over and done with."

"Richard, you're a blind fool. Their father's imprisonment was a master plan. You've no idea... Blackstone, with all his honorable notions and his host of friends, treated me like I was no better than a servant. My greatest success was to rid myself of him and his influence. Craymore's voice seethed with anger as he slammed his glass down on the side table.

"Why, I fought beside him in the war and when we returned, he accused me of cowardice because I refused to follow his orders in an attack on Napoleon's forces. The damn idiot knew we didn't have sufficient arms. But he refused to listen to reason. So I took the few sensible men who agreed with my position and got the hell out of there. A third of the men who followed Blackstone were killed and I probably would have been one of them."

Richard remained silent, not wanting to interrupt, though he'd heard some of his father's anger over his war years before.

"When Blackstone returned from the front, he made all kinds of damaging accusations against my credibility. When celebrations were planned he became the honored guest. I was ignored. I refused to allow myself to be tossed aside and my name besmirched. He forced me to resort to bribes to be adequately represented." Craymore ranted on, while almost choking on the saliva that had settled in the back of his throat.

"Like you, I presented quite a dashing appearance and knew what the ladies of self-serving aristocrats liked." He closed his eyes, grinned at the reminiscence. "I was quite the ladies' man in my younger years and I was cunning enough not to let any advantage pass me by. Lonely, embittered wives, especially those married to old men, found ways to invite me to their bedrooms to entertain them. They seemed to like the idea that my reputation was a bit sullied. In fact," Craymore gave his son a gloating smirk, "I believe it raised their level of passion to a most delightful degree. For my attentiveness, I was included in the most prestigious events.

"Blackstone didn't like it one bit, especially that I found his wife quite ravishing. I'm sure I could have bedded her too, if Blackstone weren't always hovering over her every time I was about. Why he even had the nerve to accuse me of underhanded dealings when some of the illustrious members of the *ton* complained that exquisite pieces of their wives' jewelry had disappeared." He paused, lifted the glass, rubbing the rim slowly, his voice lowered. "Not that I didn't take advantage of lucrative opportunities when they were made available." He snorted, giving his son a drunken grin.

"I didn't have to steal their precious heirlooms! Their wives were quite generous, especially the ones who had little else to offer when it came to comeliness. It was none of Blackstone's business. I wasn't born fortunate like him to come from old money and a title. I had to do what was necessary. Because of my cunning, we've done quite well and your marriage to Henley's daughter will double our fortune and secure our position in society."

Richard listened as his father ranted on, his voice slurring but his arrogance obvious. He felt sickened by the admissions but said nothing, urged him on, knew he needed to hear more.

"If I hadn't found an opportunity to drag Blackstone's name through the mud, you would have nothing. Keep that in mind, Richard, if your conscience should give you trouble. One day, you'll be the one to court the pompous members of our elite society and bed whomever you please, thanks to my cleverness," Craymore said smugly, as he finished the drink in his hand.

Pulling up a chair close to his father, Richard raised his voice and mimicked the smirk his father's voice often carried.

"Yes, Father, we've been a good team. Your efforts have proved fruitful and I've benefited immensely. Tell me, how *did* you manage to get rid of Blackstone?" Craymore smirked. With the alcohol loosening his tongue, he continued to boast. "I merely found the right contacts to help me obtain my objectives."

"The right contacts?" Richard urged him on. "Do you mean members of the *ton*?"

"No, no, that wouldn't do at all. A foolish Frenchman I met in a pub needed little prodding to play my game. I simply offered him the right price. A trollop who worked for Lady Blackstone needed only a little urging to do my bidding. She fetched me one of her master's prized volumes. With a few pounds, some pieces of fine jewelry and a few romps in the hay in the servant's quarter of Blackstone's own mansion, she gave me just the information I needed.

"When I finished with her, I placed her on a ship to America. Her relatives were already there and she'd been working to save up the money for passage. Before she left — thanking me profusely, I might add — she managed to pass the rumor that she'd overheard some private conversations between Blackstone and some tawdry characters concerning letters to France. With dramatic reluctance she told of a treasonous transaction that was to take place at the docks."

"But who would listen to a maid recounting such a tale?" Richard questioned, his tone unbelieving.

"Some of the more faithful devotees of Blackstone ignored her, but I made certain that the timid little maid—who wanted only to show allegiance to her country—was heard by the right people. After setting the stage, the authorities were notified as well as the appropriate members of the king's council. The docks were well fortified before Blackstone's arrival with officials prepared to witness the exchange." Craymore stopped, yawned into his drink.

"I'm impressed at your ingenuity, but wouldn't the authorities need more proof of the accusations?"

"Of course, I took care of it all," Craymore sneered. "Blackstone, thinking he was to obtain a rare manuscript he'd purchased months before, appeared right on schedule at the dock. Without any concern, he approached the very reputable-looking Frenchman who held a neatly wrapped package and gave the appearance of just having arrived on the packet from France. Blackstone passed an envelope to the courier, probably a very generous tip and eagerly took the package, completely unaware that he'd been given one of his own precious volumes. The fool didn't even check the contents." Craymore, despite his inebriated condition, became more animated as he told the story, obviously enjoying his own genius.

"The wrapped volume, marked with the Blackstone seal, contained highly secret information our king later found quite damaging to our sovereign nation. I personally witnessed Blackstone's confrontation with the authorities. Why the man seemed numbed and slightly confused. He mumbled that there must be some kind of mistake, but they had little interest in listening to his protests. The package was clearly marked to the attention of Lord Blackstone and, therefore, confiscated immediately and Blackstone taken into custody.

"But what of the Frenchman? Wouldn't he have confessed to the charade if he'd been accused as a spy?"

"Quite right. You're as clever and astute as your father. I foresee a grand future ahead of you, while we make a mockery of those idiots who think they have London at their feet. I've trained you well."

Richard doing his best to smile and smirk at his father's details, continued his questioning. "Did you manage to get the Frenchman on a boat back to France?"

"No, dear boy, it wouldn't have done any good. He believed I was playing a prank on Blackstone. Once he realized the seriousness of his involvement, he would've been on his knees confessing to a ruse, just as you suspected. A couple of ruthless characters willingly and for only a few pounds, created a skirmish on the docks when the authorities went in to make the arrest.

"In the confusion, the Frenchman fell off the dock, with a little help, of course. One of the two scoundrels knew exactly what to do. He jumped in right after the poor fellow giving appearing to attempt to save him. Instead, he kept him under until he could no longer confess to anything."

"You had him *murdered*?" Richard couldn't hide his shock.

"Why so surprised? A job done well must be planned to perfection. Blackstone was so anxious to receive this supposed antiquity that he trusted strangers. Now, who should be admired for strategic planning, the war hero? Because of his stupidity and your father's genius, we reaped the benefits.

"Blackstone deserved his fate. It was my turn for recognition. A man has to go after what he wants in this world if he isn't blessed at birth. It's the only way in this life. I regret that he wasn't executed. Otherwise, everything went just as I'd hoped."

"And you were awarded his estate and lands," Richard said quietly, numbly.

"The Prince Regent was most generous for my patriotism, especially when I offered to support some of his building projects with the revenue I'd surely make from Blackstone's lands. He turned the estate over to me and sent officials to remove Blackstone's wife and children, all in one night."

"I can only imagine the *ton*'s reaction. The gossip must have fun rampant."

"It took a little time for the rest of society's elite

to accept that it was now the Craymore Estate, but when the new season approached, busyness filled the gap made by gossip. The concern for Blackstone's family remained a sore spot for some. I demonstrated appropriate sadness for the whole affair, of course." Craymore yawned, his tiredness taking hold. "I even made the appropriate gestures to try and find his wife and children. Humph. I believe she would've been easily persuaded to treat me kindly in return for the care and safety of her children, but my efforts were minimal. After all, I had everything I wanted.

"Now, Richard, you must do as I ask." His voice, now barely above a whisper, still held a command. "His sons could ruin everything. Who knows what they were told growing up? We can't take a chance. Once the two in prison are out of the way, we'll need to find the younger brother, get rid of him too. Their silence will seal your fortune. Yes, my son, we've come a long way, a long way…" His father's voice grew distant, his chin falling deeper into his chest.

"Father?" Richard nudged him but he slouched deeper into the chair, his glass falling from his hand onto the thick, ornately patterned carpet.

He'd passed out.

It didn't matter. Richard had heard enough. His stomach felt pummeled, his head ached. He stood, stared in disgust at the man who raised him, who'd tried his best to create him in his own image, then turned away and walked out.

Once outside, the damp, cold air of night did little to clear his head. Walking like a man in a dream, he climbed into the waiting carriage and ordered his driver to take him to a nearby pub. His father's words, voices from the past, suspicions he'd always managed to silence were now invading his thoughts, leading nowhere, crowding in and smothering one another.

One thought dominated.

He was nothing more than the son of a murderer and a thief. He'd lived with a false identity, the heir to a stolen title, the son of a murderer. His father, so desirous of power and buried in so much jealousy, felt justified in all his actions. Worse, his father trusted him with the truth, believed that he'd carry out his orders.

Why wouldn't he, Richard thought. After all, he'd chosen to follow his father, desert his mother and planned, under his father's guidance, to gain more power and position by marrying Marielle. He'd watched his father ruin men in business. He'd even participated in unscrupulous dealings.

No wonder his father felt no qualms about telling him the whole story.

By his appearance tonight, it was obvious that his father feared the sons of the man he'd ruined. The sons might have no proof, but surely they knew of the crime. It was doubtful that they could change their fate or avenge their father's ruin at this late date. Even if the elder son is tried, Richard thought. The courts wouldn't believe a common thief and kidnapper, but it seemed his father's fear of the truth coming out was now consuming him. His father taught him that every man had his weak spot. To gain power one only needed to find it.

Tonight he learned of his father's.

The Blackstone name.

His father felt no guilt, but he certainly feared the loss of what he'd worked so deviously to gain. For only a moment Richard wished that he could have inherited more of his father's heartlessness. Instead, shame and self hatred coursed through him like poison.

To cover up his deeds, my father assumes I will murder, just as he did. I am my father's son. I even made myself believe that my disgust of my father's behaviors were signs of my own weakness.

Richard's thoughts continued to plague him as the carriage moved on to the tavern. Knowing others showed little respect for him, I convinced myself that they were envious of his power. Yet, I wanted to be free of his power over me. I believed my position secure and opportunities to build bridges of respect would be easily managed with Henley's daughter by my side.

I've lived in unreality. I've lived the life of a coward and a fool.

"Master Craymore, we have arrived. Would you prefer to return home for a glass of sherry, perhaps? This tavern is one of the worst in London. I fear for your safety."

Richard ignored his driver's concern and descended the carriage, instructed him to return home without him and disappeared into the pub.

Surprised by his young master's abrupt dismissal of him and fearing the elder Craymore's fury if his son came to harm, his driver dismissed the young master's orders and chose to wait out of sight.

The darkness within the tavern suited

Richard's purposes. Raucous laughter and the clamor of loud voice mingled together, but faces were indistinguishable in the smoke-filled room. Richard stopped at the bar and ordered a bottle of whiskey. Leaving a larger than necessary sum for the barkeeper and with bottle and glass in hand, he sought a booth in the darkest corner, ignoring the eyes that followed him.

Patrons, still capable of reason, wondered about the dignified gentleman who looked out of place in the crude establishment. Some wondered if he might desire their services, but he seemed to have little interest in attracting the attention of anyone. Richard gave no sign that he was even aware of their presence. Seated, he opened the bottle and gulped the burning liquid, ignoring the grime-covered glass. Soon he could feel the heat spreading through his veins. After his first few gulps—meant to strengthen his resolve and remove any shred of cowardice—he sipped more slowly, methodically, the liquid fire burning away his fears.

Time meant nothing to him—the past, present, or future—a void without purpose. With his mind numbed by the spirits, he reached beneath his coat and pulled out the gun he carried for protection. Rubbing the smooth wooden handle with his thumbs he looked about him. The noises from the boisterous crowd at the bar would drown out the sound.

One bullet would be enough to end the mockery and shame of his life. His father would have to deal with the Blackstones. *Let him finish what he'd begun,* Richard muttered almost aloud. *My involvement in the years of treachery are done. God forgive me.* Resting his head on one arm, he brought the revolver up and for a moment stared into its barrel. He felt tired, defeated. His mind swollen he ached for blessed relief, to feel nothing.

MARTIN PLANNED TO leave the Henley townhouse the moment Bates returned with news from Jeremy. He sat quietly, impatiently.

Marielle felt his anxiety as well as her own. Aunt Cornelia continued to recount one memory after another of the past. She sensed that her aunt's incessant chatter had its purpose. Her wise aunt, always the first to recognize a problem and amazingly quick to plan a strategy, must realize how slow the time must be passing for Martin. A couple hours remained before daylight and little would be gained with Martin out on the streets of London.

It was Alaina who finally interrupted the aunt's rambling. Her thoughts kept returning to her life in the Blackstone's former estate. Now that she knew more about the events leading to Lord Blackstone's demise, a particular memory plagued her.

"Forgive me, Aunt Cornelia, for interrupting. I..." Alaina hesitated.

"Please, go on, my dear." Cornelia felt relieved. "I'm just rattling on and on. I haven't given anyone else an opportunity to talk."

Alaina turned to their visitor. "Martin, if it is at all possible for your brother to escape, my father won't rest until he is recaptured. I realize now that one Blackstone brother in prison will not satisfy him. He'll do whatever is in his means to procure your capture. We must find some way to reveal the truth of this entire affair."

"The truth will come out," Martin said confidently. "I'll do what I must to save my brother and clear my father's name. Too much is at stake. As it is, even if we could somehow force your father to confess, my brother still must face the charge of kidnapping Marielle."

"Martin," Marielle interrupted. "At first I may have thought York to be someone to fear, but I learned differently. His safety matters as much to me, even if…" The picture of York caught in the arms of a harlot crowded her thoughts. "I could not accuse him in the courts. I'll tell the authorities what I've learned, speak in his defense."

"Your intervention is appreciated, admirable, since my brother did kidnap you. You're justified in accusing him."

"I couldn't. We became…close." Marielle realized that she might be revealing too much. Her aunt and Alaina were eyeing her. She wanted to blurt everything out, but what good would it do? It could make matters worse for York. She wondered if they suspected, but their looks carried compassion rather than judgment.

They sat quietly, each lost in their own thoughts.

Alaina broke the silence. "I remember something! Martin, there were some books…"

The excitement in her voice caught everyone's attention. They waited for her to continue, but she seemed to need some time for recollection.

Martin broke the silence. "Alaina, anything that you can remember, even the slightest detail might help."

She paused, attempted to recollect every detail. "I couldn't have been more than eight or nine. I'd become a voracious reader, since we seldom entertained and friends were discouraged. One morning, I wandered into my father's library. I was curious to see if I could find a book more interesting than the ones that were being provided for me.

"I feared my father would appear, for I'd been forbidden to enter his library unless summoned, so I sat on the floor behind his desk, hidden from view, pulling out books, only to find more hidden behind those I'd pulled out. They were recessed into the wall, for the shelves, at first, appeared only deep enough to hold a single row of books."

The room stilled, held its breath, waited.

"The book jackets were quite old, some ragged. With some difficulty I managed to pull one out." Alaina hesitated as the memory became more vivid. "The cover felt damp. I believe now it may have been just the sheer age of the volume. When I opened one, I found the Blackstone name inscribed inside the front cover." She paused, felt the suffocating silence and Martin's eyes boring into hers. She realized the import of her words, the effect they were having on him.

Her voice shook from her revelation. She covered her mouth in dismay, then returned Martin's stare. "I remember so clearly now! It was a raised seal, I recall. I felt quite afraid because of the name, knew it was forbidden. Perhaps, that's why I didn't think of it sooner. I'd been conditioned..." She paused, stood, walked about the room.

"I thought I most surely had committed a crime simply holding the book in my hands. I felt quite paralyzed by the experience, seeing, touching the name that so angered my father. Then I heard my father's voice and the fear of being caught became more overwhelming than the discovery of the books. I quickly returned the book to its hiding place, replaced the ones that had been lodged in front of it and slipped out of the room. Fortunately, my father retired to his bedroom rather than entering the library. I dared not tell anyone of my discovery. As time went by, I forgot about the incident and the books." She stopped, could see the change on Martin's face, knew her words had struck him deeply.

No one stirred. All eyes were on Martin whose head was now bowed, his elbows resting on the table, his hands combing through his hair.

Pictures of his forgotten past filled his mind — his father sitting in the arm chair, his legs stretched out in front of him, a book resting in his lap. He remembered hiding behind his father's chair hoping to surprise him, but his father knew he was there. He always did. He heard his father's voice, the voice he'd forgotten. "I smell the feet of a little sneak!" He reached around to grab the child and lift him into his lap, the book falling to the ground. The little boy giggled and wiggled about to his father's teasing and tickling.

The flash of memory startled Martin. The others could see the pained look on his face when he looked up, before he snapped back into the present.

"Alaina, if those books are still there, I must find them." Martin's voice barely concealed his emotions. "My father's library was ransacked by the authorities when they forced my family and servants to prepare to leave the estate. The officials demanded that my mother unlock a chest where my father kept his most treasured volumes. When she opened the chest, they were gone. I remember many times afterward my mother talking aloud to herself as she pondered the mystery of the missing books. She knew they had to have been stolen before my father's arrest. She believed their disappearance to be proof of my father's innocence, that someone aware of their existence had used them in the plot to frame my father.

"Mother wrote to Parliament, even took us with her to stand on the steps as she pleaded with anyone who would listen, but those who acknowledged her refused to believe that someone could enter the estate unnoticed and unlock the chest without anyone's knowledge. They ignored my mother's pleas, seeing only the grieving wife of a wretched traitor trying to save her husband. The authorities saw my father's hobby as a cover-up — we knew it was his passion. The disappearance of the valuable collection haunted York, just as it did my mother.

"York remembered a servant, one who'd only recently come to work for them, a servant whose behavior he recalled as being odd, secretive, unfriendly. Most of the servants had little problem with having two boys underfoot. This new one, by York's recollection, seemed bothered by our presence shooing us away particularly when we wandered into the library.

"The servant spent much time dusting off bookshelves. In fact, York seldom remembered him serving in any other area. The more my brother dwelt on his strange behavior, he became obsessed with finding this servant, disappearing for hours at a time, even walking the streets and watching servants leave the townhouses where they were employed. He went so far as to ask these servants if they knew of him. Many ignored him and barely listened to his description. He was barely twelve at the time, but he dreamed of one day finding that servant, a grandiose thought for a young boy, but York lost his youth after we'd been tossed into the streets.

Martin stopped, knew he'd revealed enough. His voice changed from reminiscence to stolid determination. "That is the past. Today opportunity lies before us. York must be freed from that damn prison and from his pain."

Marielle held back tears, reached out to Martin. "And you too, Martin," her voice filled with compassion. "You've hidden your bruises well. Your silent acceptance of the changes in your family seems to have been your way to deal with the tragic circumstances. You may feel that your mother and brother suffered more, but I suspect that you became the one to temper the powerful emotions that must have been brimming over during that time. York's need to protect you may have kept him from endangering himself."

"My brother, even in his most dangerous moments, never let me down nor ceased to help my mother as long as he was able to do so."

Alaina reached her hand out to Martin. "You may have given both your mother and brother a realistic hold on daily life. Being the younger one, you surely provided a space in their lives to stay in the present and nurture another. Your place in the family, I have no doubt, kept them from losing themselves in their obsession."

Marielle listened to her friend with pride. It was obvious that Martin's plight had touched Alaina deeply, for she'd not heard such softness in her friend's voice before. Alaina's own situation created a hardness and control that never allowed either Marielle or Aunt Cornelia to see this side of her.

Before Aunt Cornelia could speak her thoughts, a resounding clamor echoed through the hallway. Marielle clutched her skirt, ready to rise. Martin was already halfway to the door. Bates had returned.

Chapter Twelve

MAXWELL, EMPLOYED BY Lord Craymore since Richard was a child, not only feared the elder Craymore's wrath if some harm should come to his son, but felt protective of the impulsive young man. Observing the behavior of some of the derelicts who left the tavern gave him an uneasy feeling. He imagined that Richard might be in trouble or might be lying unconscious in an alley, or worse. He had no desire to enter the crude establishment, but there seemed no other recourse. If he delayed any longer, he might fall asleep and be clobbered himself by some drunken thief.

Once his eyes adjusted to the darkness inside the foul-smelling tavern, he spotted Richard seated in a back corner. Thankfully, he recognized his coat and not a moment too soon. Although Richard's head was bowed down, the silver on the revolver gleamed in the light of the dying candle set before him.

"Master Richard! What in God's name...?" Maxwell grabbed the revolver with one hand and latched on to Richard's collar with the other.

Richard stared up at his servant with eyes red, swollen and blurred.

"We will leave here at once, Master Richard. God forgive me my negligence for not coming in sooner." His arms went around Richard's shoulders and lifted him from the seat while pleading with him to cooperate.

Richard relented. He was too drunk to object and many in the tavern were now staring at the two men.

"Best to leave, not a place to cause a scene," Richard mumbled. "After all, I'm a Craymore with a reputation to protect." The carriage was as good a place as any to end this farce.

Richard, stumbling through the crowd, held onto his coachman, allowing him to lead him out the door and into the carriage.

Once Maxwell had him settled on the velvet cushioned seat, he paused as Richard muttered on, incoherently at first. He drew closer to listen.

"Maxwell, why have I become such useless carrion, bending always to my father's wishes, feeding off others just as he's done? I am describing my father accurately, am I not?"

His servant grimaced. His face could not deny that truth of his father's negative influence on this son.

"Oh yes, I know who and what my father is and I am his son, his heir, his flunky."

Maxwell brushed the damp, matted hair out of his young master's eyes and responded with gentle words. "You're your mother's son too, Master Richard. It might seem on the surface that you take after your father, but I know better. You're only now coming into your own. You'll shed his influence if you so desire and then your mother's heart will be heard. Give yourself time."

"My mother is dead and before her time and I did nothing to stop my father's abuse. I'm a coward even now, now that I know the truth." Richard dropped his head into his hands, his words barely audible. "Dear God, I've no desire to wake up tomorrow to face who I am."

Maxwell patted the young man's shoulder, while attempting to find the right words to comfort him.

"Whatever may have happened to cause your eyes to open, I believe that you're on a new road, Master Richard. Do not contemplate bringing harm to your person. Let me bring you home."

Richard lifted his head, slouched back on the seat and motioned for his servant to shut the carriage door.

Maxwell, still shaken by the near disaster, lifted himself into the coachman's seat and signaled the horses to move on. He decided not to return to the townhouse. Richard should not be left alone. He needed his sister now. He turned the carriage to head toward Lady Henley's townhouse. Meanwhile, Richard searched for the revolver only to realize that it was no longer in his possession.

As the Craymore coach arrived at Lady Henley's, the sun began a less than grand entrance being shrouded by gloomy clouds. Maxwell dismounted and turned the latch of the carriage, praying as he did so, that all was well with Richard. Although the gun now lay hidden beneath his own seat, he feared the young man might have found another way to injure himself.

He found Richard to be on the brink of passing

out. Fortunately, though getting on in years, the servant stood over six feet and being fed quite well by the cooks on the estate, had the strength to pull Richard from the carriage.

Richard grumbled as he stumbled along the garden path and up the steps, unaware of his destination and in his servant's tight grip.

Before Maxwell could reach the knocker, the door opened causing him to very nearly dump his cargo onto the Italian marble that graced the main foyer.

Martin and Bates found themselves being pushed back into the hall as Richard stumbled into their arms.

Aunt Cornelia, following close behind the two departing men, lifted her hands to her face in shock, then with amazing control blurted out to all present in the dimly lit foyer, "My, My, this continues to be a most unusual day."

Alaina rushed forward. "Richard! Maxwell!"

"I apologize profusely for this intrusion," Maxwell said attempting a bow while still supporting Richard. "Your brother is in need of some care — he's experienced a most difficult night. I felt it my responsibility to place him in secure hands until he comes to himself."

"What's happened to him?" Alaina gasped. She tried to lift Richard's head, while Maxwell, with Martin's help, held him up.

"I don't believe he's in any condition to explain at the moment, Miss Alaina," Maxwell said as he reluctantly accepted Martin's help. "I suggest some rest..."

Led by Cornelia, Maxwell and Martin steadied Richard and led him to a nearby couch where he immediately stretched out, his head buried in the rich tapestry cushions. Alaina and Marielle did their best to loosen his cravat and remove his boots.

"I do believe, Maxwell, apart from what appears to be your rescue of young Richard, you have arrived at a most opportune time."

"Lady Henley? I felt certain I'd be intruding. I see you have guests despite the early morning hour." Maxwell looked Martin and Bates up and down. Neither of the two strange men seemed to be of the type to be found here with the ladies.

Cornelia didn't miss his surprised look. "Maxwell, although I have barely had the opportunity to make your acquaintance, I see that you demonstrate a loyalty to your charge. The two gentlemen you see before you," looking over at Martin and Bates, "have a need for a carriage ride, for they are on a most urgent mission. Since you've arrived at such an opportune time, would you be so gracious as to deliver these men to whatever destination they desire?"

Maxwell stared at the two strangers, then back at Lady Henley, hesitated in surprise, then quickly recaptured his servant's posture. After serving in the Craymore household nothing should surprise him. It was not his place, however, to question.

He bowed, straightened. "I am at your service, Lady Henley."

"Thank you, Maxwell. I trust, also, that you are not only a very worthy servant, but also a discreet one?" Aunt Cornelia queried.

"Most definitely!"

"Well then, off with you." She stopped to reach out her hands to Martin. "We will be waiting most anxiously for news. Please keep us informed and if there's anything else I can do to help…"

Martin stooped to kiss the elderly lady on the cheek. "You've been God's angel and if for some reason we are unable to return, please know you are most dear to me."

Marielle rushed over before they could leave and gave Martin a gentle hug and whispered, "May all of God's angels be with you."

He smiled, touched her cheek, brush her hand with a kiss before following Craymore's mystified servant out the door.

Cornelia stood at the door, awed at the miraculous timing of events, watching as the men disappeared from view. As soon as the carriage was off, she heard Richard moan in the nearby parlor.

Waking from his stupor, he found himself surrounded by the three ladies, Alaina, who had not left his side and now Marielle and her aunt.

Aunt Cornelia rang for her butler, for it was quite obvious that this young man needed rest and a bath, perhaps a cold one, before she was to find out his story. As she walked away, she nodded in disbelief. The outcome of this day was of deep concern, but the activities of the past night brought with it a large dose of exhilaration. She felt quite steeped in the madness of it all. As she left the younger ones and sought out her cook to prepare breakfast, she sent up a short prayer that all would go well for both sons of her old friend Lord Blackstone.

MARTIN DIRECTED MAXWELL to Jeremy's chosen meeting place. The thick morning fog would most likely keep many Londoners inside for a time and allow them to plan. The carriage came to a stop just outside a tavern obscure enough for the men to gather at without disturbance, but very near the prison. The men stepped out of the carriage after Maxwell graciously opened the door inquiring as to whether he should wait for them.

Martin hesitated. He had no desire to put the coachman in danger, but on the other hand, how much better to escape to an awaiting carriage than to attempt to flee by foot. Out of Maxwell's hearing, he turned to Bates. Someone would need to watch the carriage, to ascertain that Maxwell stayed put.

Bates nodded, knowing what to do.

Turning back to Maxwell, he appraised him, contemplated his involvement, but Maxwell quickly put the young man at ease.

"I've been serving Master Richard for most of his life and I find myself at the moment unoccupied. Since Lady Henley has asked for my assistance and my charge is at the moment indisposed, I am without a duty for the time being."

Martin looked warily at the servant. His offer seemed genuine and he intuitively believed this man could be trusted. He couldn't pass up the opportunity to use the carriage for a speedy departure. The bell tower had rung seven times shortly before. No time could be wasted.

"I appreciate your assistance. If you're not one to step back in the face of extraordinary circumstances, I'll accept your offer to wait for our return."

The coachman bowed. "I am at your service and I assure you that I am accustomed to extraordinary circumstances in my service to the Craymores. Maxwell fully anticipated a most interesting morning. "Might I ask your name, sir?"

Martin stared directly into the eyes of the old servant before speaking. "Blackstone, Martin Blackstone."

Maxwell flinched, then nodded knowingly. "Pleased to meet you, sir." Maxwell bowed.

"If all goes well, we'll be joined by my older brother who is detained at the prison nearby."

Taken aback by Martin's words, but impressed by his honesty as well as the significance of his name, Maxwell replied, even to his own surprise, "As I said, I am at your service, Master Blackstone."

Martin nodded, looked away at the cloaked figure the now stood near the darkened doorway. Maxwell noted the interchange, understood.

Martin grasped the servant's shoulder in appreciation, turned and entered the tavern.

MAXWELL, AWED BY the strange and unusual happenings and surprised at himself—he'd just agreed to be an accomplice in a prison escape—stayed at his station thinking of all that had occurred. Lady Henley, he knew, was a woman whose reputation for being involved in the unexpected was legendary. He saw no reason to miss the opportunity to see where the adventure would lead.

As he pondered the events he suddenly remembered...the young man beaten and dragged into the stable in those early morning hours after bedlam had broken loose on the estate. He well remembered that night and later the escape. He'd heard the elder Craymore come in and speak viciously to the young man and threaten his death. He'd been cleaning a carriage, out of sight, but he heard it all.

Blackstone, the name never to be mentioned by the family, how mystifying, he thought. Shadowy details, arrested for treason, he remembered, the family thrown into the streets, Craymore's delight at the events. Servants talked, rumors passed through the doors of the estate like ghosts walking in mist, half tales, half truths. The servants never knew for certain what transpired, but all knew not to mention the name, Blackstone.

Lord Craymore elicited fear not only in his family but in all those who worked for him. His generosity to those who remained faithful and silent kept his staff dutifully blind. And now, Maxwell thought, the eccentric Lady Henley, young Marielle and Alaina all conspiring together. *I should turn this carriage around.* He looked back, caught the eye of the cloaked figure and returned to his thoughts.

But go where? To Lord Craymore?

I have either lost my mind or gained my mettle, but I believe I have no desire to become uninvolved.

Splendid, I say. I feel like a young rapscallion, I do!

Maxwell continued to muse, while the men inside prepared the final details.

Jeremy and Willie had already accomplished amazing feats within the last couple of hours. The jailer was found just as he was preparing to leave his flat for the prison. The favor he owed and a hefty sum promised for his cooperation, helped him to overcome his initial refusal. He would merely be doing his job, moving prisoners to another secured area, a job he'd already been given the night before by the head guard. The instructions for the move were already in his hands, planned for that very morning, when Jeremy approached him. Jeremy's request to allow an escape during the move was outrageous, until the request was accompanied by a tidy sum. As it was, the prison was a mess with all the construction going on, the jailer had told Jeremy, most fortunate for all involved.

By now the jailer would have already informed the prisoners of the possibility of escape if they could overcome the two guards—he would be one of them—and don their uniforms.

The jailer's suggestions became more and more creative as Jeremy continued to pepper his palm, remind him of his debt and promise more if the escape succeeded. The man knew the repercussions of his actions could be dangerous, but he'd be passed out after all. If the guards' attentions outside the prison were momentarily diverted—he had a friend who could do just that with a bit of monetary persuasion—they would be the ones most likely to be blamed.

The jailer's confidence in the plan gave Jeremy some assurance. After all, Jeremy reminded him, a favor unpaid could bring a deadly price.

Aware of Jeremy and his gang's reputation, the jailer did not ask his meaning. He knew he needed to carry this through without added complications.

Yes, it was working out amazingly well.

Martin took a moment to thank Jeremy and Willie for their help. They were the best when it came to plots and ploys and they came through admirably. They finalized last-minute details. Each knew their role. Willie already had friends acquiring needed equipment. Jeremy and Bates would be stationed at strategic points, Martin was to stay out of sight until the last possible moment.

Thanks to Maxwell's cooperation, they'd have a ready means of escape, if York and Braum could scale the walls without hindrance. If something went wrong... Martin would not allow himself further thought. He had no doubt his brother would take full advantage of any situation made available to him.

Few guards were around in the early morning, the jailer told Jeremy confidently. York would be informed of the best escape route and Jeremy's men were already preparing ropes to be anchored in the spot.

Much could go wrong, but there was no turning back.

Jeremy counted on the knowledge that his friends were masters of their trade and any unsuspecting guards within the prison walls no match for them.

Martin emerged from the tavern drawing Maxwell abruptly from his thoughts. Before concealing himself in the carriage, he directed the servant to drive slowly down the side street adjacent to the prison until he was given the order to stop. The thick fog was a welcome accomplice.

Maxwell pulled on the reins and the horses ambled slowly toward the road that bordered the north prison wall and housed the gatehouse. Suddenly the sound of another carriage moving swiftly behind him drew his attention.

"Mercy, it's Lord Craymore's carriage," Maxwell muttered aloud.

Martin heard the carriage draw up beside them and peered discreetly through the heavy velvet drape. He heard Maxwell address the passenger whose head was thrust out the window calling up to the servant.

It was Lord Craymore.

Did Maxwell betray them and send a message to Craymore? Did he err in telling the servant what was to occur? Martin wondered as he listened to the exchange, knowing precious time could be lost.

"Maxwell, what are you doing here?" Lord Craymore questioned then continued without waiting for a response. "I see he followed my directives and without any wasted time. I'm proud of that boy," Craymore said, grinning, as he looked toward the prison.

"I must admit I was a bit under the weather last night. Wasn't sure if I'd gotten my message across. Didn't seem right that I should be the one to insist that Blackstone be swiftly punished, might cause tongues to wag, you know. Yes, my son is the one who has been humiliated by that ruffian, Black... Never mind."

Maxwell absorbed Lord Craymore words. His years as his servant and footman had taught him not to display emotion and it was serving him well at the present moment.

"How long has he been in there?" Craymore queried.

Thankful for the elder Craymore's previous admissions, Maxwell spoke plainly and respectfully, but sparsely as seemed wise at the moment.

"Your son asked me to drive him here, milord. He said he had urgent business to complete. He did say something about justice being served, I believe. He's been in the prison about a quarter of an hour, sir. I imagine I'll be waiting for a time. "Would you like me to tell him that you were here and to report to you on his return, or had you planned on joining him?"

"No, Richard will handle it. Tell him to return to my townhouse immediately to give me the news. I expect that he'll have everything well under control. If not," Craymore paused, "we'll have to consider other means..."

Maxwell nodded, maintaining his subservient posture. "I will pass the message on to young Richard as soon as he returns."

"Good man, Maxwell. I may even return for a nap. I didn't sleep very well." With a nod of dismissal, Lord Craymore ordered his driver to return home.

When the carriage disappeared into the fog, Maxwell bent down towards the carriage window and with simple dignity asked, "Are we ready to proceed, Master Blackstone?"

Martin breathed a sigh of relief. He'd been praying silently during the interchange. Sitting back he envisioned his mother on her knees praying for her husband, her children and for retribution of evil. A powerful feeling akin to faith stirred within, smothering his apprehension. His fears gave way to confidence that all would turn out as planned.

"Yes, Maxwell, continue on. We should see some action very soon.

The carriage continued slowly over the cobblestone street coming to a stop at the designated site. The fog and dampness remained and to their good fortune the street remained deserted.

Martin found it difficult to wait in the carriage. He wanted to jump out and find a way to ensure his brother's safety, but he was wise enough to wait. He wouldn't take a chance of ruining what might be his brother's only chance for escape.

Chapter Thirteen

York waited impatiently in the grimy cellblock. Despite being told by a jailer shortly before of the plan in motion for their escape, he had doubts. He already knew of three men who'd escaped during a construction detail, but what were the odds of two more getting past the guards? His friends would do whatever they could—they'd worked together in similar situations—and this haphazard place shouldn't be any more difficult, but it seemed almost too easy.

He wondered how they came up with the plan and who was involved. At the same time, he needed to be prepared in case it was a trick. Yet the jailer knew Jeremy, said he owed him. It seemed to be legitimate and he had little to lose. His thoughts were broken by the appearance of the jailer looking pale and more than a little nervous.

"All right, you two," The jailer said loudly for the benefit of other prisoners. "You're bein' moved, thanks to some benefactor who seems to think you should 'ave fancier quarters." He muttered as he unlocked Braum's cell first, instructing his fellow guard to keep him "right under his nose".

As soon as the lock was turned on York's cell door and opened slightly, York grabbed his arm, thrusting him into the cell, slapping his head down to the floor. Only a muffled sound could be detected.

Meanwhile, Braum overpowered the other guard and did the same. In no time and in complete silence, they exchanged clothes with the two guards and were on their way.

Entering the open courtyard, they walked casually toward the guardhouse, appearing to anyone who observed them to be on duty. As they neared the north wall, an eruption broke out behind them, causing the two guards standing in the guardhouse to run towards the commotion.

Looking back quickly, York could see a couple of men chasing a guard dog, its chain dragging behind the animal.

The two guards who'd left their post were screaming orders to corner the dog, neither of them looking back at their station.

Hearing the ruckus, Willie and his accomplices, in position behind and below the prison walls, threw the anchored ropes over the wall at the designated area.

Both York and Braum were over the top while the guards were still chasing the dog in circles. Their friends waited below, smiling broadly when they saw them appear. Everything had gone exactly as planned and the thought of outsmarting the officials only fueled their efficiency.

Martin's good fortune of obtaining, of all things, Craymore's carriage for their departure was more than a stroke of good luck, it was a downright miracle and an irony they would be talking and joking about for years to come. The men had relished the opportunity to be involved and help York and Braum.

In Jeremy's words, "Our reputation is at stake. Leave it to the Blackstones to create the best of reunions possible," he'd told Martin earlier.

The instant York and Braum hit the ground, the men pointed to the carriage. York slammed them on their backs in thanks and took off in seconds with Braum close behind. They knew that once officials were notified of the escape, the area would swarm with Bow Street Runners.

The horses jerked suddenly, their senses attuned to the sound of possible danger. Maxwell held the reins firmly as Martin pushed open the carriage door. Braum, trembling, but sturdy enough on his feet followed York into the enclosed carriage. As soon as they were safely within, Maxwell signaled the horses and they were off while Jeremy and the other accomplices disappeared down the road.

Maxwell led the horses around the corner and away from the prison, moving briskly for a time, leaving some distance between them and the prison gates, then slowing down to a respectable trot. He knew the sight of Craymore's town carriage would not be unusual to anyone walking about.

To their good fortune, the city remained quiet under the heavy cloak of fog and now a misty rain. The decision had been made earlier in the tavern—once they'd heard of Maxwell's unexpected compliance—to return to Aunt Cornelia's townhouse. No one would suspect the kind old woman of harboring prisoners. Being well hidden in the daylight gave precious time for planning an escape out of the city by night.

Inside the carriage, the two brothers embraced while Braum's arms clasped both his friends. York and Braum, though weak and shaken by the sudden turn of events, grinned at Martin whose eyes betrayed his deeper emotions.

"Well little brother, you not only managed to free us from that hellhole, but you've done it with class. My highest compliments."

"I owed you one," Martin replied. "It wasn't too long ago that you managed to free me from under the nose of Craymore and with his horses too. This time he's graced us with his carriage and coachman. There seems to be no end to his generosity. Now all we need is the opportunity to thank him, Blackstone style."

"Aye, my boot in his face and my knife in 'is gut is the thanks I'll give 'im as soon as my strength is back," Braum growled.

"We will repay him and I suspect the day is coming closer," York said with grim determination.

Martin nodded, his emotions boiling within. York clasped the side of his brother's head and pushed it towards his own, both men sharing a moment inexpressible in words. They were quiet during the remainder of the journey. Each needed time to regain their equilibrium.

As the carriage moved out of the prison district, they heard the warning bells come to life. The local militia must have been notified immediately, most likely were already sending out patrols to scour the area. Before long, they turned into the elegant area where Aunt Cornelia resided. Maxwell pulled the carriage into the drive and around to the rear of the townhouse.

Cornelia rose the moment she heard the sound of the carriage and called for Thomas to meet their guests and lead the men into the house, before caring for the horses. Alert to every possibility, she wisely sent messages to other servants who usually arrived in the early morning and informed them that their services today would not be needed.

So much had transpired since her first sight of Martin standing in Alaina's bedroom and Cornelia suspected the excitement was far from over. The extra eyes and ears of curious servants were best gone. Only her two most trusted live-in servants remained and, of course, Bess, who seemed already quite involved and would need to be closely watched. Since she'd been party to what had already transpired, it seemed best to keep her busy in the pantry and out of sight.

Thomas was the first to reenter the house. He notified her that the Craymore's coachman, Maxwell, had left to clean out the carriage and would return later to check on Master Richard. The "unusual guests" refused to be escorted to the door. The young man Martin would remain with them. "Madam, you see the men are quite, well, their previous living conditions were most unsanitary and they do not desire to bring filth or vermin into your residence."

"Oh, why did I not consider... Of course, I suppose I wouldn't have, not having ever been in acquaintance with... Thomas, do whatever needs to be done. I did think to prepare baths. Bess is heating water, but whatever is needed to remove..."

"Do not fret, Madam, we know what is required. After all, even the horses pick up... Well, I do not mean to compare, but..."

"Thank you, Thomas. Find clean clothing for them and as soon as they are comfortable, bring them in. A warm meal and strong drink will be waiting when they have bathed and... My gracious, I am confident that you know whatever must be done."

"Yes, madam, all will be taken care of," Thomas replied. "The horse trough can be used..."

"Spare me the details, Thomas. Just get on with it."

"Yes, milady." Her servant bowed and left the room.

Earlier Aunt Cornelia had insisted that both Marielle and Alaina take some needed rest. Richard was ushered to a distant upstairs bedroom to sleep off his drunken stupor. Protesting at first, the young ladies agreed out of respect for their elder's wishes and fervent persistence, but with a promise from Aunt Cornelia to bring them any news. She believed, however, that it was best that they not see the men immediately.

Promises cannot always be kept, Cornelia thought to herself. If they choose to become upset with her, she would just have to ask forgiveness for an old woman's weak memory. *Mayhap they won't believe a word*, Cornelia thought, *but now was not the time to disturb them.* The men, she felt, needed some time together after their traumatic ordeal.

When the men were ushered into her sitting room, Cornelia noticed that even Martin had washed, shaved and wore clean clothes. Most likely his close contact with the other two men in the carriage left him physically uncomfortable as well. Seeing the condition of York and Braum, she urged them to sit closest to the fire, while greeting Martin with a warm hug.

York stayed standing and bowed before addressing their benefactor. "Lady Henley, I am astounded at what has transpired over the past few hours. We were told that an unknown benefactor had arranged better quarters. I admit that I suspected a devious hand was involved. Martin has informed us of your assistance. Our appreciation for your involvement and hospitality goes beyond words. I'm at a loss on how to repay you for your kindness and generosity."

Cornelia raised her hand to silence him. *This young man, she thought, though obviously weakened and dressed like a servant still had the presence of an aristocrat. He was most definitely his father's son, looking so much like him, she wanted to weep, but her reputation as a cantankerous old woman was not to be compromised.*

"Now listen here, young man. I accept your gratitude, but it is the last I want to hear of it. I am most pleased to be of service to you and consider it a belated gift to your dear father. Having his sons stand before me is an honor and...my goodness will you sit down young man?" While the others laughed for the first time since their arrival, York obediently took a seat.

"Madam, you place yourself in grave danger harboring escaped convicts," York said gravely.

"Shush, why you also have your father's eyes." She smiled, then glanced at the tray awaiting them. "Thomas, I see, has brought drinks and some warm scones, a nourishing meal will be served shortly. Beds, as well, are being prepared. I'll leave you now. When I return we'll discuss how I might be of help to secure your further safety. Please see my home as a safe haven to rest and be restored."

With that she turned and walked out of the room briskly, wanting them to tend to their needs rather than be concerned for her safety or reputation. She wasn't. Instead, she felt relief and pure joy to see Lord Blackstone's sons alive and safe.

Settling back on the cushions, Martin relayed the earlier events including Lady Cornelia's surprising actions, Richard's arrival and the ironic involvement of Craymore's servant, Maxwell.

York listened, taking in every detail. In his present weak state, he felt not only relief, but great pride. His brother, admirably, had taken charge.

"Perhaps I should wait until you've rested, York," Martin hesitated only briefly before going on, "but the news I have for you, I believe, will lead to a swift revival of your strength and resolve to seek justice for our father."

York showed visible shock at the change in his brother. "Do you mean that you're not going to urge me to stop my "foolish" quest?"

"No, I am as determined as you are to see Craymore suffer." Martin proceeded to tell of Alaina's discovery in her father's library.

As York listened, his heart swelled with hope and purpose. He stood and walked over to the fire turning his back to the other men. Martin and Braum watched his shoulders stiffen and his fists clench as he turned to face them.

"We must devise a plan that will not only lead us to the evidence, but that will trap and place a net around Craymore."

"We'll make short shrift of this," Braum interrupted. "Breaking in and taking out what's needed is my specialty. I feel my strength returnin' already. When those fancy wigged aristocrats see 'em, Craymore will be crawling on 'is belly. I'd like nothing better than to grind 'im into the ground..."

York held up his hand to stop Braum's visualization. "It won't be that easy. Even if we find my father's collection, it may prove nothing to those who have been far removed from the events of the past. We must get Craymore to admit what he's done."

Martin nodded. "We'll need witnesses."

"And the right circumstances to bring him to his knees. I want to talk to his daughter and Richard, since they're both under this roof. How helpful they will be is questionable."

"His daughter seems to have little respect for her father," Martin replied, "but Richard's past behavior makes him our enemy. He may need a little coercion if we're to procure his help."

"I'd be more than 'appy to take on that job,"

Braum muttered.

"First, we need to find out as much as we can. We must face the possibility that Craymore may have rid himself of the books long ago," York said grimly.

Martin and Braum looked at each other, not wanting to accept that possibility. Before more could be said, Aunt Cornelia returned.

"Why look at this. You've barely eaten and you, young man," speaking firmly to York, her finger pointing into his chest, "look ready to fall over. I insist that all of you take a few hours rest." With that, she rang for Thomas who appeared immediately to await her instructions.

"Thomas, show these men to their rooms and be certain they have whatever they need to rest comfortably. Leave a tray of food for each so that they may eat when they're ready, but get them into beds!" Cornelia demanded, not giving anyone a chance to speak. "I do not want to hear a word from any of you for the next few hours. You'll be useless to solve the mystery before us if you cannot stand on your own two feet and all three of you look as if you're ready to keel over."

The men knew she was right, but were wary. Both York and Braum felt drained from the morning's events as well as their dismal captivity, but could they trust this household? After the dingy prison conditions, the thought of a clean bed was most inviting.

Martin's loss of sleep was catching up with him, but he hesitated, stared at York, each knowing what the other was thinking.

"We're in deep debt to you and appreciate your hospitality," Martin acknowledged, "but perhaps it might be best if we took turns resting. Who knows if someone, I fear, even of this household…"

Cornelia refused to let him finish his sentence. "My dear boy, I am well able to protect myself and anyone who stays under my roof. I assure you that only those in whom I have complete trust are privy to the goings-on this morning and unbeknown to you, there are a few of your own trusted fellows roaming about the neighborhood. Nothing goes beyond my notice. I'd invite them in for tea, but I suspect they believe they're being as unnoticeable as church mice."

The men laughed at the lady's keen awareness. Bowing to Lady Henley, York followed Thomas with the others close behind.

Cornelia sighed with relief. The men were safe and would, hopefully, get some rest. She needed a nap herself. After ringing for Edith, her chambermaid and asking to be alerted if any one of her guests began to stir, she chose her most comfortable chair, meditated for only a short time then drifted off to sleep.

Chapter Fourteen

DESPITE AUNT CORNELIA'S insistence that Marielle and Alaina return to their bedchambers to rest, both found it impossible to sleep. Marielle's fear for what might transpire warred with her frustration that she could do nothing to help. It seemed that every situation she'd encountered since her kidnapping left matters out of her control. Alaina welcomed the time alone — she needed time to grasp the events of the morning and all that had been revealed.

Unable to sit with her thoughts any longer, Marielle walked to Alaina's room and tapped lightly. The door flew open.

"Marielle! Have you heard anything?" She drew a breath, waiting.

"No and my nerves are frazzled. I was going to seek out Aunt Cornelia, but Edith informed me that she's napping. I apologize if I've disturbed you."

"You've not disturbed me in the least. I've been so agitated. Do come in for awhile, then we'll go down together." Alaina walked over to her bed and propped herself up and urged Marielle to join her. They talked about the morning's events and Richard's unexpected arrival and condition. Both shared their confusion, but Marielle had more to say. She chose her words carefully.

"Alaina, I must talk to you about Richard. There's no easy way for me to say this. I've been silent for too long and I must confess, dishonest." She hesitated, before blurted out what she feared would upset her friend. "My feeling towards Richard…they're not what they should be."

Alaina reached out and clasped Marielle's hands. "I've suspected for some time that your heart was elsewhere. I haven't wanted to pry. I find it difficult, however, to believe that dishonesty is in your nature. A betrothal does not always carry love."

"Thank you for understanding. I should have trusted you more."

"I'm afraid that I, too, have kept silent and been less than honest. I'd hoped your marriage to my brother might soften him, break my father's hold on him."

"I am sorry. Richard has always treated me with consideration and respect. I'd hoped I would eventually come to love him."

"Marielle, there's more you must know. My father has coveted your father's estate and lands. He knew your dowry would be generous and the Henley Estate was his main goal. He's urged Richard on. I've struggled for a way to tell you…"

Marielle remembered York's words. He'd questioned Richard's motives.

"I should have said something earlier, but I felt Richard genuinely wanted the marriage and I so wanted you for my sister-in-law. Please forgive me for my silence."

"It seems we both have kept our secrets and

been at the mercy of others. There is nothing to forgive." She gave Alaina a reassuring smile. "Now, please tell me, how are you coping? To have your father be seen as the enemy and the object of revenge…"

"My father has no conscience. If he is the guilty one, then it's time he paid his dues. You see, I must have some of my father's ruthlessness within me."

"Not ruthlessness, but strength of will. She squeezed her friend's hand, hesitated. "Alaina, there's more. I don't know if you'll understand."

"It's York, isn't it?"

Marielle stared in shock. "How did you know?"

"I could see it in your eyes at the mention of his name.' Alaina smiled. "I wasn't sure, of course. Does he feel the same?"

"I don't know. I mean, I very much doubt it. Perhaps I created a fantasy of love. I thought…but, no, he was captured in the arms of a harlot! I fear his attraction to me was more of lust than the love I desire."

"You may be reading too much into that scenario. Why not leave a window of hope open? Assumptions are often far from the truth of what is in another's heart. Let's hope that Martin has been successful in the plan for York's escape. York may yet be your hero."

Marielle grimaced, doubting her friend's optimistic view.

Alaina knew she had little else to offer and she didn't want to give false hope. "Let's see if Aunt Cornelia is awake yet and I do want to check on my brother."

"Yes, I agree, Marielle replied, grateful to get off the topic of lost dreams. "I'll need a few minutes to refresh myself. I must look like quite a sight."

Both looked down at themselves and laughed. They gave each other a reassuring hug before Marielle returned to her bedroom to dress.

"LADY HENLEY, FORGIVE my intrusion."

Aunt Cornelia awoke, startled, as her servant rushed into the room. "Heavens, what is it Edith?"

"Lord Craymore is at the door, milady and he refuses to leave. I told him you were resting, but he insists on seeing you."

"Oh, dear. He mustn't suspect anything is amiss. Could he have seen Richard's carriage? No, Maxwell left long ago. Perhaps he told him of his son's whereabouts." Cornelia grimaced. "I must think quickly. Where is Thomas?"

"He's with Lord Craymore attempting to keep him at the door until I'd spoken with you."

"Tell Thomas I will see him. As soon as you can draw Thomas aside, both of you go upstairs and be sure our guests do not stir. I pray he doesn't know that Richard is here." Cornelia's mind raced as she waited for Lord Craymore's entrance, then quickly created her own scheme.

"Milady, Lord Craymore wishes a word with you."

"Please, show him in, Thomas," Cornelia said weakly, not moving from her chair and wrapping her shawl more tightly about her.

Thomas barely moved aside before Lord

Craymore marched in ahead of him. "Forgive me for disturbing you, Cornelia. Are you ailing?" he asked, his face masked with concern.

"Yes, I'm afraid I've been a bit under the weather. I've asked my servants not to accept visitors. If they were in any way rude, I do apologize. They are only following my orders. I'm afraid I am a very poor patient and they do worry about me."

"No need to apologize," Craymore humphed. "It is I who should ask your pardon for my intrusion, but I've been waiting anxiously for a word from my son. As I'm sure you've heard the kidnappers are safely behind bars. Richard went to the prison this morning to urge immediate punishment. He hasn't returned. I'd hoped Marielle or Alaina may have heard something."

"We've had no visitors this morning. Marielle and Alaina are still asleep and I prefer not to disturb them. They've been quite busy planning the wedding you know...invitations, shopping and parties. Why, they've exhausted me." Cornelia yawned, snuggled back into her chair. "I'm afraid I can't help you, but if Richard does stop by, I'll inform him of your visit. You look as if you could use some rest yourself, if you don't mind my saying so."

"Yes, yes, I must admit, I slept little last night. As Richard's father, I feel it's my responsibility to see that this matter is taken care of without any delays. After all, your brother has little gumption to handle such matters. I'm sure you're aware that he tends to avoid controversy."

Cornelia chose not to respond to his deliberate arrogance.

"I expect that the two kidnappers will be hanged for their treachery, if I have anything to do with it. Richard is of the same mind." Craymore paused. "Perhaps I'll have my coachman bring me to the prison and find out for myself."

"Richard is a very capable young man. I'm sure that he'll handle the matter efficiently. He may need more time."

"Yes, yes, of course. I'm weary of this entire situation. Rumors and scandal abound. The marriage should put a stop to it and protect Marielle's good name. I'm sure you agree."

"Why, of course. Now I don't want to be inhospitable, but I do need to rest." Cornelia wrapped her shawl around her more tightly before ringing the bell beside her. Within moments, her servant appeared.

"Thomas, please see Lord Craymore out." She gave a weak smile to her visitor. "It was a pleasure to see you…perhaps another time."

Craymore hid his scowl at the obvious dismissal. "Again, my apologies for disturbing you. I hope your health improves soon." Bowing, he followed Thomas out the door.

"EDITH, WE WANT to speak with Aunt Cornelia. Why do you insist on primping us now?" Marielle questioned with obvious irritation.

"Your hair, dear ladies, looked a sight. There, much better now, but how about this comb? I think this pearl one for you, Alaina."

"Enough, Edith." Marielle scolded. "We are going downstairs."

Edith threw up her hands, then closed them in a prayerful position hoping that Lord Craymore had left the premises.

When Marielle and Alaina entered Cornelia's sitting room, they found her pacing back and forth, her fingers pressed tightly to her lips.

"Aunt Cornelia, Edith told us that you were resting. You look to be preparing for combat."

"I fear that has already occurred, Marielle, but without combat, perhaps a little acting on my part."

"What's happened?" Alaina queried.

"Your father just left."

"Father was here?" Alaina asked, her voice raised in alarm.

"Yes, looking for Richard. It seems he has not been notified of the escape yet. He'll know soon enough. When he returns home, his servants will no doubt be abuzz with the news."

Marielle drew in a deep breath, her hand rising to her throat, her voice wavering with apprehension. "The escape was successful then?"

Before Aunt Cornelia could reply, Richard appeared in the doorway.

"What's happening here?"

The ladies turned to see Richard, his clothes askew, but his manner of more substance than his first appearance in the wee hours of the morning.

"Did I hear you speak of my father?"

"Yes, Richard," Cornelia answered, her eyes narrowed, unsure what to expect from him. "Your father came looking for you, wanted to know if you'd returned from a visit to the prison."

"Yes, he sent me on a mission." Richard clawed through his hair, mumbled before finding his voice. "He'll be most disappointed to know I ignored his request. Instead I went to the tavern and got soused. I suspect Maxwell kept my confidence?" He didn't wait for a response. "I apologize for my abrupt visit. You had other visitors, if I remember correctly."

"Richard," Alaina interrupted, "There has been a turn of events. When you arrived, you were not only inebriated, but quite distraught. Maxwell was most concerned for your safety. You said many things. Do you have any recollection of what you told me?"

Richard ignored formality, walked slowly to a chair, sat down heavily, staring up at his sister. "Perhaps you need to tell me. This past night has been a living nightmare. I heard things...found out things. He paused, stared squarely at his sister, glanced at the other two women who stood behind her. "I don't know where to begin. I think it would be best if you told me what I said."

As Alaina and Richard talked, Cornelia and Marielle stood in the background listening quietly. Cornelia was pleased with his words, assuring herself that Richard had indeed found himself and may be exceedingly helpful in whatever was to come. When the moment became too intense in the renewed relationship between brother and sister, Marielle and her aunt quietly left the room.

"I'll tell Edith to prepare the breakfast table.

The others may be down soon."

"The others?" Marielle stopped, glared at her aunt.

"Oh, heavens. I never finished telling you. The escape was quite successful. York and his friend are resting in the upper bedrooms."

York is here?" Marielle gasped. "Is he well? I mean, are they both well?"

"Weak from the conditions of that hideous place, but well enough. They are, hopefully, getting some sleep."

"Yes, I..." Marielle felt overwhelmed with relief and overcome by the reality that York was so near. She wanted to escape, to calm her pounding heart. "I need to go to my room. I..." Before her aunt could question, she rushed from the room.

Cornelia didn't try to stop her, even though the girls had just left their bedrooms a short time before. She could see the change on Marielle's face, knew that York's name affected her deeply. She wouldn't pry, at least not yet.

Marielle rushed up the stairs, almost tripping on her skirts, but it was too late. As she turned the corner, she slammed into York.

His hands grasped her arms. Both caught their breath. Braum swerved out of the way with Martin close behind.

Marielle was stunned into silence—York's face so close, his eyes dark, piercing into hers.

"Marielle, a pleasure to bump into you once again."

"I just heard. I..."

York ignored his conflicting feelings and his

desire to sweep her into his arms, spoke in a measured tone. "I suspect that you thought I was safely behind bars." He sneered, the words of the arresting officer, now in the forefront of his mind.

Marielle looked up at him, bewildered by the coldness in his voice, the hardness of his expression.

Martin, seeing her discomfort and hearing his brother's abrupt response, interrupted. "York, we must go downstairs and see what's developed. There'll be time later for a reunion."

York took in her expression of surprise, brushed past her and followed his brother down the hall.

Marielle watched him disappear down the stairs, the picture of his face, gaunt, tired, his cruel words scorching her. How was she to react? She wanted to follow him, confront him—instead, she walked mechanically to her room slamming the door behind her.

She felt relief that he was safe and rage at his dismissal of her.

What did he mean? I have more reason to be insulted at his rakish behavior, she thought bitterly. She gritted her teeth and stalked out of her bedroom.

AUNT CORNELIA MARVELED at the strange gathering. Richard, having summoned the courage to face the Blackstone brothers, now sat across from them. "Unimaginable," she thought. After their original confrontation, the men had spent more than an hour behind closed doors. The women waited anxiously, sometimes cringing at the muffled voices obviously raised in anger, at other times curious at the quietness. When the men emerged, they'd come together, a tenuous truce accomplished. Now, seated around the dining room table, they were actually working together, though cautiously.

Richard knew nothing of the books Alaina had discovered in their father's library. York questioned his ignorance of the volumes, but gave him the benefit of the doubt.

"I'll go to the estate, Richard offered. "If they're there, I'll find them."

"We will go to the estate," York cut in, narrowing his eyes. "If Alaina's memory is correct, they'll be there. With the Blackstone seal, they would be difficult to dispose of in any market." He refused to believe otherwise.

"But their existence will not be enough to prove your father's innocence," Richard said grimly. "Too much time has past."

"Do you have another suggestion?" York asked, menacingly.

"Yes, I will bring my father with me, to confess."

"You would do that?" Martin asked, surprised and suspicious. How do we know that you'll not have sympathy for your father or for yourself and turn it to your own ends?"

"My word may seem of little worth, but I give it to you." He looked around the table measuring their reactions. They were wary of him. He expected no less.

York, still feeling the remnants of fatigue, knew he it was best to put his resentment aside if anything was to be accomplished. He needed more information. "How many servants remain on the estate?"

"A butler, a cook, a footman, two stablemen, that I recall. Other servants and hired guards were dispatched to London as messengers or to collect information...for your capture."

"And how do you plan to convince your father to return to the country?" York asked, already weighing alternatives to getting him there.

"If I told him that the escapees might return to the estate..."

Braum interrupted. "So 'e can set up a trap? I wouldn't trust 'im, York. 'e's 'is father's son, a Craymore. A leopard don't change 'is spots. I say we get our men to grab Craymore, drag 'im there, make 'im confess and it'll be done with."

York reached out and grabbed Braum's arm whose fist was being held too close to Richard's face. "We need to think this through.

"Richard, Braum has a point. Your father's demise will also be your undoing. You may no longer be the heir to your father's holdings. If we can prove my father's innocence and the truth is made public, you have the most to lose."

Before Richard could reply, Alaina, who'd been listening from her chosen seat by the window, rose and stood behind her him. "I believe that my brother has recognized my father for who he is, but to assure that he'll carry out his part, I'll accompany him to the estate on the pretense that I must collect articles in preparation for the wedding."

"I'll also be coming." Cornelia interrupted. "You'll need objective witnesses if there's to be a confession."

"Aunt Cornelia, it's much too dangerous for you. If anything goes wrong, you might be injured or worse," Alaina pleaded. "You have done more than enough. The situation is between the Craymores and the Blackstones."

"If you think I've interfered to this point without seeing it through to the end, you do not know me very well, my dear."

"She's right." Marielle moved away from her spot by the door, stood before them. "My aunt would never pass up an opportunity to participate in a situation that held any element of danger. I, too, will be going." She crossed her arms about her, lifted her chin, expecting an argument.

"I've waited too long for this to turn into a circus," York snapped. He watched Marielle's expression, could see the hurt and anger well up, but ignored her reaction. The situation would place them all in danger. He'd done enough to cause her anguish. He wanted her safely away from the confrontation.

Struggling to control her rage, she snapped back. "You will not stop me. I am as much a part of this as anyone in this room."

York knew her stubborn side too well. He'd make sure his men were well hidden and ready to intervene, if needed. "If the ladies must be there, they should go together and ahead of Craymore."

He turned to Alaina. "Perhaps, you could usher Marielle and Lady Henley to a safe place before your father and brother arrive. You may be able to help us gain admittance without too many casualties."

"York, you're trustin' that they betray their father and lose everything. 'ave you gone mad?"

"No, Braum, but if we're being betrayed," he glared at Richard and Alaina, "Marielle and Lady Henley could be in danger as their passengers."

Marielle narrowed her eyes, surprised that he was considering her safety.

York continued. "If we're betrayed, I have no doubt that our friends will take matters into their own hands. If you are true to your word, Richard, I have no desire to make life worse for you. It appears to me that having Craymore as your father has been punishment enough."

Richard met York's glare, spoke boldly. "I cannot bring honor to the name of Craymore. It's been damaged beyond repair, but I desire for myself and my sister, who has somehow been able to forgive my weaknesses, a life of dignity. I'll do whatever needs to be done to bring about justice. If not, you have every reason to kill me and in truth I will have deserved it."

York nodded, turned to the others. "Let's make the final arrangements and get on with it. Our prime concern at the moment is getting out of London unnoticed."

"I've already thought of that." All stared at Richard in surprise. "It seems Maxwell has done a fine job escorting you from the prison. He should have no problem getting you out of London. I'll have him drive me to my father's townhouse, then send him here. Marielle and Alaina should leave earlier in Lady Henley's coach. I'll have one of my father's coaches prepared for our journey. If you leave immediately upon Maxwell's arrival, I'll wait at least an hour before my father and I leave London."

"Are you certain, Richard, that you'll be able to convince Father to return to the estate?" Alaina asked.

"He'll be there. I'll convince him that it's the safest place to be considering the circumstances. It's my turn to take the upper hand and I believe he's taught me well."

York took a final assessment of Richard. His vows seemed genuine and he could already taste his impending revenge. "I agree that a confession, if possible, would be the best and witnesses will cement the truth, but one thing must be clear." He stood to make his point, glared at Richard. "I will deal with your father."

The men looked up at York, understood his resolve, nodded.

"Then let's get on with it," York said firmly. Everyone nodded, except for Aunt Cornelia.

"Alaina, I told your father a small lie in order to make him leave here quickly. It seems I've been quite ill. He may question my sudden good health."

"We'll be sure to bundle you up well for the trip," Alaina replied, smiling at the tiny woman's feigned expression of illness. "We'll let him know that, despite your illness, you insisted that we needed a chaperone. I believe he's aware of your stubbornness." Everyone laughed as Cornelia winked in agreement.

Richard stood to leave. "I'll need to return home for a change of clothes before seeing my father. Lady Cornelia, will you and the young ladies be ready to leave within the hour?"

"Most definitely. Come ladies, gather bonnets, shawls and reticules—as well as your courage and we'll be off."

Richard hesitated, faced York. "Both our families have suffered, albeit to different degrees. Perhaps fate has made it possible for us to grieve the past and create a better future."

York took in his words, nodded solemnly, as Richard left the room.

"I put no stock in 'is words. 'e might be a better manipulator than 'is father. You ain't going to trust 'im, are you, York?"

"Yes, I believe it is in our best interests. Where's Bates? He'll need to get a message to Jeremy to ensure our backup."

"I have no doubt that Bates is about. He seems to have found a little side entertainment right under this roof," Martin said, grinning, as he looked over at Lady Henley. York stared at both of them with curiosity.

"I'll fetch him for you," Cornelia smiled knowingly. He's already provided me with some interesting entertainment that I've missed in my later years. Who knows what position I might find him in this time?" She teased, a mischievous glint in her eye, before giving the ladies a gentle push towards the door to begin preparations for the journey.

Chapter Fifteen

HOW CAN THEY have escaped? There has to be a mistake. Lord Craymore shoveled through papers on his desk, inwardly cursing. He hadn't been able to think straight since his servant brought him the news. Leaving the scattered papers, he went to the window, his fury overcome by the fear of the Blackstones' reprisal.

Everything should have been taken care of this morning. The entire mess would have been over and done with.

"Pardon me, milord."

"What it is now?" Craymore snarled.

"Your son has returned," his butler said nervously, aware of his lord's rage. "He is in the courtyard speaking with the coachman. Shall I let him know that you have been anxious to speak with him?"

"Of course, tell him to see me immediately. I hope he has more news than you've been able to conjure up. Worthless servants, "he muttered under his breath.

"What took you so long?" he demanded, when Richard appeared. "I expected you to arrive hours ago. Maxwell must have known that I would be waiting to hear. Instead, I returned home to find that the prisoners escaped! Did you even speak to the officials?"

"Yes, Father. I'm as shocked as you are. I felt confident that measures would be taken...I can't imagine what happened," Richard said gravely. "After leaving the prison, I took care of some other business, then I stopped briefly to see Marielle."

"I stopped there myself looking for you, spoke with Lady Henley. There was no mention of your visit."

"You must have arrived before me—I stayed only a short time. When I arrived home, I was informed of the escape. I immediately returned to the prison, spoke with Hurley, the head guard. He was outraged as well as embarrassed. It seems that the men may have been aided in their escape by someone within the prison." Richard grimaced, swore, glanced at his father, noted his avid attention to his words.

"I was shocked, having worked out a scheme with him only hours before. It had been easy to persuade him to do our bidding," Richard stopped, smirked. "I suggested that getting rid of the prisoners before trial might be very beneficial to him. Hurley agreed. The men who run the prison are no better than the prisoners themselves. Offer them a few pounds and they'll starve a prisoner or beat him to a pulp. I don't know what went wrong after that," Richard said wearily. "It seems the Blackstones had other connections working against us."

His father cursed as he walked to the window and looked down at the street. "I've ordered our men to join the search. They must be recaptured as soon as possible and this time there'll be no question. They'll be hanged immediately!"

"The foot patrols are out in full force. I suggest we go to the estate, Father. As it is, Alaina and Marielle are returning to the country this afternoon. Lady Henley will be accompanying them. With the prisoners on the loose, they shouldn't be alone."

"Why are they going to the estate? Cornelia said she was ill. In fact, she gave me only a few minutes to speak with her. I don't appreciate having her snooping around."

He's setting himself up. This will be easier than I thought.

Richard walked to his father's side. "I agree, Father. Lady Henley has a tendency to put her nose where it doesn't belong. We're of no use here in London. News of their capture will reach us soon enough at the estate.

"I doubt any of those women would be able to discern any of our dealings, but you may be right, Richard. Why are they returning anyway? I heard nothing about it."

"Something about some needed items for the wedding. I didn't question. I'm sick of hearing about all their irrelevant details."

"Perhaps you'd better go with them, Richard. I'll wait here for news."

"They would have already left. They were preparing to leave during my visit."

"Since Alaina's been in London and not under my thumb, she seems to think she can do anything she desires. I should never have agreed to let her stay with Cornelia and Marielle. When she returns,

I'll have her things moved here."

"Father, I've already spoken to your coachman to prepare your carriage. I'd assumed that you'd want to be there in case the kidnappers chose to retaliate for their arrest." Richard could have sworn that he saw him shudder. He had definitely found his father's weakness.

"Yes, I should leave London. The estate is preferable, if there's a problem. I'll need to contact a few of my men to return and set up guard posts."

"I've already thought of that. They're on their way as we speak."

"You're thinking more and more like me, son. Is Maxwell waiting?"

"No, I told him to return to my townhouse," Richard replied, relieved that his father trusted him so completely. "He's been driving me about since early morning. The horses needed attention and I thought yours would be fresh for the long drive."

"You have everything well thought out. I'll have the cook prepare food for the drive and we'll be on our way."

Richard nodded to his father, watched him as he left the room. The others should be well on their way and now he was preparing to lead his own father into a trap. There was no doubt in his mind that his sire deserved the consequences. With just one word to the authorities, he could have the kidnappers recaptured. Things would be back as they were, but he couldn't go back. The truth had cut through to his core — he'd heard too much.

He thought of the night before when Maxwell appeared, just in time. If he hadn't come in, he'd be dead now, almost a pleasing thought, but then what? His father would continue his tyranny. He knew that money and a title would not free him from the truth. Affirming his resolve, he left the study to check on the carriage.

Within a half hour they were settled in the carriage for the trip to the country estate. As they drove through the London streets, they noticed clusters of people gathering on corners.

"There's excitement in the streets, son. Perhaps we should stop and see what's happening. Maybe they've been captured."

"Richard reached over and closed the curtain. "The news of the escape will, no doubt, be on everyone's lips, the eventual capture as well. Let's leave London to its problems. We have enough to think about."

Craymore sat back, shrugged. "You're right, son, the authorities have been humiliated by the escape, they're sure to have every man and hound available to capture the tyrants. I'd prefer to be out of town when the news arrives of their capture and avoid all the gossip. There may just be a wedding and a hanging on the same day," he paused, humphed. "I, personally, can't wait to see Blackstone's sons dangling from a rope."

Richard nodded in agreement, aware that his father's words did not hide what Richard read beneath them. His father feared the sons of Lord Blackstone.

"We're a good team my boy and you have a secure future before you." Craymore patted his son's arm, then leaned back and closed his eyes.

Richard settled back and feigned a yawn. He hoped to avoid any more conversation. He had too much on his mind.

The ladies' coach turned into the long drive leading to the Craymore estate. Storm clouds had replaced the gray-blue sky and rain pounded down on the coach. They were relieved to have finally reached their destination. Each had been lost in thought for the last few miles, but now they were animated, anticipation and dread evident in their voices.

"Maxwell shouldn't be far behind," Alaina said, her heart is pounding."

"What if Richard did not succeed, or worse, if the carriage was stopped, searched?" Marielle knew she'd been imaging all sorts of horrors along the way.

Cornelia spoke with more bravado than she felt. "Now, my dears, it's natural for us to feel anxious, but we need to stay calm. We must keep our heads clear and focused. Alaina, are you certain that your servants will abide by your instructions and not be in the way?"

"I've thought of little else for the past half hour. I think our plan is solid. Marielle has drawn up her list of items. I'll send two of the servants to the Henley estate with the list and Marielle's instructions. They'll be told to wait there for her arrival."

"My list is extensive enough that it should take some time for my chambermaid to prepare. I've written a note to Matty to offer refreshments. She'll most likely assume that I want everything prepared ahead, so that I'll be able to return to London as soon as possible."

"Sounds like a fine idea," Cornelia said jovially, despite her uncertainty. Are there any other servants whose attention may need to be diverted?"

"Yes, one in particular, my father's ancient and blustery butler, Baldwin, who I swear despises women as much as my father. He found much pleasure in tattling like an old woman whenever I disobeyed my father's wishes. I can think of no way to force him to leave his post," Alaina said grimly.

"Just leave him to me. I'll corner the old coot and drive him to distraction. I'll have him hiding in the cupboards to escape me."

"I have no doubt that you'll do just that Aunt Cornelia," Marielle chided as their coach halted at the front steps.

Once the passengers descended, Cornelia presented her driver with the basket of fresh fruit and drink that she'd brought along while Alaina directed him to wait some distance away in the far corner of the estate, as planned. The ladies hurried up the steps, thankful that the rain had let up momentarily.

Alaina noted the strange silence about the place. Without her father's presence, the servants were most likely taking advantage of their freedom. "The servants could be taking a late afternoon nap. I assure you, however, that as soon as we step foot into the house, Baldwin will be shuffling through the hallway to find out who might be disturbing his peace."

She was right. The ladies had barely closed the door behind them, when an ornery-looking elderly man appeared dressed in respectful, but rumpled attire. The lines on his face created a permanent scowl as he hastily brushed aside the few thin strands of white hair that fell over his brow.

"Lady Alaina! Your arrival...quite unexpected. If I'd been notified you were returning...uh hum...I would have prepared for you and your guests." Baldwin's voice held surprise, a touch of consternation and feigned politeness.

"I need to collect a few things. You may go about your business, Baldwin," Alaina said coolly.

"Indeed, Lady Alaina. I'm at your disposal!" He turned to the Lady Cornelia and Marielle. "May I take your wraps ladies and escort you to the sitting room? You must be quite tired after your ride from the city. Our staff is scant, what with his lordship in London, but I will see to it that a light repast is prepared for you and a fire is started."

Aunt Cornelia scooted her tiny frame in front of Marielle and Alaina and immediately introduced herself to the butler. "I believe we've never met. I'm Cornelia Henley, Marielle's aunt. I'm so pleased Alaina invited me along. She's been quite busy, you know, with the whirlwind of affairs and parties the *ton* offers during the season. With Marielle's upcoming wedding, there seems no end to the busyness."

Baldwin attempted to interrupt to gather wraps, but she ignored his efforts. "I thoroughly enjoyed the ride away from the city. The weather, however, has not cooperated in the least! Why, I've built up quite an appetite. Good man, I think we shall leave the girls to their business. I'll accompany you to the kitchen to see what delicacies your cook might have to offer." Cornelia wrapped her arm around his. "Is there a cook available since his Lordship and the family have been in London for the season? Why, of course, there must be. After all, Lord Craymore wouldn't leave you without a worthy cook to keep his servants healthy now would he?"

Baldwin attempted to pull away from her grasp, overwhelmed. "Milady! I beg you to wait in the sitting room until I have checked…"

"Oh, nonsense, Baldwin. That is your name, I believe, such a dignified name. Why don't you lead the way and we'll rouse the cook?"

Alaina and Marielle watched amazed as Aunt Cornelia wrapped her arm more tightly his and pushed him onward. Before they disappeared, Alaina called out to Baldwin, who was muttering unintelligibly, while Aunt Cornelia continued to chat away without allowing him to complete a sentence.

"Baldwin. Before you leave, please tell me where Rodney and Darby can be found. I need them to do an errand."

Aunt Cornelia, in her enthusiasm to rid them of the butler, realized that she was moving too quickly and not allowing Alaina to work out her plan. "Oh dear me, forgive this old woman her lack of sense. I just find if I don't eat at the proper time, I can become intolerable. Now, Baldwin where can Alaina find...who is it my dear that you are looking for?"

"Rodney and Darby, I require them to take a wagon over to the Henley estate to collect some of Marielle's items for her trousseau. Once they're off, she can help me gather my belongings and we'll meet them there. We want to return to London as soon as possible."

"Milady, I believe they're in the stables, but you might find them napping at this late hour in the afternoon, I'm afraid. They were up at the crack of dawn with those new horses your father acquired. I'll go and find them for you."

"Oh, don't be silly. You and I must be off to the kitchen," Cornelia interrupted. "I'm certain Alaina will have no trouble fetching them and sending them on their way."

Before Baldwin could argue, Cornelia nudged him on prattling about her hunger. Both disappeared into the kitchen area leaving Alaina and Marielle with their hands cupped over their mouths stifling their laughter.

It took little time for Alaina to find the two men sitting on stools in the back of the stable, arguing over a hand of cards and sharing a bottle of whiskey. Both were stunned at the appearance of Alaina and one fell off his stool. The other grizzled-looking servant, who looked like he hadn't bathed since she'd left, looked fearful as he asked if the master had accompanied them. The men knew they'd neglected their chores, since they hadn't expected anyone to return until after young

Craymore's wedding.

Alaina glared with distain as she handed them Marielle's list and ordered them to prepare a wagon immediately and be gone within a quarter hour. After being assured that the men would be out "lightning fast", the ladies returned to the main house to await Maxwell and his passengers.

"BLASTED WHEEL!" MAXWELL swore, forgetting servant posture. "When we hit that rut back there it must have caused more damage than I thought."

York, Braum and Martin stood outside the carriage assessing the damage while the wind and rain whipped about them. Blinded by the mist, the horses swayed to the side of the road minutes before. One wheel had struck a sharp rock jutting up as they made a turn, now all stood in the mud surveying the damage before them. The cracked wheel settled into the mud in a lopsided position. The men faced the obvious. Their only hope was to unhitch the horses and ride to the estate. While they decided on a plan of action, they heard the clopping of horse's hooves in the distance. York yelled up to Maxwell to warn him, while the passengers jumped into the carriage and shut the curtains, armed and ready for a confrontation.

The Craymore's carriage rounded the turn and slowed to a crawl when the driver saw a problem up ahead. Richard drew the curtain aside and could see a carriage pulled to the side. He glanced quickly at his father who was, thankfully, still asleep. Lifted himself up through the window of the carriage, he called out to his driver. "What do you see, Harry?"

"Looks like a carriage broke down. The rain and fog is blindin' me. We'll be on top of them before we know for sure what's happened."

"What is it, son? Must have fallen asleep."

Richard grimaced, but his father hadn't moved from his spot. "Nothing to worry about. Just an old carriage stranded at the side of the road. We've no time to stop and give aid."

"Let them find their own way home. We have more serious matters to be concerned with," Craymore muttered closing his eyes.

When they reached the crippled carriage, Richard peered out again. His fears were realized. As they crawled beside the carriage, he stared up at Maxwell who sat in the driver's seat as dignified as usual despite the rain. With a brief wave of his hand, Maxwell pointed to the wheel and motioned him to go on, praying that he would simply pass by. Richard suspected the men would find a way to reach the estate. The Blackstone brothers were not ones to be defeated. He motioned his driver on. He would need to divert his attention once they reached their destination. The last thing he needed was for Harry to query about Richard's carriage and driver stranded on the road.

"How long did I sleep?" his father muttered, "Will we be arriving soon?"

Richard could see that his father was still groggy and showed no awareness of anything amiss. "We should be arriving shortly. You may as well relax. The rain has grown heavier, but we shouldn't have any problem now that we're so close."

"I'm glad of that. The ride's been far from smooth and the chill in the air makes my old bones rattle. I think I may need another sip of that brandy."

Richard found the bottle tucked between them in the seat and handed it to his father, greatly relieved that he was none the wiser.

MARIELLE'S ANXIETY GREW as she watched for York and Martin's arrival. Alaina had left her to search for the hidden volumes. Time seemed to stand still. *Where are they? They should be here by now!* As she glanced back hoping that Alaina would return, she heard the sound of a carriage coming up the drive.

She watched as the driver descended to help his passengers out. Through the fog and darkening sky, she strained to see who it was from her position at the window. It wasn't Maxwell. *Oh heavens, what's happened? I must find Alaina.* She rushed down the long hallway in the direction her friend had gone realizing she had no idea of the location of the library. "Alaina, where are you?" Her voice was barely above a whisper. *What if Baldwin returns? S*he returned to the main entrance. *What on earth is taking her so long?*

Within moments the main door opened. Marielle stepped back out of sight as Richard and Lord Craymore entered.

Once father and son were in the house, Craymore immediately took charge. "Where is Baldwin?" he growled. "He should be here to greet us. We've become soaked just walking from the carriage!" As he turned, he spotted Marielle.

"My dear. He stifled his surprise and irritation. Forgive my rudeness. I didn't see you standing there. Where are my daughter and Lady Henley? Perhaps your aunt decided not to accompany you?"

"She's..." Marielle, momentarily at a loss for words, stared up at Richard. Richard reached out instantly and took Marielle into his arms. "Darling, I am so glad that you arrived safely."

He turned to his father. "The weather changed so rapidly, I was concerned that the ladies' journey may have become difficult."

"I quite understand, son. After all, your wedding is not that far away. We must keep Marielle safe, she's been through enough." Lord Craymore smiled at Marielle, feigning sincerity. "I assume you've had a safe trip? Now, where is my daughter?"

"I believe Alaina went in search of Aunt Cornelia and your butler," Marielle attempted a smile, praying her fear was well hidden. "They'd gone to the kitchen to see about refreshments. Aunt Cornelia finds it difficult to be still. Since we weren't expected, she offered to be of some help in the preparation."

"Hmm, I'm not surprised. I know how busy your aunt keeps herself these days."

"Yes, she does like to be in the middle of things. She's most likely making some suggestions to the cook right now." She searched for more to say, hoping to detain the men until Alaina returned. "With the wedding fast approaching, we realized our need to collect some last-minute items. There seems no end to the details."

"I find it surprising that my daughter took it upon herself to return without notifying me," his lips thinned as he stared down at Marielle.

"Father, she did inform me," Richard interjected. "I believe she's old enough to make those decisions for herself without bothering you." Giving his father a furtive smile, he turned to Marielle. "We decided to join you. After all, getting away from the city is a welcomed reprieve with all the commotion. Have you heard the news?"

Craymore gave him a steely look. "We needn't burden Marielle with issues that do not concern her, do we, Richard?"

"True enough. I'll enjoy spending a relaxed evening with my bride-to-be. You must stay the night. The weather is turning worse."

"I planned to visit with my father this evening. I've been waiting for the weather to clear so that we could arrive there before nightfall." She hesitated, wanted to say more, to delay them. "Did you say that something happened in London?"

"We will discuss it later," Lord Craymore said brusquely, not wanted to deal with Marielle's reaction to the news. "I'm sure the two of you would like a few minutes alone to greet each other properly. I'm going to find Baldwin." Craymore walked briskly away before Marielle or Richard could intercede.

"Richard, Alaina's in the library!" Marielle whispered frantically. "The others haven't arrived!"

"Their carriage broke down. I've no time to explain. Come! We must find her before Father does."

Chapter Sixteen

"WHAT IN DAMNATION are you doing?" Craymore glared at Alaina as she crouched on the floor of his library with books strewn about her.

She looked up, shocked to see her father's face twisted in rage."

"I was just looking... I...I thought I might bring some books with me to London. I just couldn't seem to choose which ones I wanted." She knew her excuse was weak as soon as she uttered it. Before her father could release his rage, Richard and Marielle rushed in.

"Father, what's going on in here?"

"You were correct in your presumption that your sister might be snooping about. She seems to be looking for something and I expect her to explain herself immediately."

"Might it be best to discuss this later and privately?" Richard urged, hoping to delay the inevitable. "After all, Marielle is our guest. It isn't necessary for her to become involved in family issues."

Craymore forced himself to stifle his rage. He had to find out what Alaina was after, but not with Marielle present. "I agree. Why don't you and Marielle go and check on Lady Henley. See to it that they're given a room to refresh themselves.

Marielle will want to look after her, I'm sure. When they're settled, rejoin your sister and me."

Craymore turned his back on Alaina to speak to Richard, giving her the opportunity to scramble up from her position and move towards the door where Marielle stood. She was not going to be trapped in the room with her father.

"Come, we will go together to find your aunt," Alaina said, wrapping her arm around Marielle's.

"Alaina, you will stay here," Craymore ordered.

"Father, perhaps we can speak later. I must attend to Marielle's aunt. She's not feeling well and we have left her for too long." Ignoring her father's enraged countenance, she grasped Marielle's arm and left the room.

Craymore made a move to go after her, but Richard stood before him blocking his way.

"Bring your sister back here immediately. I must know what she was looking for. If she knows of those old manuscripts, who knows who she may have told? You don't understand the seriousness."

"Father, calm yourself." Richard held his father's arm. "You're not making sense. What manuscripts? I have no idea what you're talking about." Richard managed to close the door of the library, as he questioned his father, his brows furrowed, waiting to hear more.

York, Martin and Braum stayed off the main path leading to the estate, following instead a narrow stream and passing through a wooded area bordering the main lawn. Jeremy and his cohorts, having arrived earlier, spied the three men as they emerged from the brush on foot having concealed their horses. York showed no surprise at seeing them. He knew they'd be watching, waiting and removing any obstacles.

Bates had passed information back and forth before the men left Cornelia's townhouse. York and Martin had already outlined strategic places where the men would have a good view of the estate without being seen. Before they took their positions, Jeremy disclosed the previous arrivals. One of Jeremy's men agreed to ride back to where the carriage was left to help Maxwell.

York and Martin planned to enter the estate nearest to the pantry. Braum would conceal himself in the garden just outside the library to wait for a signal. One signal would let Braum know that all was well, another that they needed some assistance.

York insisted that Martin wait with Braum, but he vehemently refused. They were in this together. Separation in the past had caused one or the other to be imprisoned. Martin stood his ground. They'd both face this situation together.

"I don't like this at all," Braum muttered, as they neared the house. "My guess is that 'is son is setting up a trap. 'e's lived a charmed life, York, 'elpin' you brings 'im no gain."

"You may be right, Braum and we'll soon find out." York and Martin continued cautiously on their way. To their advantage, the rain was letting up and visibility improving.

Richard bent down to pick up some of the scattered books, while his father ranted. Thankfully, he'd stopped him from going after his sister, at least for the time being. He didn't know how much longer he could keep him occupied.

"I don't believe her story. I need to find out what she was looking for!" the elder Craymore raged.

"We have no reason to doubt her. She's always been a voracious reader and rebellious enough to choose them from your library," Richard answered more calmly than he felt.

"Son, do you have any idea of the valuable secret I have kept in this library all these years?"

"Father, what are you talking about? You mentioned manuscripts earlier?" Richard queried, choosing his words carefully and expressing appropriate surprise.

Craymore humphed. "You remember that I told you how I was able to procure Blackstone's arrest by using one of his own manuscripts?"

Richard nodded, stayed silent, waited.

"Those manuscripts carried great value. It seemed a shame to only remove one and then allow the authorities to confiscate the others. I made sure that before the Blackstones were driven out the rest were removed. One of his newly hired servants was easily bought and well taken care of afterward. The books were safely hidden until we were settled into the estate."

Richard feigned surprise. "Are you saying father that they're here, now, in this room?"

"Yes and they're of even more value now after

all these years. They'll bring a grand price someday, perhaps in France. When I suspected that your sister may have been sneaking in occasionally, I moved them. I'd kept them here, behind these books, in the exact spot where Alaina was searching. I became concerned that she might come across them, so I moved them up a few shelves and out of a child's reach, or anyone else's who might, even innocently, pull a book from the shelf. The collection is hidden behind that shelf, the one above the window."

Craymore pointed to shelves above the burgundy and gold velvet valance that decorated the window looking out into the garden. "I moved them there myself — no easy task at the time, for some were quite heavy. I climbed up the ladder taking one book at a time until all were safely stored. I suspect that Alaina knows about them. I don't understand why she'd be looking for them now. Does it make any sense to you?"

"You may be reading too much into her behavior, but let's assume that she knows of them. She would most likely have no idea how they were obtained. Alaina desires to stay in London permanently, not an easy path for an unmarried woman to take and still keep her reputation. She's intelligent and resourceful. If she suspected that a few books of value might bring her a sum of money to live on, she may have thought they would not be missed. What other reason could she possibly have for taking them?"

"You could be right, however, Richard, they carry the Blackstone seal! She may have told your mother, or, perhaps, your mother found them herself. On the other hand, if Alaina is ignorant of who they belonged to, she wouldn't realize the implications if she did try to sell them. A knowledgeable book seller would question how she came into possession of them. After all we've accomplished, this could become a major obstacle to being free of the Blackstones. Alaina must tell what she knows. I have little trust in where your sister's loyalties lie. If she suspects they were wrongfully obtained, she must be silenced."

"What are you saying?"

"I'm saying that your sister could ruin all we've worked to attain."

"She knows nothing of what happened between you and Blackstone. If she saw the seal, she most probably believes that the books were left as part of the estate. She needs only to be told that they are not to be removed or spoken of."

"I have no idea what she and your mother talked about or if your mother shared her own suspicions about my involvement with Blackstone. Alaina resents me and would most likely enjoy seeing me suffer. She's become a danger to us, Richard."

"Father, you're being irrational."

"Don't talk to me in that tone of voice," Craymore snarled. "If it wasn't for my resourcefulness, you would have nothing! I was not irrational when I devised my plan to be rid of Blackstone. I took what I deserved and you've benefited. Your mother helped to poison Alaina's mind against me and if she talked to her about the

Blackstones' demise, who knows what your sister may be planning? She spent many hours at your mother's bedside. We cannot take the chance." He glared at his son, resting his hand on his arm. "Soon you will be the master of the Henley estate and, someday, all of what I have will be yours. We must not allow a conniving woman to disrupt our plans."

Richard nodded, attempted to keep his composure, until he could figure out what to do.

Craymore's voice softened. "I'm sure you realize by now, son, that women have little use except for procreation and to pleasure a man. Apart from that, they are foolish and ignorant." Giving his son's shoulder a squeeze, he walked across the floor and picked up one of the books Alaina had strewed about. "Besides, son, my plan to marry her off, may not go as well as planned, for I fear she's already soiled."

"What are you saying? Why would you think such a thing?"

"Don't be so shocked. I've seen her carousing with my men and the way they've looked at her. She's no doubt tumbled in the hay with one or more of them."

Richard turned away so his father couldn't see his face, for it would have reflected his sheer hatred of him.

"Richard. I want you to take Marielle and her aunt over to the Henley place now, before dinner, with the excuse to gather her belongings. With Marielle and the aunt about, it will be too difficult to gain Alaina's full attention. Once you're gone,

I'll have Baldwin send for her. Do you understand Richard? I must find out what she knows. When you return, we'll discuss the outcome."

"Father, I don't see the necessity for my leaving just yet. Let me talk to my sister."

"Don't argue with me. I want time with Alaina, *alone*. I'll take care of this myself. Well, what are you waiting for? I want them out of here before Alaina says anything to them. Who knows if she hasn't already told them of the books? She has no appreciation for the wealth she's enjoyed." Craymore hesitated, lost for a moment in thought.

"Don't worry, Richard. No harm will come to your sister," he patted Richard on the shoulder. "I'll assure her that she'll be well taken care of if she chooses to reside in London. I'll be glad to be rid of her. If she knows of the Blackstone manuscripts, I'll convince her that they became my property with the estate." His voice took on a more conciliatory tone. "I admit when I saw her in here, I was outraged, but I believe she and I will come to a compromise, profitable to her and adequate for me."

Richard feared for his sister, but now was not the time to create more havoc. He nodded to his father in feigned resignation and left to find the women. He must warn Alaina of their father's persistence on the matter. She'll need to be more convincing. *York and Martin should already be here. By God, they better be or I'll take care of him myself.*

His father's erratic behavior since the Blackstone brothers were identified was growing worse. The plan was to keep his father in the library. He had little doubt his father would stay there to contemplate his talk with Alaina. Baldwin would most likely notify him of their departure. Richard felt he had no recourse but to go along with what his father requested, but he would not be gone long.

CRAYMORE STOOD STARING up at the shelves above the large window. *Alaina won't tell me the truth. She cannot be trusted.* He paced back and forth knowing what he needed to do, playing out all the angles in his mind until he was satisfied. *Yes, I'll have Baldwin send some tea up to her room, with a hint of laudanum. After all, she did look a little peaked when she left. It must be done, Richard. You have always been a dutiful son. It will seem harsh to you, but in time when you begin to enjoy the fruits of our labors, you'll see it was for the best. Who knows what she may have already said to Cornelia and Marielle. I'll consider what to do about them later.* He sat down in his chair, poured some brandy and rang for Baldwin.

RICHARD ORDERED HIS father's coachman to bring the carriage around to the front before speaking with the women who'd gathered in Alaina's bedroom. Neither Marielle nor Cornelia wanted to leave Alaina, but he assured them that they would return soon. He urged them on, reminding them that she was well aware of her father's wrath and has always, to his amazement, been able to deal with it.

Marielle was not convinced. "I feel very uneasy leaving her."

"I agree, Richard, I could stay behind in my

room," Cornelia added.

"My father expects us to leave together and will no doubt assure himself that we're off. Alaina understands that now is not the time to defy him. York and Martin as well as his men can't be far away."

Alaina nodded. "Richard needs to follow Father's instructions. I'll be able to handle the situation until you return."

"We will not go far." Richard tried to reassure the women. "My father must have no doubt that I'll follow his directives. Alaina, stay here until he sends for you. It may gain us a few minutes. If he brings up the manuscripts, feign total ignorance. When I suggested that to him, he openly admitted that he may have overreacted, assumed too much. Apologize for trespassing in his private domain and, most likely, he'll harangue about your rebellious nature. Alaina, if we're to be successful, you must keep him in the library."

"Richard, trust that I know what to say. I'll apologize most heartily and offer to clean up the scattered books. I will behave as ignorantly as he assumes that I am."

"You might ask him if he'd allow you to have a few of his books. Perhaps, ask him if he wouldn't mind helping you to choose them. He'll be disgruntled, but there's little else he can do. You've been a fine actress in the past, this may be your greatest role. Do you think you can bring it off?"

"I will do my best." Alaina could see that her brother was concerned, didn't want to leave her and was trying his best to help her. She reached out, hugged him, tried to assure him by her expression that she could handle the situation.

"If only we had some evidence that York and Martin have arrived," Marielle said, shaking her head, inwardly frustrated that, once again, she could do nothing.

"We must hope that they are close by," Richard said evenly. "They most likely altered their plans after the trouble on the road. We'll ride only a short distance, then I'll give Harry some excuse to turn back. By then you should be in the library. You won't be alone with him for long. Keep the door ajar and keep the conversation going. Pour father another drink, whatever it takes to keep him distracted until we return." With a final reassuring nod of support to his sister, he ushered Marielle and Lady Henley from the room.

His father met them at the bottom of the stairs. "Please give your father my best, Marielle. I'm sure that you are anxious to see him and, of course, those animals of yours. After all, they are what started this mess, aren't they?"

Marielle didn't miss his sarcasm, but only nodded as Richard opened the door for them and led them out.

Craymore watched as Richard helped the ladies into the carriage and waited until they disappeared from view. He'd already ordered the tea to be sent up to his daughter and told Baldwin and the cook to retire for the night once the tea was delivered. After time enough had passed, he climbed quietly up the stairs, dousing two of the candles at the top of the staircase.

There was no one left to disturb them.

Assured that their partners were on alert and had taken care of any interference, York and Martin proceeded to the back of the estate and towards the pantry door—a place he and Martin often hid in their game-playing as children. They passed quietly through the kitchen, surprised that there were no servants about. Soon they were walking down the familiar hall to the library. The door was ajar and no one saw them slip in.

"Strange," York commented looking around the empty room. "It's too quiet, Martin. I'm going to investigate. Stay hidden. You know what to do if a problem erupts."

Martin preferred that they didn't separate, but knew it would be no use to argue with York. He positioned himself behind the velvet curtains. The oil lamps in the room would give enough light for Braum to see his shadow. While he waited, he prayed that his brother wasn't walking into a trap.

"Harry, I must ask you to turn about," Richard ordered. "I'm afraid I've forgotten a package I meant to bring along."

The driver grumbled. He was already soaked to the skin and they'd almost reached the long drive that led to the Henley's. He was looking forward to finding some shelter while they took care of their business. "Master Richard, the rain's startin' again. I'd be glad to get where we're goin'."

"No doubt, Harry. We may need to delay the trip until morning. You'll be able to warm up soon enough." Relieved to hear that it would be the final trip of the night, he pulled on the reins to turn the horses back toward the Craymore estate."

"Bring us to the side entrance," Richard called out as they traveled on their way. The ladies will be able to avoid getting drenched climbing the veranda."

The occupants of the carriage sat silently, each concerned for Alaina and wondering if York and Martin had arrived and, perhaps, already confronted Lord Craymore.

Craymore knocked on his daughter's bedroom door and waited for a response. Startled, Alaina walked to the door without opening it. "Yes?"

"Open the door, Alaina."

Fear rose in her. She'd stalled too long in her room. "I was resting, Father. I just need a few minutes…I'll meet you in the library."

"I must speak to you now. Open the door immediately." She knew it would be of no use to refuse. She opened the door slowly.

"Father, please, I'll join you momentarily in the library."

Ignoring her request, he pushed the door open. Alaina stumbled back. He reached out and grabbed her arm.

"You're hurting me."

"You seemed to have lost your footing. How are you feeling? I sent Baldwin up with a cup of tea. I thought our talk may have upset you." Craymore looked across to see the teapot and empty cup. Let me pour a cup while we talk."

"I have no desire for tea." Alaina prayed her voice did not reflect he fear. "I do apologize for trespassing in your library. In my rush to choose a few books, I'm afraid I left quite a mess. I didn't want to keep Marielle and her aunt waiting. I would have picked them up. I'll go down immediately and return them as I found them."

"Alaina, you seem distressed. Here, take a sip of tea. It will relax you. Then we will discuss the books." He held one of her arms tightly as he pushed the cup into her half-opened hand.

Her hand shook as she lifted the cup at his urging, brought the cup to her lips, barely sipped, her eyes transfixed on her father's.

"What were you looking for, Alaina? Were you aware that I have certain books that hold a great deal of value to me?"

"I have no idea what you're talking about. I only wanted to borrow some reading material." She tried to push away from his grip, but he held her arm more tightly.

"Tell me, Alaina, what did you and your mother discuss when you sat by her bedside night after night?"

"She was often too weak to talk. I usually read to her. I don't know what you are suggesting."

"Ah, but I think you do know. Drink your tea and we'll talk some more."

"I don't want tea. Please, let's go down to the library, Father. I'll show you the books I'd like to borrow."

Craymore could no longer hold in his simmering rage. Grabbing her by both shoulders, he pulled her to him. Alaina dropped the cup, the tea splattering both of them. He stared down at her, his eyes glaring at her heaving breasts and the tea stain on her bodice.

"You remind me more and more of your mother when she was young—the way she looked when she was your age, full of life and lust. But, like you, she could not be trusted." Loosening his grip, he slowly pulled at the soft fabric covering her shoulders, pulling the material down her arms until more of her breasts were exposed. Alaina froze as his fingers traced the edge of her sleeve.

"Father, I beg you. Leave me alone," Alaina pleaded, her voice quivering and barely above a whisper. She tried to pull away but he pulled her closer.

"Tell me what you know of those manuscripts."

"What manuscripts? I only wanted to..."

Craymore pulled her against him, the material of her gown being pulled down until her breasts were almost totally exposed. He leered as he reached behind her with one arm and grabbed the back of her hair, pulling her head back. "Tell me what you know or I'll treat you as I did your mother, before I kill you."

The horror of what her father was saying washed over her. She realized now, too late, why he ordered Richard and the others to leave the house. He planned to kill her. She tried to pull away, to scream, but it was no use.

"Don't fight me, you bitch. You've never appreciated anything I've given you. You're just like your mother." He pushed her toward the door.

"If you harm me, everyone will know—you'll be ruined. I don't know anything about manuscripts. Please, I'll go to the library and put everything back in its place and it will be as if it never happened. I just want to live my own life."

"You're my daughter. You belong to me, just like everything on this estate belongs to me. You must die—an accident, of course. I'll grieve appropriately. He carefully lifted her sleeves, straightened her bodice. "Come, let's take a walk." He moved behind her, pushed her through the door, one arm around her waist and the other covering her mouth as he led her into the hallway.

The butt of the gun slammed down on Craymore's head before he could react to the sound he heard behind him. He collapsed, releasing Alaina as he fell. She pulled herself away. York kicked his bowed head against the balcony railing. He fell sideways and lay motionless. When he was certain Craymore was sufficiently immobilized, York rushed to Alaina's side as she clenched the opposite railing.

"He was going to kill me." Her body shook as he lifted her, carried her back to her bedroom and laid her on the bed. She stared up at York, speechless, in shock.

"Rest here, I'll carry him down to the library. Martin is there. No one else is about. Why the hell did Richard leave with Marielle and her aunt?' York seethed. "Will you be all right for a short while?"

Alaina nodded still incapable of answering

him.

York reached down to place the coverlet over her as he left the room.

Craymore still lay in a heap in the hallway. York lifted his limp body and carried him down the stairs and through the hall to the library, just as Baldwin came rushing towards them.

"Who are you? What has happened to Lord Craymore?"

York didn't have to answer. Richard stood behind him, opening the door of the library to allow York to pull Craymore through before ordering Baldwin to bring Marielle and Lady Henley, who stood nearby, to a nearby sitting room. Baldwin, unable to comprehend the situation, tried to follow his orders, but the ladies refused to move.

Richard grimaced, but knew the ladies would not leave. Ignoring their presence, he helped York carry his father to the large leather chair by the draped window, while Martin kept watch by the door.

"Marielle," York said sharply when he saw her standing by the door, "Alaina's in her bedroom. Go attend to her." Marielle hesitated, agitated again at his dismissal, before realization struck her. She rushed from the room, fearful for her friend.

York stood a few feet from Craymore, unmoving. He was here, in his own father's library, facing the monster who had ruined his family. His strangled emotions scorched his insides. He wanted nothing more than to squeeze the life out of him but, first, he wanted a confession. He wanted

Craymore to look him in the eyes. Instead, he sat shriveled up like a cripple.

Richard bent down and lifted his father's head. Even after all he'd seen and heard, he couldn't deny that the man who sat pitifully before him was still his father.

"Father, can you hear me?"

Craymore groaned, opened his eyes.

"Richard," he said weakly, unaware of anyone else's presence in the room. "Why did you stop me? Don't you understand? She will ruin us. Foolish boy, you let your heart get in the way. You must harden your heart, so that you'll remain strong. You must do it now so your strength of mind will return."

Do what, Father?"

"Kill me," Alaina said softly as she stood in the doorway staring numbly at her brother. "He tried, unsuccessfully. York stopped him."

"Who?" Craymore lifted his head until his eyes stared into York Blackstone's stony face.

"Blackstone? What are you doing in my house?" Craymore gasped. "Richard, call the authorities." He began to flail his arms wildly about him attempting, without success, to stand. "Grab him, Richard. Send Baldwin for my men." Richard stared down at his father coldly. Everyone in the room stood silently about until Craymore stopped his crazed outburst and sunk, helplessly, into the chair.

York walked closer to him, calmly and in control.

Craymore cringed in his seat. "Blackstone? You

were supposed to have rotted in prison. You've returned too late. It's all mine now."

York paused, lifted his brow, then smiled. Craymore believed he was his father. The man he'd dreamed of tearing apart slowly, watching him die a gruesome death, had become a mindless fool. He felt a strange disappointment. His attack must have made him delirious. He wanted Craymore to be of a clear mind, to fully realize the time had come to suffer for his deeds.

"I thought you were dead. I made certain that you were imprisoned long enough to kill any man. You were always too tough to die, even on the battlefield. You and your self-righteousness—it brought you nothing," Craymore snarled. "I can still see your face when they arrested you, your arms wrapped around your own manuscript—one I filled with treasonous information. You thought to ruin my reputation, but I won, didn't I? You lost everything and I won it all. Go back to the grave and grovel in the dirt."

Craymore stopped, shook his head, rubbed his eyes and turned slowly to his son. "Richard, you hit me too hard, I'm hallucinating. Help me to my room. Richard, do you hear me? Get me out of here!"

"Father, it's Lord Blackstone's son who stands before you. He's come to claim what is rightfully his. He is not an illusion."

Craymore glared at Richard in disbelief. "Rightfully his? You've gone mad. What have you done?" Craymore coughed loudly. Dropping his head, he reached into his pocket to pull out a handkerchief. While Richard looked up at York, Craymore reached down into his boot, this time, for a small revolver. He lifted it, pointed it towards Richard.

The shot came from across the room. Craymore stiffened, looked straight ahead, stunned, then hunched over and fell to the floor. His own gun fired as he fell, the bullet lodging in Richard's arm.

All eyes turned to the door where Alaina stood. The gun, dangling by a finger at her side, fell from her hand. A wave of nausea overcame her, just before she lost consciousness.

Martin rushed over to her as Marielle attempted to stop her fall.

York stood silently over Craymore's body, while Richard knelt down beside his father. He turned the crumpled body over with his one good arm, while blood began to seep through his wound and spread down the other.

His father gazed up and mouthed his final words, audible only to his son. "You betrayed me." He closed his eyes. His body shuddered and became still.

Richard lifted himself up, standing tall above the man who no longer owned him.

Martin opened the curtains and signaled to Braum, then moved to his brother's side, both acknowledging to one another that it was finally over.

Cornelia strode quickly across the room, passing York and Martin, ignoring the body of Lord Craymore. Richard's arm needed tending.

Chapter Seventeen

THE MORNING FOG lifted and it promised to be a pleasant day. Aunt Cornelia sat in her parlor musing over the events of the past few weeks. The parliamentary procedures were ended. Her testimony and those of the children of the late Lord Craymore, as well as the manuscripts bearing the Blackstone seal, were more than enough for the courts.

The late Lord Blackstone's title and lands were granted to his eldest son. His accounts, which had become part of the king's treasury after his arrest, were released. York and Martin had well earned their regal reward. After the hearings and the king's declaration, both men chose to return to the cottage for a few days to rest.

For York, the realization that the quest was finally over and the Blackstone name once again carried wealth, title and honor, brought a strange combination of emotions—at times elation and pride, at other times, a bittersweet satisfaction. York's unattained desire to be the one to kill Craymore, gave way to the reality that Craymore's children were also victims of a man obsessed with power and revenge. Now each needed a time to heal.

Cornelia had taken it upon herself to offer her

services and contacts to York for the hiring of new servants and for refurbishing and redecorating the estate. York gratefully accepted. Before returning to the cottage, he hired her solicitor to handle money matters and to find a townhouse in London to rent for the time being. They would reside in the city for awhile, allowing Richard and Alaina needed time to remove their belongings from the estate and to work through their own grief.

Alaina agreed to stay on with Marielle's aunt until matters were settled. Aunt Cornelia felt that she needed motherly affection and she was grateful to provide it.

The disposition of their father's accounts was with the courts, leaving Richard with much uncertainty. Many of his father's business connections were murky and rifling through his papers, he realized there were some he knew nothing about. His faith, however, in his own abilities with business affairs gave him some measure of peace. He would need to reestablish trust among the influential in London and mend bridges his father had severed.

Cornelia felt a great sense of satisfaction for her part in the adventure. She felt especially pleased with the reaction of the *ton*, after their initial shock of the disclosure. The talk about town was intriguing to say the least. The newspaper had created such a grand mystique about the young Blackstone brothers that available daughters were pleading with their mothers to throw parties inviting the two young men. Cornelia had already received more invitations than she could handle, as well as many unsolicited visits from the ladies of the *ton* who hoped to be fed information for the gossip mill. She smiled as she thought of their trivial excuses to come for tea.

This morning, thankfully, had begun quietly. It gave her time to consider what still needed to be done. Some unsettled business needed her wise interference and Alaina was her first concern.

The poor girl has barely eaten enough to keep a kitten alive. I must figure a way to bring her out of her malaise. After all, she saved her brother's life. Her father's bullet only grazed Richard's arm, but it would have been fatal if she hadn't brought the revolver down with her.

Although she praised Alaina for her wise action, nothing seemed to move her.

Her brave front has all but dissolved since her father's death. It's doubtful she's mourning his demise, but she refuses to talk about her last meeting with him. He was her father, Cornelia mused, *despite his evil nature.*

And then there's my dear Marielle, Cornelia shook her head in dismay. *She's not faring much better, though she has been a great comfort to Alaina. Thankfully, she postponed the wedding. The gossips expected no less, what with the shocking revelations. But, more is going on than meets my eye and if my perceptions are accurate, that handsome York has a great deal to do with her unhappiness.*

THE DAYS SPENT at the cottage were a welcome reprieve for York and Martin and an opportunity to see George and settle personal business. When their faithful servant heard that he would once again be employed at the Blackstone estate, he was overjoyed. York encouraged Braum to join them also and offered him a lucrative position. Braum refused, preferring to return to London.

"You ain't getting me in any of those fancy clothes," Braum said. "You'll know where to find me if you'll be needin' any 'elp."

York understood. He offered Braum an attractive amount for his aid. Although it took much convincing for Braum to accept, he relented when York let him know how handsomely he repaid Jeremy, Bates and the others.

"Well, if those blokes are goin' to be rubbin' their rewards into my face, I may as well celebrate your good fortune with 'em," Braum said before wishing them well in his own awkward way. Before they went their separate ways, they pledged to keep in touch.

York and Martin returned to London, ready to begin their new life. A townhouse had been rented until a suitable one could be bought. Once they were settled, York prepared to take care of some unfinished business.

MARIELLE COULD SEE the twinkle in her aunt's eye when she opened up the note brought by the messenger. "Why Aunt Cornelia, you have a look of mischief about you. Who's this one from? You've received so many of late."

"Oh, it's another tea and one I believe I will attend." Cornelia immediately changed the subject. "How is Alaina doing today?"

"Not very well, though she agreed to walk in

the garden with me. I thought the sunshine might help. I imagine that her father was quite brutal to her before York interfered. I found her shaking and so distraught in her room. When I told her that York was confronting her father in the library, she almost jumped from the bed to retrieve the revolver from her nightstand. She seemed to be in shock even then. Since she's refused a doctor's care, we can only hope that time will heal her pain."

"She's young and strong, but hiding in this house is not going to help her to heal," Cornelia asserted. "Perhaps a ride in the park might be a nice beginning. I think I'll arrange it and I know just the person who might oblige."

"Aunt Cornelia, what do you have going on in that head of yours?"

"I'll keep it in my head for now, until I've created a plan. I'm going up to change. I have a tea to attend this afternoon."

Marielle watched as her aunt left the room. Her steps seemed sprightlier. *What is she thinking up now*, she wondered, before getting lost in her own thoughts. She wondered how York was faring, heard he'd returned to London. After all had been settled with the authorities, York and Martin were consumed with details surrounding the proceedings, as well as the crowds that hung about the courts daily wanting to get a glimpse of the Blackstone brothers. She and Aunt Cornelia left quietly on the final day, after being assured that everything had turned out well, then York was gone.

Her father insisted that she return home for a

few days to rest and she felt relieved to have the time away from London and the gossips. Matty and Gerald were delighted by her visit and Beatrice chased the carriage up the drive. The pups had grown and were scattered about the estate, various servants taking on the responsibility and seeming to enjoy the pups' antics.

Even her father had changed.

When the news reached him of Lord Craymore's guilt, he was distraught, not over Craymore's death, but at his own weakness. He'd allowed the man to manipulate him, even with Marielle's future. He was at a loss for words when he heard of the Blackstone affair. He'd always had his doubts of Lord Blackstone's guilt, yet he too had joined the ranks of others who accepted the sentence.

He asked Marielle for forgiveness for his neglect, though she'd told him more than once that it wasn't necessary. She was pleased that he was taking more of an active role with estate business and even attending *ton* parties. It seemed that now that tyranny was uncovered and justice served her world was in balance again...except for one thing, her heart.

CORNELIA'S VISIT WITH York turned out better than she could possibly imagine. Returning in her coach, she reviewed their discussion. He is a devil and a most handsome one and that brother of his, a close match. She was most pleased that Martin agreed to send a note asking Alaina to join him for a ride in the park and York's plan for Marielle should be a most entertaining spectacle, she mused.

The note arrived the next morning addressed to Alaina. Aunt Cornelia received the note, hesitated, placed it in her pocket and returned to her needlework. Marielle managed once again to encourage Alaina to walk in the garden with the excuse of picking a bouquet for her aunt. The garden was alive with color and the fragrance of roses filled the air. Marielle could see that her friend was taking notice and breathing in the sweet scent.

"I'm glad that you urged me to join you, Marielle. The warm sunshine does lift my spirit and the flowers are so lovely. I've been selfish in my behavior."

"Please don't talk like that. You have every right to your feelings. A weaker person might not have survived. The courage you've demonstrated over these past few months has given me such strength. If I am able to be a source of strength for you now, I'm grateful." Alaina reached out to embrace her and Marielle beamed at seeing a genuine smile on her friend's face.

"And what about York? You change the subject every time I mention his name."

"I hardly think of him. Why, look at this lovely cluster of daffodils!"

Alaina didn't believe a word of her denial.

"Now let's make that bouquet!" Marielle said cheerfully, ignoring the twinge in her heart.

They both kneeled to gather an assortment of flowers, while quietly respecting each other's wishes.

"Ladies, we have a visitor and I am afraid he should not be an unexpected one."

Both looked up surprised to see Martin walking alongside Aunt Cornelia.

Martin smiled as he approached them, taking in their beauty as they knelt among the flowers. "It's my pleasure to be here. You both create a lovely picture in your sunbonnets."

Marielle stood and smiled, walked over to give him a brotherly hug, happy to see him, although his likeness to York was bittersweet. "Are you now settled in your London home?" she asked.

"Actually, we arrived just a few days ago. I'm indebted to your aunt for everything was in order. I must admit having a butler, a cook and a coachman, not to mention other servants at our disposal is a strange experience. I'm afraid I have not been accustomed to such royal treatment since I was a child and then I simply took it for granted."

"Bathe in the luxury, young man," Cornelia interrupted, "You well deserve it. Now I am afraid I have a confession to make to Alaina." Cornelia sheepishly reached into her pocket and handed her a small envelope. "This arrived over an hour ago. I should have brought it to you immediately, but I was in the middle of a row of stitches. I totally forgot it. It seems that Martin sent it to prepare you for his visit."

Alaina gave him a shy smile as she opened it and read the short note.

Dear Alaina,

May I have the pleasure of your company for a carriage ride in the park this afternoon? My cook will prepare a picnic lunch. If I do not hear from you, I'll assume that you accept and I will arrive at noon.

Martin Blackstone.

"Oh, dear, I really do appreciate your invitation, but I haven't been feeling well and I ..."

"Alaina," Cornelia pleaded. "This is such an embarrassment and it is entirely my fault. I'm certain you'll have a lovely time and it would be so good for you. Since Martin is here, please, I beg you to accept his invitation. You already have color in your cheeks from your time in the garden and you look the picture of health today. My embarrassment will be compounded if you do not accept."

Alaina could see no way out. Cornelia had been so good to her and she couldn't miss Martin's look of disappointment when she tried to refuse. "It is a lovely day and I am feeling better. I would be happy to accompany you." She smiled at Martin, while brushing off her skirt and tucking away a strand of hair that had escaped her bonnet. "If you'll just give me a few minutes to get my wrap, I'll join you in the foyer."

Once Alaina and Martin were off, Cornelia was prepared to put the next part of her plan into action. She'd already given instructions for a lunch to be prepared and for the carriage to be brought around.

Marielle was busy arranging the bouquet of flowers when she entered the parlor.

"Everything is set my dear. I've decided that you and I would benefit with a ride in the country.

Don't you agree? You look too lovely today to spend your time indoors." Cornelia already had Marielle's wrap in hand. "The ride will do us both good. Come dear, the flowers are perfect. We mustn't stay in the house a moment longer."

"But, Aunt Cornelia, your tea?"

"Didn't want to go anyway, just a bunch of old matrons complaining about their aches and pains. Why, I'd much prefer to spend the afternoon with you."

Marielle couldn't get a word in as Cornelia scurried around to gather her shawl and bonnet. Martin's visit must have energized her, she thought. She could see how excited her aunt was to go for a drive. How could she say no?

The days since her return from her visit with her father had been dreary. She, like Alaina, had no desire to leave the house. Richard was no longer a regular visitor. They'd seen very little of each other since that horrible night. He had his own demons to reckon with and she'd had too much time to think. She couldn't imagine that she would ever marry and she wanted nothing to do with social events. She thought of returning to the country for good. She did miss riding Silk through the countryside and life there would be very different now that she and her father had reestablished their relationship.

"Marielle, come dear. Everything is ready." Cornelia stood at the door still holding Marielle's cloak, a broad smile on her face.

"I'm coming." She gave her aunt a bright smile. "I'll enjoy a pleasant drive."

"Then we'll be on our way."

Thomas opened the door for the ladies and took their hands as they descended the steps to the carriage awaiting them.

"Aunt Cornelia, you've awakened."

"Forgive me, dear. I haven't been very good company. I must have dozed off." Marielle smiled. Her aunt fell asleep soon after they left the city.

"I'm glad you were able to rest. Let's see what Edith has packed for us." Marielle chose a couple of pieces of fresh fruit and handed one to her aunt.

"Oh dear, what is that noise?"

Marielle tried to look out the window but couldn't see anyone, though she heard the horse approaching at a good speed. Both could feel the carriage slowing down.

"Who could that be?" Cornelia asked, acting ruffled, her role played expertly.

The carriage came to a complete stop. Marielle squeezed her aunt's hand to calm her before turning to peer out once again.

Suddenly the door was pulled open and York stood there, wearing a devilish grin, his hair in disarray.

Marielle gasped.

"Well, well, look who we have here?"

"York! What on earth are you doing here?" Marielle snapped, clearly stunned and trying desperately to collect her wits. "You scared us half to death! I thought you gave up highway robberies?"

"Some hobbies are just too enjoyable to set

aside, especially when the prize is so delightful." York leaned against the door, wearing a shameless grin. "Come, Marielle. I think we should be on our way."

"What? The hell we will!"

"Such language from a lady, I'm shocked." York reached into the carriage and lifted Marielle out before she could protest.

"How dare you! Put me down!" She tried to swing at him, but he ducked in time.

Swinging her around, he lifted her up onto his horse and mounted quickly, holding her snugly against his chest. Marielle couldn't see her aunt's smile of delight as they rode away.

When Marielle gained some modicum of control, she screeched at him but to no avail. He rode swiftly leaving her no choice but to allow him to hold her firmly against him. Once they had gone a distance, he slowed the pace, giving Marielle an opportunity to voice her outrage.

"Why the audacity to think you could take me at your pleasure. Have you lost your mind?"

"Ah, Marielle, I would love to take you at my pleasure, only in a much more comfortable position."

"How dare you. I demand that you return me to my aunt immediately!"

"But, my sweet Miss Henley, we have much to talk about and I know the perfect place for us to work out our minor difficulties."

"Minor difficulties? Haven't you put me through enough? I thought once you regained your title, you'd become a gentleman. Why, you're still a rogue!"

"A rogue? My lady, I can remember when you were quite reluctant to leave me." Marielle's anger flared brighter with his words.

"I was your captive. Now, you've succeeded in your goal. What do you want from me?"

York's voice grew softer. "I want only to talk with you, unless you want more. You must put your head down, before your eyes are scratched out by the brush."

Marielle remembered similar words spoken months before and prepared to argue.

York leaned forward pressing her head down with his own and not giving her a chance to rebel as he led the horse down the path towards the cottage.

"Oh, no—not this again."

"Ah, you remember." York reached the opening that led past the stream. The cottage sat in the distance beyond the ridge. Marielle lifted her head to see the place she thought she would never see again. No smoke came from the chimney this time. It looked quite deserted.

"Is there no one living there?"

"Not at present. Braum has found a comfortable flat in London and George is now delightfully ensconced as my personal valet. He is quite content."

"But then there is just the two of us. What could my aunt be thinking of your outrageous behavior?"

"I'm afraid your aunt is well aware of where you are and she quite approves."

"What?" Marielle turned, glowered at him. "Aunt Cornelia is part of this little scheme? I thought I was obliging her by going for a drive. I can't believe that she'd turn on me. How could she? I will never... Why she..."

"I see you still have the habit of not finishing your sentences."

"You brute!"

York grinned at his spunky captive, as he approached the cottage, dismounted and reached up to lift her down despite her stiff refusal. He started up the steps ahead of her only to look back to see Marielle standing there, rigidly, her arms firmly wrapped around herself and an expression so full of fire it could blind a man.

"Are you coming, my sweet?"

"I am not your sweet. I demand that you bring me home."

"I believe I've heard those words before. Come, you can be just as angry inside." He moved closer and nudged her up the steps, while she followed, reluctantly.

Once inside, Marielle looked around at the familiar surroundings. Memories engulfed her. She felt a chill in the air, but not in her heart. She watched as York knelt in front of the fireplace, his broad shoulders stretching the fabric of his coat as he prepared the fire. She stared at the errant curls slipping over his collar and wanted to give in to the desire to let her fingers run through each strand.

How could he still hold this power over me? He'd shown his true colors. It took him little time to run to a harlot to meet his needs, while I grieved his separation from me. He didn't love me and even if he professed love, he'd most likely keep a mistress. He'd proved what kind of man he is, she thought angrily.

York felt her eyes upon him and wondered if he could again stir the passion they had shared once. He'd never stopped thinking about her, dreaming of her in his arms. She was meant to be his and damned if he would let her go again. But, first, he needed his questions answered. Had she betrayed him or was she coerced into revealing what she knew?

Once the fire started, he stood, turned to her. Her back was to him now. He saw her tremble. Was she truly afraid of him?

"Marielle, look at me. I want to know your thoughts."

"What do you want from me, York?" she said softly. "You've accomplished what you set out to do. I was merely a pawn for you to move and now you have your inheritance and your father's name has been cleared. I should think that you would be savoring your victory, content to enjoy the fruits of your labor."

"Is that what you think? That I saw you only as a means to an end? Have you so soon forgotten?" He moved closer. For each step he took, she backed away until she had nowhere else to go. The heat of his body near hers made her heart feel as if it would explode. She turned away only to have him reach out and draw her too him.

"No! Do you think I can forget that you were captured with a prostitute and right after you held me in your arms? In my vulnerability I believed your promise to return to me. I should have realized that a man so full of hate and mistrust could not love with any sincerity." She hadn't meant to mention the word love. That was her stupidity. He desired her, had never offered love. She tried to pull away, but he held her more tightly.

"Is that what you've believed, that I returned to London only to satisfy my lust? There has never been a day when the memory of you has not either given me strength to go on or tormented me. You're mistaken to think that I would have desired another woman."

She turned away but he grasped her chin, gently, turned her face to his.

"Now it's my turn, Marielle. Is it true that you aided the authorities in my capture?"

"You were captured in a brothel in a compromising position, were you not? Save me from your lies. This time I truly want to go home and forget all that transpired here, to forget you." Marielle's voice wavered as she looked up into his eyes, knowing that she lied with every word she uttered. "And what do you mean about aiding the authorities in your capture? Why I never..."

York pulled her closer.

She tried to pull away, her fists clutched against his chest, anger simmering in her eyes.

Suddenly York began to laugh. It didn't matter — nothing did — as long as she was here in his arms. He lifted a hand to nestle them into the soft waves that fell about her shoulders.

"You beast! How could you laugh?"

York stopped her words as he crushed his lips to hers.

She struggled for only a moment until she tasted the sweetness and felt her own hunger. Lifting her arms, she wrapped them around him.

He parted her lips with his tongue, no longer able to contain his desire for her. She responded, as fire coursed through her. He lifted her, carried her to the bed that they had once shared, never lifting his lips from hers. When he finally broke the kiss, he was bent over her, his arms still wrapped about her.

"It seems that we were both misled. Isn't it time for us to put the past behind us?" he whispered. "Let's savor the present and become reacquainted."

She tried to speak. He stretched his body over hers, stopped her words with another kiss. She could no longer hold back her own desire.

She wanted him.

He forced himself to control his need to take her right then, though he felt the heat of her body and a need that matched his own. As his hands caressed her, he did his best to explain to her the events of the night of his capture.

She listened, her heart accepting his words and the truth she saw in his eyes. Her body molded to his, surrendered.

She believed him, her tears speaking to him more than words. His lips grazed her ear and sent shivers down her spine.

When she finally spoke, she could only manage a whisper. "York, I could never speak of you to anyone. I could never... Oh God." She no longer had any control over her mind or body as his touch sent shivers racing through her.

Her body tingled, while she struggled to tell him what she needed to say. "I could never have turned against you or want you to be captured. I don't understand how you could believe... Oh, York. I..."

"Shush, enough my love. Forgive me for believing wrongly. I..."

Marielle silenced him with a kiss, her passion flaring beyond her control.

YORK AWOKE FIRST. He rose slowly, reaching for a quilt to cover her while he went to add more wood to the fire.

Marielle began to stir and turned to find York gone, but soon felt his presence as he stood over her. He reached down and kissed her.

"York... How long have we been here?"

"Don't worry, love. I don't think Aunt Cornelia will be sending anyone to search for you."

"York, I, I mean we, well..." York could only laugh at her confusion.

"Why you are laughing at me. Here I lie in a strange bed with a highwayman turned gentleman. I believe I've become a bird of paradise!"

York's laughter filled the air as he drew his body over hers. "You, my midnight miss, are definitely a most passionate and beautiful bird of paradise.

"I suggest that we find ourselves a parson as soon as possible my little bird, or I fear you'll be the talk of the *ton* in no time."

Marielle's eyes grew wide at the reality of his words.

"I hadn't expected that I would be proposing marriage in this position, but I find it most delightful and it seems that your lust for my body appears to be as strong as mine for yours," York teased.

Marielle blushed at his words. He was right. She wanted to taste every part of him. His maleness mixed with a smoky scent filled her with an even greater desire to touch and tantalize him. She gloried in the freedom she felt in his arms to give and receive. Yet, she needed to hear more, to hear the words a woman needs to hear from the man she loves.

"No, I believe I may need to face my deflowering without the benefit of a marriage contract."

York twisted his body to her side drawing her to him. "What in good heavens are you saying, woman? You refuse to marry me?"

"It seems you have forgotten something that should accompany a marriage proposal."

"Forgotten something? In the position we are in at this moment, there seems little else to say except..." York smiled with the revelation of what she needed to hear. He sat up and drew her up to him and held her in his arms as gently as if she were a delicate flower.

As he looked into her eyes, she could see that his own looked misty and full of love. She knew without him saying a word and he knew, as she smiled and her eyes glistened with unshed tears.

"My sweet Marielle. I believe I fell in love with you the moment I first saw your face in the moonlight. Your innocence and the fire in your eyes were like magnets drawing me to you. I felt the desire to want to protect you, even then, though I was carrying you off. I may not have seemed like a prince, but I could never have hurt you. I would be honored to have you as my wife to share my life, my bed and to carry our children. Will you do me the honor of becoming my wife?"

Marielle laughed with delight as she reached out and hugged the man that she knew was most definitely her prince.

Epilogue

AUNT CORNELIA SAT in her parlor sipping a cup of tea and feeling quite pleased with herself. The wedding was delightful. Thank goodness they'd stopped home and agreed to wait a couple of weeks to marry. She was thankful for the chance to plan an informal ceremony in her own home. Marielle made the most beautiful bride and York couldn't have looked more dashing. The reception was just a small gathering of family and friends, just perfect considering the unusual circumstances.

After all, the news of the wedding did cause a few old crones of the *ton* to choke on their tea when they were told of the upcoming nuptials. The newspaper columnists had their fun and mothers who'd hoped to push their daughters into York's path at the next big event of the season were none too pleased.

Cornelia grinned to herself as she thought about how quickly the news spread. The old birds were waddling up to their noses in their wild imaginations. Or was it so wild? *Oh, how I do enjoy when society's conformity takes a back seat to passion!*

Alaina should be returning soon. Her outings with Martin have been so good for her. I do believe that another romance may be budding. We shall see if I might be able to push that along a bit. Then I need to focus my attention on that brother of hers…

MARIELLE AND YORK snuggled together enjoying the garden of their new London townhouse. The scent of rosemary and primrose permeated the air, but the couple paid little heed to their beautiful surroundings. Both were entranced as they gazed into each other's eyes while their minds dwelled on the miracle of their coupling and their future together. The smallest of her pets, Chance, was busy gnawing at a bone on the stone path nearby.

Just a few weeks had passed since their time at the cottage, but long enough for Marielle to know that their new life together would be filled with more surprises as she whispered into York's ear.

"Are you quite certain? It's been such a short time."

"Yes, my love, I have little doubt. It only takes a moment in time and I would bet the moment happened in a little cottage in the wood...where it all began."

York's eyes lit up. "I think it's time for a celebration. In an instant, she was in his arms as he carried her inside and up the steps.

Laughing, she snuggled closer, her body responding to his desire. She felt warm, safe and marvelously loved.

Thank you for reading *h*... enjoyed it. If you did, please help... this book by writing a review. To fi... new releases, message me and 'like' my... at www.facebook.com/elaineviolette.author .

s and Alaina's
ise

One

...er bedroom mirror... lavender dress she ... old, but it should appease her benefactor. Lady Cornelia Henley or Aunt Cornelia, as she preferred to be called, had insisted that she cast off the darker shades of mourning now that a year had passed since her father's death.

Whatever she wore made little difference. She seldom left the house, except on an errand or a brief shopping trip. Invitations sent to Aunt Cornelia seldom included her. Even when she'd been invited, she found it was more out of the hostess' curiosity at her condition or to give her other guests someone to whisper about. The Blackstone-Craymore scandal remained fresh in everyone's mind and embellished stories that held little likeness to the true circumstances continued to circulate. No one knew that she'd been the one that shot her father to death or that she still woke up shivering in the night at the enormity of her crime.

She held that truth in her heart, but they knew that her family name had been dragged into the dirt, that her father had wrongfully accused a noble aristocrat of treason out of greed, and many believed that the Craymore children were a party to it, simply because of their name.

Alaina had feared that Cornelia would pay dearly for taking her in, but thankfully, the sprightly elderly lady refused to let others' judgments concern her. She'd been a calming influence throughout the scandal and knew all the sordid details since Marielle Henley, Alaina's oldest and dearest friend, was Cornelia's niece and York Blackstone's wife.

Marielle and York had fallen in love during his struggle to regain his inheritance. Aunt Cornelia was party to all the details. Her niece and her husband were now settled into the Blackstone Estate, happily wed and with a new baby girl. It was Marielle who had approached her aunt concerning Alaina's welfare after her home had been confiscated by the authorities. Cornelia had opened her heart and her home to her despite her family's fall from grace. How could she ever thank her?

She'd agreed to the change in wardrobe, but refused the invitation to visit York and Marielle, though Cornelia encouraged her to go. She wasn't ready to return to the estate that had been her childhood home as well as the place where her father had died at her hands. Further, York only reminded her of his younger brother, Martin, since the two looked so much alike. Once the court proceedings were over and the estate returned to York Blackstone, its rightful heir, she and Martin spent time together under Aunt Cornelia's watchful eye. Martin had been understanding and had helped to shield her from being questioned by authorities.

She could never forget his kindness or his grey eyes searching hers nor the few minutes that they were alone on the Blackstone veranda, when he reached out to her and held her. They'd been talking about putting the worst of the past aside. He had encouraged her to hold her head high when society cast her off as the child of a tyrant.

Then he'd kissed her, not a kiss between friends, but in her memory of the moment, a kiss of promise. He'd made her feel whole and young and hopeful when her insides felt bruised and shamed.

Oh, Martin, I hoped for too much. How could I have expected that you would fall in love with the daughter of the man who destroyed your family? She'd always be a reminder of the years he and his brother spent trying to survive when he should have been enjoying a life of regal dignity. *No wonder you chose to leave England and find adventure in America.* She tried to understand but still felt devastated that he'd left unexpectedly, and without taking the time to visit her and say good bye.

He'd sent her one letter after arriving in Boston. She'd read it over so many times that it was barely readable now, especially stained with tears. He had promised he'dreturn to London one day, but there was no mention of returning to her. What else could she have expected?

She fisted a hand to her lips to stop the anguishing memories and stifle the anger she felt at the unfairness of it all. She'd allowed herself to believe that Martin's kiss meant something more. No doubt he knew that she'd adored him when they were children, but she'd been a pony-tailed nuisance. The kiss obviously didn't mean the same to a man anxious to leave a tragic past behind.

She thought of her brother. At least Richard had been able to reestablish himself in business over the past few months. Fortunately for him, a man's past is more easily forgiven than a woman's. How could she not be happy for him? He'd been everything to her after their mother's death and he'd been her protector against her father's abusive tirades.

Aunt Cornelia's voice from the other side of her bedroom door shook her out of her dismal musings. "Come in, I was just about to come down."

"My, my, don't you look lovely," Cornelia said as she entered. "That color becomes you."

"I thought you would be pleased." Alaina tried to return her benefactor's cheery smile. "I so appreciate everything you've done for me over the past year, Aunt Cornelia. And it's been a year that I have taken advantage of your generosity. I wish I could repay you in some way." She reached out and gave the older woman a gentle hug before turning away. She walked the few steps to her window and pushed the curtain aside, staring out into the street. "If I could find a position, perhaps as a governess, out of London, where my family's disgrace might be unknown, I would no longer be a burden to you."

"You have never been a burden. Please, never say that again."

Alaina continued to look away as tears threatened. Her previous thoughts only increased the gratitude she felt for the dear woman. "I have caused you undeserved criticism, even from your closest friends."

"Nonsense. I have enjoyed your company. I may have originally taken you in at my niece's request, but I have benefitted by your companionship. I have come to love you like a daughter. I am well aware of the unfairness of Society's judgment. I refuse to be party to it and cater to other's favor, friends or acquaintances. I am too old to concern myself with their pettiness."

Cornelia waved a hand in the air as if to brush off their small-mindedness. "You have not deserved their cruelty, Alaina. You have a heart full of unselfish love. I know how you cared for your mother during her illness and your allegiance to your brother. In my eyes, you have paid the heaviest price for your father's crimes for too long. I pray in time, the shroud many have placed over you will be removed. Perhaps we need another scandal to fill their ears."

Alaina chuckled at Cornelia's attempt at humor while her heart burst with overflowing gratitude at her vehement loyalty.

"How can I ever thank you?"

"By allowing me to take you shopping for some new gowns. Styles do change, you know. And I do want you to come along to more events with me. You must admit that when you have accompanied me, gentlemen have attempted conversation with you. I remember well, that young man, Mr. Darrow, Lady Townscend's nephew. He's asked if he could visit. He had no intention of visiting me, young lady, but you have wanted no male attention. Society has been cruel, but time heals and you are too lovely, my dear, for handsome gentlemen to stay away."

Alaina smiled tolerantly at her. The dear woman never gave up. She couldn't share her feelings for Martin with her. They were too deep and too precious. She needed to hold her longings close to her heart.

"My goodness, I am going on and almost forgot to tell you that your friend, Priscilla Dunfly, has arrived. Did you expect her?" Cornelia asked, her chin jutting out just enough to display her disfavor of Alaina's friend.

"No, but as you know, Priscilla has a tendency to stop in without notice."

"Yes, I have noticed.

"It has been nice to make a new friend," Alaina said gently, knowing that Cornelia had not taken well to Priscilla, a young widow Alaina had met while out for a walk a couple of months earlier.

"You are quite right, my dear. I should not judge her." Cornelia looked down at her small, wrinkled hands now clasped tightly to her waist, her posture revealing contrariness. "It is just that she seems to be over zealous in her desire to befriend you — not that you do not deserve to have many friends. I also noticed that she had her eyes on your brother Richard when he arrived during one of her visits."

"Are you suggesting that her continued friendship with me might have some ulterior motive, perhaps to get closer to my brother?"

Cornelia shrugged. "No doubt she enjoys your company and that may be all there is to it. I simply question her overzealousness in befriending you. She is a widow with a questionable reputation, I dare say. Your brother is extremely handsome and available. A close relationship with his sister is advantageous to that end. Perhaps, she hopes that you will encourage a relationship between them," Cornelia smoothed the lace that edged the cuff of her long sleeves. "I do want you to make friends, Alaina, there's just something about her... Well, I am off to my tea. Thomas and Edith are here if you need anything, my dear."

"How nice of you to stop in," Alaina said as she walked into the parlor to greet Priscilla.

"Alaina, you have finally shed those dreary dresses. You look beautiful."

"Thank you. I welcome your visit though I admit I am surprised to see you again so soon. I fear I may have little to talk about. My days are quite mundane."

"I desired some cultured conversation," Priscilla said, untying her frilly yellow bonnet. "Please come and sit. I was forced to spend the morning with that dreadfully boring Lady Dresden. I feel wrung out from her repetitive stories and woeful complaining about her husband," she said while tossing her bonnet aside. "She should accept that he has a mistress, most do. Honestly, you would think she'd be happy that he leaves her be. With his looks I would be on my knees thanking God for finding him a woman who'd keep him out of my bed."

Alaina sat beside her and listened patiently to her friend's dramatic outpouring.

"What she ever saw in him in the first place is beyond me, though no doubt his title had something to do with it. She did nothing but complain about him even before she found out about his affair."

Alaina smiled at her friend's chatter. Priscilla seldom allowed a moment's pause in conversation or accepted a refusal without pouting for effect. "How delightful you are. Your visit has brightened my day."

"Excuse me, Miss Alaina." The butler stood at the door of the drawing room.

"Yes, Thomas?"

"A gentleman is here to see you. A Mr. Harrington."

"A gentleman?"

She looked at Priscilla who, to her surprise, made no comment, instead, seemed more concerned with straightening the ruffles on her skirt.

"I have no idea who Mr. Harrington is and I received no calling card," Alaina said, rising from her seat. "Perhaps, another unfinished affair of my late father. I'll go and see what he wants and send him on his way. Richard insists on taking care of all unfinished business and he is out of London for the next couple of weeks." Alaina turned to leave.

Priscilla popped up from her seat. "Oh, no, please invite him in. I…know him."

"You know him?"

"Yes, we've met on a number of occasions."

Alaina noted that Priscilla appeared suddenly on edge. Her earlier conversation with Cornelia popped into her mind. *He may be someone Priscilla has an interest in as well.*

"If it's a business call, it may be tedious. Perhaps, I should see him alone." She took a few steps to the door.

"I shall leave immediately if it appears I am intruding on business not of my concern, I promise."

Priscilla almost appeared to be pleading and did not follow her as Alaina had expected. Instead, she returned to her seat.

"...if you insist," Alaina said finally, feeling uncomfortable at her friend's odd behavior but not certain how else to deal with her at the moment.

"Please show him in, Thomas."

She returned to her own seat and before she could ask Priscilla how she was acquainted with the visitor, the gentleman appeared.

"Mr. Phillip Harrington," Thomas announced. Alaina stayed seated as Harrington entered the drawing room. She couldn't help but notice that he was quite handsome—tall and slim, though she noted a severe tightness about his mouth that she found unflattering. She thought he might be close to thirty-five. He was well dressed in a single-breasted waistcoat in a subtle taupe with darker brown trousers. His neck cloth, a snow-white, was neatly tied without undue starch. Quite impressive. His good looks must be the reason for Priscilla's desire to be present."

"Miss Craymore, it is a pleasure to see you once again," Harrington said as he stopped a few feet from her, bowing slightly, and ignoring Priscilla.

"Once again? I am afraid you are mistaken. I don't believe I have made your acquaintance before."

"You were a mere child when I visited your father. Unfortunately, I needed to return to America soon after. You were extremely lovely then. You have grown into an even more beautiful woman."

Alaina's cheeks flushed. It had been a long time since a man complimented her appearance. Mr. Harrington was a flatterer. Still, there was something about him that made her uneasy. Perhaps it was his connection to her father that disturbed her. "I understand you and Mrs. Dunfly are acquainted."

Priscilla sat stone still, staring at Harrington while he simply nodded.

Alaina didn't know what to make of it. She felt uncomfortable talking about business in front of Priscilla and her friend made no move to lessen the strained atmosphere. "Mr. Harrington, you mentioned my father. If this concerns—"

"I would like you to see this as a social call," he interrupted. "A long overdue one, I am afraid. Do you mind if I have a seat?"

"Of course." She waved toward a chair near the settee that she and Priscilla shared. She glanced at Priscilla who looked tense, her lips clamped together and her eyes averted.

"And the reason for your visit?" Alaina asked, deciding to get it over with so he would be on his way. She wanted to question Priscilla about her peculiar behavior, but not in front of this stranger.

"I realize that I have been errant in not contacting you sooner or courting you properly but I have lived in America for the past few years."

"Courting me? You are extremely forward, Mr. Harrington, as well as improper. I do not even know you. Furthermore, I have a guest."

"Alaina," Priscilla interrupted." I think you need to allow Mr. Harrington to explain."

Alaina looked from one to the other. "What is this all about?"

"Please." Priscilla reached out a hand and urged her to settle back.

Harrington rested his elbows on the arms of his chair and folded his hands. "I asked Mrs. Dunfly to be here today since I was unaware of how you would take the news I have to present. I thought her presence might be a comfort to you in case your father did not tell you about our contract."

"My father? He has been deceased for over a year."

"Yes, I do offer my condolences. I am disappointed, however, that he did not see fit to tell you of our signed agreement."

Alaina's body tensed. Just the mention of her father brought painful memories. She didn't know if she had the strength to know any more of her father's dealings.

Harrington removed a folded sheet of paper from his coat. "I fear that this will come as a shock to you. The contract was drawn up over five years ago." He paused long enough for Alaina to lose her patience.

"Mr. Harrington," Alaina held out her hand.

Harrington gave her the paper and sat back, obviously waiting for her reaction.

Alaina unfolded the aged and wrinkled document, examined it, saw her father's seal and signature and began to read. She stopped suddenly and drew in a ragged breath. "Betrothed?" The word struck her like a blow.

"I see that this is truly a surprise," Harrington said, wearing a look of concern.

"This is outrageous. You certainly do not expect me to honor this." Alaina tossed the paper aside and rose from her seat. She nearly laughed aloud. Hadn't her father done enough to belittle her as a woman? Now, even in his grave, he could still have power over her life. Only an hour before she'd been thinking of Martin, wishing that like, York and Marielle, they could have had a future together. That he would love her, miss her, return to her. How foolish to think she'd ever be free from her father's tyranny.

Harrington rose from the chair to retrieve the discarded document. "I had no idea your father hadn't discussed our contract."

Alaina's insides churned, not just with the shock, but with tremendous sadness. She'd tried to place her father in a different light after his death, even at times attempted to have mercy on him, to try to understand his need to claim what wasn't his. But, once again, she was reminded of his callousness and lack of feeling.

"How dare you assume I would be desperate enough to marry a complete stranger?" she asked before turning to Priscilla. "How long have you known about this? Is this why you befriended me?"

Priscilla cast her face down. "I agreed to help him. I cannot say more. Please believe that I have enjoyed our friendship."

"Stop!" Alaina snapped. "Aunt Cornelia was right. She questioned your motives and your unexpected visits, but I thought I'd found a friend."

"I am your friend. I had—"

"That is enough, Priscilla," Harrington interrupted.

Regaining her control, Alaina met Harrington's eyes. "Why should I be shocked? My father's underhanded ways should not surprise me." She pointed to the document he held. "And when did you and my father decide to plan my future?"

Harrington refolded the paper and placed it in his coat pocket and sat down. "Your father and I were in the midst of discussing my compensation for our business arrangement in America when I saw you. You had just attended your mother who was seriously ill as I remember. You came to his study to deliver a message to him. I remember he was quite irritated at you for interrupting. I was party to the rather abrupt communication."

"And I became the subject of your conversation," she said with no attempt to hide her bitterness.

Harrington continued. "I couldn't help but notice your beauty and vibrancy even at such a young age. I told your father just that. You were perhaps fifteen at the time and obviously unaware of my reaction to you. Your father seemed pleased. The agreement was made."

"I was thrown in to seal a *bargain*?"

"I prefer not to see it as coarsely as you suggest, Miss Craymore. Your father, I am certain, was looking out for your best interests. I am a man of some means and our partnership seemed certain to increase my prestige."

"My interests were never his concern, and I assure you, Mr. Harrington, I am perfectly capable of deciding my own future. Perhaps you might tell me why you have chosen to come and present me with this useless information after all this time."

Harrington's lip curled as he met her glare. Alaina observed the tightness about his mouth that she'd noticed earlier. She waited, sensing the change in his mood. He stared at her for a moment without speaking. His eyes appeared to darken.

"Miss Craymore," Harrington said quietly. "I had a faint hope that you might possibly entertain the idea of marriage, considering your age. It would have made things easier. I even wished that I could have moved more slowly, perhaps, been able to take the time to persuade you of the advantages. After all, I am not unpleasant-looking and am sufficiently able to support you." Without warning, his voice took on a sharper edge. "However, I haven't the time to waste on an extended courtship."

"Then the matter is settled," Alaina said, squaring her shoulders.

"The matter of the betrothal for the time being, perhaps, but we have other matters to discuss that you might take more seriously." Harrington leaned forward and clasped his hands together.

Alaina hadn't noticed how tightly she was gripping the arms of her chair until she forced herself to stand. "I believe it is time for you both to leave. Our business is done." Before she could call Thomas to see him out, Harrington stood and grasped her arm.

Alaina shrugged back from his touch.

"Miss Craymore, I suggest that you hear me out. You might want to sit back down."

Alaina drew back at the warning note in his voice. Before more could be said, a servant tapped at the open door.

"Miss Alaina, I apologize for the interruption but could I have a few minutes of your time? We have a problem in the kitchen. I wouldn't bother you while you have guests but Lady Henley isn't home and Cook is in frenzy."

"I'll be right there, Edith." She turned to her visitors. "I believe we are done here."

"Please, attend to your housekeeper's problem," Harrington said, returning to his seat. "We'll wait until you return."

Alaina stiffened her jaw. She wanted both him and Priscilla gone, but she didn't want to rouse Edith's concern. She followed Edith out the door, wondering what more could be said that would make her day any worse."

HARRINGTON HAD OBSERVED Richard Craymore for

a week before visiting his townhouse. He wanted to get the measure of the man he'd hoped would be willing to represent his father's interests. Instead, Craymore agreed to only a brief introduction, telling him to leave the papers he needed to discuss with him, to his butler. He was too busy preparing to leave on a business trip, Harrington mused, as he watched Alaina leave with the servant. He'd left London without a word, though he'd left the address of his hotel with his servant. He most likely hadn't even glanced at the documents he'd left behind to his detriment. Miss Craymore could not refuse.

The Chinese businessmen that he and Lord Craymore had wooed for months before his death were ready to sign a trade deal that would make Harrington among the wealthiest men in Boston. He was not going to let Craymore's death stand in the way of completing the transaction.

The men traveled twice a year from China to America and back so Craymore's death went without notice. Only recently when he had completed most aspects of the trade agreement had they asked for Lord Craymore to be present at the signing. Despite the language barriers, the men were shrewd and inflexible. Having done business with British traders in the past, they trusted a Lord of the Realm more than Harrington, a Boston businessman with few credentials to his credit. Yet, it was he that had done most of the groundwork over the past year, while Craymore lay in his grave.

He turned to Priscilla. "Stop shrinking into the fabric of that settee. You look like a frightened mouse. You know what I expect of you. You must help me convince Miss Craymore to travel to America with me. If not, you know the consequences."

"She does not deserve this."

"If her brother had been more like his father, I would not have involved her."

"And if I had not been fooled by your friendly façade when we first met, I wouldn't be a party to your scheme."

"True, but you have little choice in the matter now, unless you care to defy me."

Priscilla's shoulders shuddered. She looked away.

He smirked. He'd created the desire affect.

He turned his back to her and reviewed the entire situation in his mind to be sure he hadn't missed anything. Lord Craymore had believed that trade between China and America was a great avenue of wealth, especially since the elite Bostonians desired the tea, porcelain, silks, and coarse cottons from China that had been imported to Britain for years. With America's new freedoms fought for in the Revolutionary War, businessmen were able to take advantage of the lucrative market but in decades since, they had done little. The Chinese expected to have trade go both ways. America had little to offer them. Lord Craymore wasn't one to ignore profits, even if they needed be gotten through underhanded means. He knew the Chinese had a taste for opium and Turkish markets were ready to do business.

Harrington had spent the year firming up

agreements and courting Boston businessmen who could back his endeavors, and all after Craymore died. His reputation would be in shreds if he didn't keep the beneficial promises he'd made to them.

He also hoped to bring an end to his other business, one he had to admit, he enjoyed, but of late it had become more difficult to stay in the shadows, despite his alias. If it were found out that he was involved in the disreputable enterprise, he would become a pariah to the purists in Boston.

He'd already wasted close to three months figuring out a plan which including this trip to England. He had to be on the next ship out of Liverpool. Once he arrived back in Boston, he would have only a few weeks to complete the deal. If the Chinese representatives become dissatisfied with his efforts and give the contract to someone else, all he'd worked for would be lost. It wasn't going to happen.

Telling them of his betrothal to Craymore's daughter was genius. He saw immediately that they were impressed that a British Lord would think so highly of him as to let him marry his daughter. Regardless, they wanted proof of Craymore's continued involvement.

Richard Craymore would have been the perfect substitute but he refused to take the time to listen to his offer. His other business took on more importance, imprudent man. Alaina, Craymore's loving daughter and his devoted fiancé, must be the convincing factor. Even that might not be enough. If she could convince them that her father was ill but dedicated to the project and thought enough of closing the deal to send his own daughter in his staid, it might suffice. It was a last ditch effort but if in the end they sign the contract, it was worth dragging her to America.

Gaining her participation was the most difficult obstacle he'd had to overcome. He should have made a point to become better acquainted with her sooner, He'd hoped she'd be ripe to seduce. In his investigations into the Craymore scandal and the gossip surrounding it, he'd learned that her reputation was in most respects ruined in proper society due to her father's deeds. No suitors were knocking at her door. To his disappointment, the news of the betrothal infuriated her.

Her devotion to her brother was his next card. He was gambling on her love and loyalty to him.

"Phillip."

Priscilla drew his attention. He frowned when he looked her way. She appeared to still be cowering on the couch.

"Phillip, is there no other option? I fear Alaina will refuse to go with you or she might tell Lady Henley. Your plan could go entirely wrong."

He didn't miss the desperation in her voice. He took the few steps toward her, leaned down until his face was a few inches from hers. "You befriended her, gained her confidence. It was you who told me how much she adores her brother, looks up to him. I trust your information is accurate. If she refuses me, then you must use your wiles to convince her to be on that ship to America."

"I said I would try. That must be enough," she

whispered.

"Trying is not enough," he seethed. "You will succeed or find another way to pay your creditors. He leered at her, noting as he had in the past, her curvaceous figure. He stood and strode away from her, leaving her to think of her own dire situation and what she needed to do to overcome it.

It had taken some time on his last visit to encourage her to befriend Alaina. He knew what persuasive tactics to use for each unique situation. In fact, he was a genius at his work. Priscilla was sliding swiftly into debt by her own admission and hounded by creditors who were demanding more than money. He had promised her generous compensation and protection. He smirked at the thought of her vulnerability. Once he left for Boston with Alaina, he would be done with her.

The door opened and Alaina walked in, looking agitated. She shut the door firmly behind her, but took only a few steps into the room. "Mr. Harrington, you say you have another issue to discuss with me. Please get it over with. I want both of you gone from my sight as soon as possible."

Miss Craymore was behaving like a termagant. It was time to end this charade of courtesy. She was getting under his skin with defiance and he needed her under his thumb. "The matter is of great importance and I must have your assistance."

"What could you possible want from me?"

He paused before answering, clasping his hands together. "Your immediate and congenial cooperation to travel to America as my fiancée and, obviously, your name, Miss Craymore."

Harrington's pronouncement received the affect he'd hoped for. Her mouth dropped open as she took an abrupt step back.

"You must be insane. First, you present me with a betrothal of which I had no knowledge, and now you want me to go to America with you? Please leave." She reached for the door handle.

"The matter concerns your brother's freedom, his very life." His lips turned up in a sneering grin. He'd gotten her attention. He reached into the pocket of his topcoat and pulled out the documents he'd purposely held until the last. He held out them out to her. "I am sorry to have to do this. If I had any other recourse...."

"I believe your contriteness to be as false as whatever papers you hold in your hand."

"Decide for yourself." He shrugged as he placed them in her outstretched hand. As she scanned the papers, he gauged her reaction. She seemed to be trying her best to hide her emotions but she wasn't fooling him. Her face grew pale and her chin trembled as she studied them.

"Where did you get these?" Alaina demanded.

"Your father enjoyed bragging about his escapades, particularly when we sat and enjoyed the excellent brandy he procured without having to pay revenue to customs. He told me how the system worked, barrels of fine liquor sunk off shore and at night retrieved and placed in caves away from the eyes of collectors of revenue. Of course, alcohol was only one type of contraband. Your father had no scruples when it came to possessing items of value that could be imported without customs handling."

"You and my father were involved in smuggling too?"

"Notice that my name is not on those documents. Your father liked to boast of his gains. Because I felt the need to have security over my investment of time and labor, I found it quite easy to pocket some of the papers he enjoyed flaunting, just in case he conveniently forgot to pay me for my services. One must never be too trusting, you know. I couldn't help but notice when I perused them at my leisure that your brother's signature appeared on many of them. Your father, of course, has escaped prosecution. Death is sometimes convenient. Your brother, on the other hand, I understand is doing fairly well at this time, trying to overcome the blackness of your name. That is according to your friend Priscilla who you have so conveniently confided in. Harrington nodded toward the couch where Priscilla sat.

Priscilla looked away.

"Perhaps if you possessed some papers with your brother's signature, Miss Craymore, you would see that these not only hold the proof that your brother trafficked in uncustomed goods but that he took part in bribing customs officials to overlook contraband."

"I *know* my brother's signature."

"Then you must see the obvious."

He saw her body shudder. *Good.*

"If these papers were to get into the hands of the authorities," he continued, "they'd present more than enough proof of your brother's criminal involvement in a sophisticated smuggling operation, punishable by imprisonment or even death.

"Richard is not a smuggler," Alaina said between clenched teeth. She glared at Priscilla. "You knew of these accusations?"

Priscilla nodded, looking ashamed. "I respect your brother, Alaina. You have told me how hard he's worked to re-establish himself and regain his reputation. When Phillip showed me these papers, I had to hear him out. I feel wretched over this."

"You have no conscience," Alaina snapped. "I trusted you."

Harrington sighed. He had no time for women's emotional outbursts. "Your brother signed these requests and bills of lading. I preferred not to be involved in your father's more covert affairs, though he urged me to take advantage of opportunities. My only concern was our collaboration on a trade agreement with China that promises to make me a very wealthy man. Unfortunately your father died before it was finished. I continued to work toward procuring the agreement, obviously without your father's aid, though I had no choice but to use his name and reputation. Now, my interests are in jeopardy unless I can demonstrate your father's continued commitment.

"I care nothing for your interests, Mr. Harrington, and my father is dead."

"Be that as it may, the men are not aware of your father's passing. I tried to contact your brother. Rather than taking the time to examine the evidence, he left London and is now unreachable."

"He is out of town on business. He won't return for weeks."

"And I cannot wait. I've been given a deadline I must adhere to or lose a fortune. My associates are impatient. The voyage back to America will take a month. That leaves me, perhaps, two weeks, maybe three to meet their deadline once I return. I need to be on the next ship leaving Liverpool and have a Craymore in attendance as your father's representative. You are the only one available. I need you to accompany me as my fiancé, with a chaperone, of course."

"I cannot just pack up and leave. What would I tell Lady Henley? My reputation as frail as it is would be beyond repair." She shook her head. "No! You must realize what you are demanding is unconscionable."

"Miss Craymore, perhaps I have not made myself clear. If you don't agree to help me, these papers will be in the hands of the police before I board ship. Do you understand?" He took a step closer causing her to step back. "I am not culpable for your brother's illegal activities. If I go back to Boston alone, these papers go to the authorities and your brother will be arrested immediately upon his return to London. "

"My brother...you must understand." She lowered her eyes and folded her hands to her lips.

Harrington observed her confusion and obvious fright. He was pleased that he had succeeded in breaking through her protective wall.

"Of, course, if you have little regard for your brother and choose your reputation over his ruination, than I will leave immediately."

"You do not know my brother! A father carries great influence on a son. Richard sought to please him. He worked by his side." She looked away, murmuring more to herself than to her audience. "He was very young, ambitious. He could have signed papers without the knowledge of what they contained. He came to realize my father's deceitful nature. He distanced himself, refusing to be party to his unscrupulous activities."

"That is all well and good, my dear. We often regret our past actions. However, the damage was done. Being a party to smuggling carries severe penalties. I doubt that you want to see your brother imprisoned," he stopped and rubbed his chin, "or his swollen body tied to London docks, though that practice, I believe has been discontinued. Imprisonment or banishment is enough to destroy any man."

Alaina hand went to her throat. Priscilla rushed to her side and tried to reach out to her. Harrington held Priscilla back. A bit more coaxing and he would have his way.

"You must calm yourself, Miss Craymore. I have become desperate myself. Otherwise I would not resort to such measures. I am in business to make profits. I have tried to handle the situation civilly, but have gotten nowhere. I can wait no longer. I must leave tomorrow evening for Liverpool. *If* you involve anyone else, these papers go immediately to the authorities before I board the ship. I understand that you no longer hold a place in society of any true value. Sad state of affairs and, no doubt, your status is undeserving. If we marry, the Harrington name will erase your stigma of being a Craymore. You can reestablish yourself as the wife of a wealthy man."

"I would never marry you nor will I believe that my brother is a criminal. He couldn't have known what he was signing."

"Without question, bacon-brained freebooters are hired to do the dirty work, but that does not exonerate your brother, as you must realize. These papers prove his involvement."

"And you would blackmail me into cooperating?"

He gave her a tight-lipped grin. "Unfortunately, I am left with no other choice. I do not resort to violence to obtain what I want. I am a businessman and negotiator by nature. Information used to the best advantage, I believe, holds more force than a fist and is far less messy. Once the agreement is signed, you can return to England on the next ship. Though, you may change your mind about leaving. You might prefer the hospitality in America over the stuffiness of the English."

He straightened his waistcoat and flicked off a tiny piece of lint from a sleeve. "A coach has been hired for tomorrow evening and a chaperone acquired to accompany you. Priscilla will help you with your travel needs and inform you of my arrangements. I recommend that you accept her assistance since no one else can be told of the reasons for your departure."

"Please, I cannot leave Mrs. Henley without a word."

"If that is your position, I have no alternative than to visit the police immediately." He pulled the papers from Alaina's hand and tucked them into a coat pocket. Your brother's arrest and imprisonment will rest on your conscience." He turned to leave.

"*No*, if you would only wait until my brother returns. I beg you, he will straighten everything out."

"And all I've worked for will be lost." He buttoned his coat. "Priscilla, are you coming?"

"Alaina, please reconsider," Priscilla pleaded. "Phillip promised me you need only to play a part for a short time. You would come to no harm and can return once these contracts he talks of are signed. I know how much your brother means to you." She brushed tears from her eyes. "I care about him too. I realize you may feel that your reputation would be beyond repair but I would help you in any way I can. Richard's *life* is at stake. You mustn't let Phillip do this. My betrayal may be unforgiveable, but he will follow through with his threat and Richard will suffer for it."

Alaina crossed her arms tightly about her as if the room had suddenly grown cold. Harrington watched, unmoving, waiting.

"Think of your brother imprisoned," Priscilla pleaded. "Your reputation in society will mean nothing with your brother locked in a cell."

Alaina looked at Priscilla before nodding, her lips trembling, her expression resigned.

Harrington drew in a breath, concealing his relief.

"You are wise, Miss Craymore. You will need traveling clothes, especially warmer wraps for the ship voyage and sturdy shoes or boots. Priscilla will return tomorrow afternoon and help you to gather what I suggest. Tomorrow at midnight, I will wait in a carriage up the street. He pointed in the direction of where he would be. "I expect that you will be on time. Your chaperone will be with me. When we arrive in Boston, we will shop and add to your wardrobe."

"I don't want her help." She glared at Priscilla. "I want nothing from either of you."

"And how do you plan to pack a trunk under the eyes of your benefactor and her servants and carry it out in the middle of the night?" Harrington goaded. "You must be sensible. I will instruct Priscilla on the most useful items. You can determine how best to transfer items to her carriage without notice during her visit."

"Lady Henley attends her sewing circle on Thursday afternoon, if I recall," Priscilla said. "I'll come while she's gone. We are of similar size; I'll add some of my own gowns later in a trunk to be brought to the ship. Alaina, please accept my help. Your sacrifice is noble."

"Get out of my sight." Alaina muttered, turning away.

"I'll arrive at two and help…"

Harrington waved a hand for Priscilla to say no more and follow him out the door. He ignored the tears streaming down her face. Enough of women's hysterics. He had nothing else to say to Miss Craymore whose back was turned to him.

He sneered, aware that sometimes silence speaks louder than a final word.

ALAINA SAT ON her bed, tears dried. She'd barely moved a muscle over the past few hours. Harrington's revelations and threats, Priscilla's betrayal, her father's visit from the grave — at least that's what it felt like--had swept her into a storm tide of rage and disbelief. She'd finally regained some control. It was time to prepare for what she must do.

She would leave letters for Aunt Cornelia, Richard and Marielle, her dearest friend. She would tell them of her surprise when she heard of the betrothal and her decision to accept, and that her fiancé, a successful businessman, had to return to America post haste. The letters would appear shallow and, her decision, rash. They were aware of her despondency over the past year. Perhaps, they would see her leaving as an avenue of escape from society's treatment of her since her father's death or, more likely, that she'd snapped and lost her mind. There was nothing else she could say to ease their minds.

She exhaled a tortured breath as some of the horrors of the past hour returned. What if he wanted more than just her presence? What if he expected her to marry him, or ruin her in other ways? What if she didn't survive the crossing to America? She'd never been on a ship and she'd heard of deaths on long journeys. She shook her head. These thoughts had held her prisoner for the past few hours. She had to block them out, go forward, or witness her brother's ruination.

But how could she just walk out the door, perhaps never return? Leaving meant tossing aside the possibility that society would accept her someday as someone other than her father's daughter. It meant giving up the dreams of Martin returning and wanting to be with her. In her secret heart, she'd yearned to see him again, had held out hope that he would return to her and they could heal from the past together.

She pressed her hands to temples. She wanted to scream but everyone was asleep and unaware of what she was going through. She'd pretended all was fine, that she had a headache and wanted to go to bed early. Fortunately, Aunt Cornelia was tired from her day's activities and retired after dinner.

She went to her writing desk, thinking about what she could possibly say to ease the shock of those she would leave behind. *If I could only wake up from this nightmare. If there was another way.* Her gaze fell on an unopened letter on the desk. Edith must have placed it there earlier. Her visit with Harrington and Priscilla had distracted her from ordinary events of the day.

"Oh, *God*," she breathed, realizing it was a letter from her brother. She broke the seal, her heart pounding as she unfolded his letter, holding out the smallest hope that an answer might be enclosed. Her brother had saved her from grief so often. *I need your help more than ever, Richard.* She read, each word causing a deeper ache in her heart.

My dearest Alaina,

I hope this finds you well, though the news I am about to disclose may jar your spirit and cause you immeasurable anguish. Regrettably, I must prepare you for impending events. An unexpected visitor brought documents that I ignored in my anxiety to leave for my appointment in Chelsea. I took them with me to read on my route from London. The information contained has caused much despair and, I fear, implications beyond my power to ignore. I prefer not to go into the details in a letter, for what I must tell you will be disheartening enough. I know no other way to break the news, my dear sister.

When my business is done and I return to London, I expect that the authorities will be at my door with a warrant for my arrest. Information of a criminal nature will be in their hands by then. The evidence they hold will be difficult if not impossible for me to explain away. Therefore, it is a certainty that I will be detained and possibly imprisoned. I have no idea what the eventual outcome will be, though I will do my best to prove my ignorance of the charges. My concerns have been and always will be for your well being and in a matter of weeks you will be forced to face another scandal. I send my deepest regrets for having to forewarn you, but I feel I must. I pray that God will be your protector during the months ahead, and you will eventually be freed from the dishonor you have been forced to bear.

With sincere devotion,
Richard

She crushed the letter to her breast. Richard knows of the charges and takes them seriously, enough to expect arrest. She could no longer hope that Harrington's proof had no basis or that her brother would be saved from the accusations.

She could not allow him to face the humiliation, the disgrace, and worse, imprisonment. She had no doubt that Harrington would carry out his threat. She'd recognized her brother's signature, implicating him in crimes against the crown. He spoke of ignorance. Then it was true. He'd most likely signed papers without true knowledge of their contents. She had to believe that. How can he possible prove innocence?

I'll not let him rot in prison as Lord Blackstone did. Never! She thought of the times her brother protected her from their father's wrath. Now she could protect him. She could not choose her own life over his. Priscilla had been right. She could not choose her position in society over her brother's imprisonment.

She had to accept Priscilla's aid in her flight from London, despite her betrayal. She believed Priscilla when she said she cared for her brother and feared for what Harrington might do. It was obvious that she was distraught over the entire situation. Still, she could never forgive her. She'd confided in her, shared stories of her and Richard's lives under her father's dominance. She'd believed she'd truly found a friend amidst society's rejection. Instead, Priscilla had planned their meeting, had worked with Harrington while pretending to be a trusted friend. Aunt Cornelia was suspicious of her friendship and tried to caution her. The sweet, old woman had wisdom and foresight that Alaina lacked.

She cringed as she considered the future in a land she knew little of and with a man she knew less, only that he, like her father, chose wealth over virtue. Yet, how different could it be, she thought. *After all, I've lived most of my life under the rule of a tyrant.*

More Books by Elaine

A Convenient Pretense
A Kiss of Promise
The Journal of Narcissa Dunn
Coming soon: Seeds of Hope

Author Biography

Elaine writes and loves to read Regency Romances and Women's Historical Fiction. A veteran English teacher, she presently teaches public speaking part time at a local community college. She is a PAN member of Romance Writers of America, CT Romance Writers (CTRWA), and Women's Fiction's Writers Association. As a lover of the ocean and its energizing beauty, she happily resides on the Connecticut shoreline with her golfing husband, Drew, and delights in being a wife, mother, and grandmother.

You can visit Elaine's website at www.elaineviolette.com

CPSIA information can be obtained
at www.ICGtesting.com
Printed in the USA
BVOW04s1637261116
468969BV00001B/6/P